T0195749

The Bloodline Chronicles

Vol. 2

JOE H. SHERMAN

 www.trafford.com
North America & international
toll-free: 1 888 232 4444 (USA & Canada)
fax: 812 355 4082

The Bloodline Chronicles: Volume I
Joe H. Sherman
Trafford Publishing, 333 pages, (paperback) $15.99, 978-1-4669-9351-8
(Reviewed: September, 2013)

This novel, set in a pseudo-medieval fantasy world à la Fritz Leiber's iconic Nehwon realm, is a fast-paced, fun read that should appeal to fans of adventure and sword-and-sorcery fantasy.

The storyline revolves around two brothers, Taurwin and Sorram, who awake to find themselves buried as if dead. Smelling of rotting corpses, they unearth each other and begin to unravel the mystery of their situation. The last thing Sorram remembers is that Krotus—one of the most powerful battle mages in the empire—told him that this would be their last test; if they survived, they passed. Malodorous and hungry, they set off to hunt down some sustenance and some soap!

Meanwhile, unable to pay the high taxes for their farm, Jerhod and his family have just been evicted. Homeless and hopeless, they meet up with other dispossessed families and struggle mightily to formulate a plan that will lead them to food and shelter. That's when Jerhod encounters the two brothers in the woods. He is immediately taken aback by their appearance: Their bodies are covered in scars, their teeth are sharp, and they're extraordinary hunters. They quickly come up with a mutually beneficial deal—some soap for two recently killed deer—and the brothers decide to accompany the homeless families to the empire's capital city. There, they begin to unravel the mystery of their bizarre existence.

Powered by a duo of dynamic characters, this novel is the beginning of what could be an excellent series, depending on where the author decides to take the storyline and how deeply he delves into the potentially profound themes surrounding the two unlikely heroes (the inner conflict between their human nature and animalistic instincts, the examination of what it means to be human, etc.). The story suffers from minor editorial flaws, including awkward sentence structure at points and some conspicuous typos, but overall the narrative provides a strong start to a potentially extraordinary series.

Also available as an ebook.

CONTENTS

Sandra Burns graduated from Edison State Community College with an Associate of Arts. She currently lives in Covington, Ohio. She enjoys quilts, crocheting, and playing with beads. Sandra works in digital media as well as with pencil, oil, and watercolor traditional, but plays constantly with pastel and colored pencil trying new techniques. Some techniques work and some do not. A little of her work can be found on Deviant Art under the name "Eftemie". Her advice "Art flows where it wishes to go. Don't try to control it."

Books include The Whispering Sycamore, The Great Horned Owl, Roscoe The Volunteer EMT, Leafy Finds A Home, Little Witnesses, The Stillwater River, The Bloodline Chronicles Vol. 1.

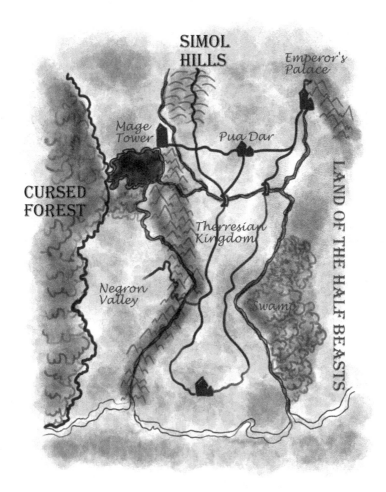

PROLOGUE

Hoovar couldn't believe how things worked out by the day's end after looking back at how he had come to arrive there. He had been summoned to the imperial capital city Pua Dar, only to be notified that he would have to forfeit the lands of the western quadrant of his estates to the pompous neighboring lord, Roaran Pizolla; he was told it was due to his lack of utilization of the valuable land. After an extended stay in the city, things were finally looking better. It had taken longer than he had ever imagined it would to find a few farmers. Nor did he want to admit that he would still be "shit out of luck" if it weren't for those two strange and gifted young men. Sure, it took some time for Hoovar to come to a tentative agreement with the farmers of the boys' camp, but he was sure it was a fair agreement that would benefit everyone. Now all there was left to do was to return to his estates.

Daven knew he was in debt to Sorram and Taurwin once again. How much was he going to owe those two before the year was out? First, they fed him and his family when they were desperate for meat. Second, those two boys not only fed him and his family, but they also provided enough meat to feed all the families that had been traveling with them to the capital city to look for work. Of course, they wouldn't have been traveling or be in need of meat if they hadn't been evicted off their farms for not having enough to pay their taxes. Then once they arrived at the city, the boys created jobs by hunting the bison on the northern plains. Between the butchering of the bison and the construction of the icehouses to store the meat, everyone was able to find work. Everyone in the group profited from those two in one way or another. Daven suspected there wasn't anyone in the group who didn't have more gold now than they had ever dreamed of before they met those two. Now those two managed to find someone looking for farmers to develop their lands. He realized that not everyone would want to return to farming in the country, but he suspected there would be very few who would remain at Pua Dar.

He for one couldn't wait to return to the simple life of farming where all he had to worry about was the weather. Well, that wasn't quite accurate. Nevertheless, it was simple compared to living near the city. Not to mention the fact that he had enough coins to smooth over any rough times or drought now. It was still hard to get over the difference from just a year ago. Penniless and hungry to wealthy and it wouldn't have been so without the chance meeting with two strange, scared boys living in the wilderness. That first trade of deer for a bar of lye soap was the deal of the century.

Sahharras was delighted with the way things were turning out. She would be allowed to finish her training under Cornelius's instruction, but more importantly, she would be able to watch over Sorram and Taurwin as they matured.

She felt that the friendships the boys had developed with the farmers would be beneficial as well. If she weren't mistaken, she would say that they had adopted the Hyzer family as their own. She knew they treated Sylvy as a sister, and Garnet and Daven often played a parental role. She didn't think they were quite as close to Jerhod, but she could be wrong. These were relationships that she was sure would help them cope with their animalistic urges and tendencies. Yes, it was a miracle, but things were actually going to work out after all.

SURPRISES

"I hate to admit it, but they did pick a good spot to stop for the night," Lord Hoovar told Thommaus as he dismounted and began to stretch his aching muscles. The group of farmers, which he had hired to develop the western quadrant of his estates, had travelled farther than he had expected them in one day. These farmers had surprised him again. They hadn't travelled with the precision and uniformity of a well-trained army, but that would be impossible with all the livestock to contend with constantly. Still, they did keep a more than respectable pace. He would even rate their progress as impressive.

"We are only stopping long enough to water and rest the livestock. Then we are leaving apparently," Thommaus informed his longtime employer as he too dismounted in order to stretch his legs. The long day in the saddle reminded him just how long their stay in the city had been. He hated the thought that he had gone soft during his stay there.

"What? That doesn't any make sense. It will be nearly dark before they can get all the livestock watered. They don't actually intend to attempt traveling in the dark, do they?"

Hoovar protested vehemently. Yeah, these farmers were impressive in many ways but very odd. He hadn't even known this water hole was here until they had shown it to him. How they knew it was here was beyond him. It was a little farther from the road than he would have normally camped, but it was more than adequate for their needs. The water was good and fresh out of a spring. There was even some early spring grass sprouting here and there for the animals to graze upon during the night.

"Yes, they do. They plan to travel all night actually. They decided to push on as hard as they can until they reach the north road. Then they plan to rest there for a day or so before heading north," Thommaus told him as he grabbed his canteen. He shook it and realized he would need to fill it before he remounted.

"I just don't understand. First, they refuse to leave for two days for no apparent reason and now they move at a pace that an army would be hard to keep. It is as if they think the Fallen One himself is on their trail," Hoovar complained. Well, that was an overexaggeration, but to continue during the night was completely mad.

"I explained that already. Sorram and Taurwin told them not to leave or enter the city until they returned. They would not leave without them, especially after they had given their word," Thommaus replied. He understood Hoovar's frustration, but it wasn't going to do any good to get upset. These people did not follow orders without question as a soldier would. They didn't follow orders at all, now that he thought about it.

"They are behind this latest bit of insanity too, aren't they?" Hoovar complained. "You have got to be kidding.

Why do they take advice from those two boys as if it was a command? They are fine boys, but how much could they know about marching?" he ranted as he began pacing. He was glad Thommaus didn't mention their work at the smithy, their performance at the Arena, or the fact that they can hunt bison without getting themselves killed. He knew those two had crafted his fine enchanted weapons, and he still wasn't sure how they had accomplished it. Hell, he had no idea how they were able to hunt the great bison on the northern plains without being trampled either. He hadn't actually witnessed their performance fighting in the Arena, but the way he heard it, it was equally as impressive. Those two boys seemed to know more than they should as it was. He wasn't about to believe they were some sort of marching expert too. There was a limit to how much one person could know.

"Lord Hoovar, I thought I would offer you a place in our wagon if you require rest. The offer is open to your men as well," Daven Hyzer offered as he approached. He knew the man was upset, and he was hoping he hadn't interrupted at a bad time.

"If you don't mind, could you enlighten me as to why you have decided to travel in the dark like a mad man?" Hoovar demanded as he turned toward Daven. "You can't think you will make very good time in the dark. You risk breaking a leg on the pack animals for what, a few more miles?" he added in protest. His first impressions of this man were approving, but the man was nearly as crazy as he was competent.

"Well, there were a few reasons for pushing on. You had said yourself how beneficial it would be to arrive there early and start settling in before it is time for spring planting. Then Sorram and Taurwin asked us if there was any way if we could cover more ground in a day. This was the best plan that we were able to come up with in such a short time. We decided we would travel as we have all day except Corney and his apprentices will light our way in the darkness with something called a light orb or a heatless flame. I seem to be unsure about what they plan on using, but they did say they would be able to do it. If we can keep the animals to the paved road and utilize those lights, the risk of lame livestock should be minimal. Corney and apprentice will take turns through the night and rest in one of the wagons as we continue during the day. Sylvy is supposed to help them when she can, but there seems to be some doubt how much she can handle. I think my daughter has it in her head she can do more than Corney will allow her to attempt.

"I wish I understood more, but there it is. Those with herds will have to take turns sleeping in the wagons as well as the wagon drivers. I think we should have enough people to allow us to continue in two- or three-hour shifts for at least three or four days. The livestock will have to rest when we stop to eat. That is why I am offering you and your man a place in our wagon. Thommaus's wife has already volunteered to take the reins of our wagon for the first shift. That would put us at the north road in just over a week if we don't have to stop for too long for lunch and dinner. Of course, we will try to utilize the jerked bison to limit stops. Once we arrive at the north road, we plan on stopping, resting, and resupplying there for at least a couple of days. We will be there in time for spring planting with time to spare. You have my word on it," Daven promised and hoped the man accepted his explanation. He wasn't sure why the boys had wanted them to travel as fast as they could, but they wouldn't let it go until nearly everyone had promised. Half of these people owed those two boys one way or another. Well, that may have been the understatement of the year now that he thought about it. It was probably more accurate to say that all of these people owed those two a great deal, but that was beside the point. Half of him was curious about their reasons, but the other half was afraid those two might confide in him. Too many of their explanations gave him an upset stomach. If it continued for too long, he was going to end up with ulcers.

Hoovar had never thought of using light orbs for that purpose. He wondered if that was Corney's suggestion or one of his apprentice's ideas. The endless uses for magic never stopped impressing him. It was a shame the guild of the magi dedicated so much time to learn new ways of destroying everything with magic instead of finding new ways to improving people's lives. "That is fine, but why do they want you to press so hard?" he asked again. There was no need to say what he meant by *they*. *Is there any way to safely place light orbs permanently?* he wondered to himself. He would have to talk with Corney later if he could keep the crazy old mage's mind from wandering. He really hated to see his old friend ramble as he did sometimes. It was just another reminder just how ancient the two of them had become over the ages.

"I am not sure, but I suspect they want us to be as far from the city as possible. Certain elements in the city guard were less than cordial toward us at the end of our stay. I think the boys were concerned for our safety. The boys could be right. It may be safer the closer we get to your lands. We agreed to travel as fast and by any means possible until their return, and that is what we will do. You don't have to travel

5

with us. You could camp here for the night and catch up easily tomorrow if you wished," Daven explained. They had agreed to travel as quickly as possible, but with the livestock to care for, anyone mounted as Lord Hoovar was could easily outpace them.

"Concerned for your safety? They are going away again. Where are they going this time? Where did they disappear to last time for that matter?" Hoovar demanded to know. That was why those two wanted the farmers as far as the farmers could get from the city. It was because those two were not going to be here to watch over them.

"They are already gone and I didn't ask them where they were going or where they had been. You can ask them yourself if you wish when they return, but I would advise against it," Daven answered calmly. He had almost made that mistake himself, but the look in Taurwin's eyes had stopped him. It was amazing how much that boy could say with just one look.

"Why? Why wouldn't I want to question their actions?" Hoovar inquired. He never was one to subscribe to that "ignorance is bliss" bull. It was always best to be well informed. That was one of the reasons he had always spent so much time with the scouts when he was in command of the empire's armies. He did the same when it was still a small kingdom. That was before it became the massive cancer the empire was today. Well, that was different though, wasn't it? He wasn't that man anymore, and he had better start getting used to it.

"Because some things you are better off not knowing," Daven replied with a sigh. He wasn't sure if that was an accurate statement. There were things about those boys he wished he didn't know. He wished he didn't know about their cruel imprisonment by the tower of the magi. He didn't want to know about the cruel tortures they had to endure or about the sick experimentation on them either. He never desired to know the imperial magi did any of these things, let alone know to whom they did it. However, would not knowing have been any better? He seriously doubted it.

"What? What are you talking about?" Hoovar asked but decided it didn't matter. He didn't even wait for an answer. "Is there anything I can do to convince you on a different course of action?" Hoovar asked as he studied Daven.

"I don't think so. Those two have convinced everyone here to travel as fast as possible in order to get as far away from Pua Dar as quickly as feasible," Daven admitted. He knew it must sound crazy to take advice from a couple of kids. Of course, he wasn't about to tell Hoovar those boys were supposed to be about seven to nine years old either. The man would call him a fool for sure if he did.

"I have commanded armies that numbered into the thousands. Planned and fought battles that lasted days and yet I can't seem to direct a few farmers and their families. I am starting to believe you are as mad as the bureaucrats," Hoovar ranted as he shook his head. He wasn't even sure why he cared. After all, it would benefit him if they were able to pull it off and arrive earlier.

"First of all, we are free men and women, and we go as we see it in our best interest. The boys said it is not safe here and we believed them. I don't believe you and that your one man can offer us any more protection than we can ourselves. Therefore, it is in the best interest of my family to keep moving. We will farm your land and pay taxes as we have agreed, but you must let us do what we must. We have to care for our families. You must see that. Don't you?" Daven told Hoovar. It was all he could do to hide his frustrations with the man. After all, what did the man expect? They were farmers, not soldiers. They had to scurry around and scrape out a living when and where they could. Safety was a luxury that they had yet to experience.

"Yes, you are right. I should apologize. I am afraid I am new at this lord thing, but I promise to try to do right by you and the rest. I guess I am not used to my new role and people doing as they wish instead of doing as I have ordered," Hoovar apologized. He couldn't help but think how much simpler it would be if they did though.

"I can understand and respect that. To be honest, I wouldn't have expected a lord to apologize to a simple farmer either. I should apologize to you as well. I probably shouldn't have raised my voice to someone in your station," Daven replied after he realized what exactly he had just done. He had heard of people being severely punished for talking to a lord with that tone. He had never seen it or knew anyone it had happened to personally, but that didn't mean those stories were not true nevertheless.

"I still think those two boys should let me know what they are doing though. After all, I did agree to take them on so they could stay close to Sahharras while she serves her apprenticeship with Corney. They are under my employment, are they not?" Hoovar said thoughtfully. Thommaus may not tell him what he was doing every second of the day, but if the man was going to be gone for a few days, the man would notify him, wouldn't he? The last time Thommaus went . . . He couldn't remember Thommaus ever going away for a couple of days. Sure, he may go hunting for a day, but that was about it. Surely, the man had taken more time for himself than that. Maybe he just couldn't remember it. Damn it, if he wasn't becoming more like Corney every day, how long did he have before he would begin to ramble?

"I don't know what your agreement with them entails because I wasn't there when you made it. However, it wouldn't surprise me if they see the agreement differently from what you may have intended. I assure you, whatever they are doing, they believe it to be the right thing to do," Daven tried to reassure him. "What they say has a lot of weight to it with most of the people here, I am afraid. They have been a blessing for my family like many others here. If you wish to dissuade the group from following their advice in the future, it may prove more than difficult because of the way people here revere those two. It may be to your benefit if you two were to take a more active part in the discussions and help with the some of the other decisions the group faces. Your experience and knowledge with military matters could give us a different perspective on many issues we face. For example, we were concerned about security and safety when we set up our farms. Once I realized our destination, I thought I might try to return to the farm I had left. However, if I did, wouldn't I be at risk to fall victim to thievery as I had only a year before? When you are isolated and rely on whatever defenses you and your family can muster up, it can make you and your family easy pickins. Now, what if a couple of families joined me and built their farm in close approximation to mine? Couldn't we help defend each other?" Daven said, partially to explain but equally important to lead the conversation in a different direction. After all, it was really a stupid question. Of course, they could, but what he really wanted to know was if there was any way to enhance their defensive positions by strategic placement of the farms' buildings. It wasn't as if each farm could have a wall with archery towers built around it now, could it. He was just bating Hoovar. If Daven could get the man talking, all he would have to do is listen and learn.

Hoovar thought that several of Daven's suggestions had merit to them. His years in service had taught him how important building construction and placement could be in terms of defensible positions. He found it rather intriguing that a farmer would even think of it. It was one more example of how strange these people were and at the same time reminded him how often he had underestimated them.

"Yes, you could. There is always safety in numbers. I would be more than happy to help any way I can, but you must realize I don't know squat about farming. I have no idea how much livestock you can put on a sector of land without overgrazing or how much hay should be cut and stacked for winter months. I think you are right about my agreement with the boys as well. I remember Sahharras suggesting I take them on and I agreed. However, I don't remember what exactly I took them on as or what compensation I was to pay," Hoovar told him with a laugh. "Well, you know the old saying, there's no fool like an old fool," he added and both men laughed. One of these days, he was going to have to ask Daven to tell him the story of why the man had vacated his previous farm in the first place.

*   *   *

At first, he didn't know why he had woken up early, but after wiping the sleep from his eyes, he saw that he wasn't alone. The two uninvited guests stepped out from the shadows of his bedchamber without making a sound. They kept their faces hidden deep within the hoods of their cloaks. It didn't look like either one was armed, but he seriously doubted these two were from housekeeping, especially since he didn't have any. He was in serious trouble. His own sword was out of reach in his closet with the rest of his armor. He was already regretting all the things he hadn't done in life.

"You are Sergeant Avary, the one who arrested a little girl named Sylvy Hyzer for the assault of three guardsmen a while back, are you not?" one of the intruders asked.

"Yes, it was the law and I did my duty," Avary answered truthfully. He wished he had lied as soon as the words were out of his mouth. The truth was an honorable thing, but what good does honor do for a dead man?

"We wanted to thank you personally for how you handled it and for the help you gave to make sure she was safe and comfortable during her incarceration. We put some gold in your footlocker for you and the prison guard named Frackur. It is time the two of you think about retirement," the strange man replied quietly.

"That is kind of you, but you don't have to do that. I did what was the right thing to do. The world would be a better place if more people tried it once in a while," Avary explained nervously. Accepting bribes wasn't the right thing, but this wasn't really a bribe now, was it. He could accept it just this once, especially if there actually was enough to retire.

"You will not be able to report for duty tonight or the next couple of days," the man stated as he took a step closer.

"What? Why not?" Avary protested in his confusion.

"You are going to have an accident. It may hurt some. Can you refrain from calling out, or will we have to restrain you?" the intruder continued calmly.

"What? I thought you were here to thank me, not assault me," Avary protested as he began to panic again. The man was calm enough to be discussing the weather. Maybe he misunderstood the man. Surely, he hadn't just been threatened.

"We have thanked you. Now we will make sure you can't report for duty for a few days. We wouldn't want you to be killed by accident. This was the only way we could think of to keep you off duty for sure. Would you like some herbs or something to dull the pain?" the intruder continued, flat and emotionless.

"Killed?" Avary objected as his mind raced. The fog in his head cleared, and he knew who he was talking to now. It had to be one of the two fighters from the Arena. "I see. You are going after Maypes and his cronies and you don't want to run into me by accident. The little girl said you would go after him. Somehow, I knew she was telling the truth. I guess I didn't expect this. You realize murdering Maypes won't solve anything, son. You two will become fugitives, to be hunted for the rest of your life for your trouble. You don't want that now, do you? You should let it go, son. He ain't worth it," Avary advised with genuine concern. He argued for Maypes's benefit, but his heart wasn't in it for the waste of flesh. He knew the man was as corrupt as the foulest depths of the abyss could be. He couldn't understand who protected the man in the first place. How the man kept his job as a city guardsman was beyond him. Maypes was a disgrace to the guard, and that was all there was to it. Nevertheless, he felt his advice was sound and in the young men's best interest to let it go.

"You were right when you said the world would be a better place if people tried doing the right thing. Maypes is like a rabid animal, and he should be put down like the diseased vermin he is. If we don't put him down, he will continue to hurt others. Then we would be as much to blame as he. Besides, we will not be any more of a fugitive than we already are because we don't plan to leave anyone alive who will complain, unless the one who complains is you. We will not kill you because we are in your debt," the intruder explained as he stepped closer. When he reached the foot of the bed, he reached down and seized Avary's leg and foot.

"Are you ready? I will make it quick," the intruder promised.

"Yes. Go ahead if you must," Avary answered as he braced himself for the pain. Then there was a crack and a sharp pain up his leg. "Mmm, that does smart," he groaned through the pain.

"Would you like a hand wrapping it before we leave?" the intruder asked with concern.

"No, I think I can manage," Avary grumbled at the preposterous situation. This was insane. First, they thank him and then they break his ankle. Well, if it kept him alive, he wouldn't complain. Well, at least he wasn't going to complain anywhere he could be heard anyway.

"We are truly sorry for this, but we have to be going. There is much for us to do," the man declared and he went to the window where his silent partner had just climbed out of. Then the intruder silently departed through the window.

The first thing Avary did was crawl to his footlocker to see what the strange intruders had left inside it. To his surprise, he found it locked and secure. He fetched his key from its hiding place and returned to open it. There inside were two large leather sacks. He opened one and marveled at the gold, silver, and gems inside. There was more wealth in one sack than he had ever dreamed of before this. It was more than adequate for him to retire. Maybe he would go visit his son out in the country. With this kind of wealth, he could spoil his grandchildren and live in luxury for two lifetimes. He couldn't wait until he saw Frackur's face when he gave Frackur his share.

* * *

"Come on, Trentos. There is nothing going on here tonight. We will have to find some new musicians to hire. They have only been gone one day and I already miss them," Sharletae admitted with a sigh. She wasn't sure why she had said it. It wasn't as if Sorram and Taurwin had been gone a long time. There had been times she wouldn't see them for a week at a time before they actually left the city, but just knowing they were close made her feel . . . safer.

"Things will pick up by week's end. It is always slow early in the week," Trentos replied with doubt. The lack of activity in the saloons could be a coincidence, but somehow he doubted it. Those two were good for business, and that was all there was too it. The strange part was the fact that those two had been good for all kinds of business. The bison they hunted caused the construction of the icehouses. The empire had to have some place to store all of what it had purchased after all. Between those two things alone, there were enough people not only employed but also paid so well that all the businesses had been booming. Those people spent their coins at the taverns, dress shops, and smithies all across the city.

"Not this slow. This is ridiculous. There are only seven men here, and there were not many more than that at the Arena," Sharletae complained in disgust. She could always tell how business was faring by how many men wasted their coin on drink.

"Sharletae! Sharletae!" a voice called from the door.

"Rossea, what are you doing here? Where is Hawkuas? He didn't leave you out here by yourself, did he?" Trentos questioned. He would do more than dock the man's pay if he had abandoned her.

"He . . . he has been taken away. He . . . they beat him something awful. They will hang him, I am sure of it," Rossea replied hysterically before she began to cry.

"What are you talking about, Rossea? Who beat him? Hang him?" Trentos asked quickly. He was alarmed now.

"Get ahold of yourself and tell us from the beginning," Sharletae demanded as she tried to comfort the poor girl.

"I had picked up a customer at the White Stagg, and Hawkuas was escorting us back to the house when we were stopped by some guardsmen. They told my customer to 'get lost' and said I was under arrest. Hawkuas asked them, 'What for?' and they told him it didn't matter. Then they said they would make sure I lived to tell the others what they did to me. Hawkuas fought them the best he could, but he was outnumbered. He took an awful beating. When they dragged him off, he was still alive, but I am sure he killed at least two of the guardsmen. I ran to find you as fast as I could. There are more guardsmen in the fore gate than I have ever seen before tonight. There are four waiting outside right now. Sharletae, they will hang him if those guardsmen are dead. What are we going to do?" Rossea exclaimed in a rush in between sobs.

"Sounds like we better get out of here. We will head for the house and see who is missing and go from there," Trentos ordered as he wrapped Sharletae in her shawl.

"Sounds like a plan to me," Sharletae agreed. "You lead the way and we'll follow. Don't slow down or stop for anything and don't you worry about us. We will be on your heels the whole way," she added as she pushed him toward the door.

Trentos stepped out the door and turned to the right to go back to what had become home for him. He saw the four guardsmen following them at a distance, but at least they were not trying to catch up to them. It wasn't until he had rounded a corner that he understood why. There were more waiting for them up the street. He continued until he came to an alley that led off the street. If they could get through to the next street and circle back around, they could go in through the stables at the back of the house. He had led them halfway down the dark alley when the sound of a sword sliding out of its scabbard stopped him in his tracks. Then he saw a man step out of the shadows. It was hard to see the man's face in the shadows, but he caught a glimpse of the side of the man's head from the dim light that came from the street. The man wasn't wearing a helm today, and he was missing an ear. Trentos knew it had to be Maypes, and there were two more men behind him.

"Maypes, what is the meaning of this?" Trentos bellowed in his anger.

Maypes laughed and replied, "It has been decided to make everyone involved in the theft from the city coffers be punished, and that includes you. You and anyone associated with those two vermin are going to pay in blood. I would like to have been able to get my hands on them myself, but others will get the pleasure. I guess I get to carve you up as a consolation prize."

The full moon was playing tricks on Trentos's eyes. He thought he saw more movement in the shadows along the rooftops of the alley. How many men did Maypes bring to kill him? He drew his sword and waited for Maypes to approach. "Sharletae, when the fighting starts, see if you can get around them and get to safety. I will hold them as long as I can," he ordered while his heart pounded in his chest. It was the only plan he could come up with under the circumstances. He hoped he would be enough so the women could get to safety. He had his doubts whether there would be any place safe for them after tonight.

Then something thing happened to make his blood run cold. To Trentos, it looked like shadows leapt from the building onto the men behind Maypes. He heard the sound of a splash before he felt a wet spray as one of the men behind Maypes fell. The other guard started making gurgling sounds and then he too went down to thrash around on the cobblestones. The commotion caused Maypes to spin around to see what had happened behind him, but his reaction was too late. Maypes stood there stunned for a moment as his attacker held Maypes's sword immobilized. Trentos heard the bones, in Maypes hand pop and crackle as the bones shattered under the fierce grip of the shadow. The darkness made it hard to see, but he couldn't mistake the sound of Maypes's sword falling to the ground with a clatter. Then he couldn't turn away as he watched the shadow continue to squeeze Maypes's hand. He could have sworn he saw the fingers on his hand explode as the pressure had become too great while Maypes stood their gasping for breath, but that was impossible. Maypes finally caught his wind. He let out a scream that attracted the attention of the guardsmen at the mouth of the alley who had herded Trentos and the women there.

The guardsmen clambered into the alley to come to the aid of Maypes. Trentos heard them coming, and he spun to greet them as he disregarded the mysterious shadows. "Quick, behind me!" he shouted to Sharletae and Rossea, but there was no need. He could hear something scramble along the wall above his head as a shadow moved toward the oncoming guardsmen. It was over in seconds. Some of the fools never even drew their sword. They lay on the ground thrashing and gasping their last breaths before they even knew what had attacked them. Hell, he still didn't know what it was. However, it was coming back toward him and the women. He kept his sword at the ready, but he felt like he would be little protection for Sharletae or Rossea. He watched as the terrifying shadow slowly made its way with a fluid grace toward them. Even if he could hold this shadow at bay for the women, there was still the other shadow that held Maypes to contend with somehow. They were good as dead.

Sharletae had known fear before, but somehow this time it felt different. Things had been going so well. She never had the luxury to plan for her future as she had since Sorram and Taurwin had bought her and the rest of her girls and then set them free. It seemed cruel to have hope for the first time in what seemed forever and have it all taken away. She decided she would not go without a fight this time. Maypes and the guards would have to kill her first before she submitted to them. She may sell herself to pigs like them, but she set the price; she decided the terms. She would not let them take that right from her again, never again. She clutched at the knife she had taken to carrying concealed into the folds of her dress as she stood behind Trentos. She waited for her chance to help Trentos, but the moment never came.

Sharletae saw the shadows descend from the roof of the building onto the men behind Maypes. She thought she saw a shadow attack the man in front of her and the man fell with his throat ripped and torn to shreds. She saw the man use his hands to try to stem the flow of blood from his ruined throat, but it was of no use. What light there was made the man's blood appear black as it pooled onto the cobblestones. She knew he was dead, but obviously, the man just didn't know it yet. No amount of healing would save that man. She saw the other shadow move toward Maypes like the wind and then heard Maypes cry out. She knew the guards at the mouth of the alley would come to his aid and the three of them were going to be caught in the middle of the killing field. There were guardsmen on one side of the alley and something more dangerous, much more dangerous, on the other. She couldn't imagine a worse place to be. She heard the clamor of armor coming toward them, but she couldn't take her eyes off the shadows. The second shadow appeared content to hold Maypes, but the one in front of her began to move back up the side of the building. She lost sight of it in the darkness, but she could catch glimpses of it as it scurried down the alley toward the oncoming guardsmen. She could make the glimmer of swords drawn, but the shadow descended down behind them so quickly and silently that they apparently didn't see or hear it coming. She didn't even see a single guardsman strike out at it. The speed in which the shadow tore through them was unbelievable. Within moments, there were men scattered across the alley. The men were well on their way to becoming corpses. She wondered that if she had blinked, she would have seen any of it.

She began to tremble uncontrollably as the shadow started to make its way back up the alley toward them. The shadow didn't appear in a hurry as it moved slowly toward them. The light from the street gave her a better view of the mysterious shadow. The shadow had the silhouette of a man. Well, at least it walked upright on two legs, but it couldn't be a man. No man could do what she had witnessed. She saw it land behind the running guardsmen without making a sound. Then it ran up behind them and began to tear through them as if they were made of tissue paper. It used its long fingers to tear flesh away and fling it aside. The sight of the carnage made her stomach turn. It was everything she could do to keep from emptying her stomach right there in the alley. They had to get away from there, but there was nowhere to go. She wondered if they could get around the shadow holding Maypes before the other one came for them. No, it was already too late. It was walking right toward them.

Rossea thought she was scared when the guardsmen had beaten up Hawkuas and then dragged him away, but that was nothing compared to this. First Maypes had promised retribution for their roles in the Arena fight. Then the shadows appeared to come alive and attack the men at

Maypes's back. She wasn't sure what had happened to the guard on Sharletae's side, but the one opposite of her was definitely dead. She saw the shadow drop from the building and come down on the guard she had been facing. She heard a disgusting sound that made her think of an overripe melon being smashed. She could make out the guard's body standing for a brief second with his head simply gone. Then gravity took over and the man fell to the ground, limp as a boned fish. She didn't even want to think about what had made that sound.

The shadow moved fluidly toward Maypes and so fast the man didn't even have time to turn completely to defend himself. She wasn't sure what had happened to Maypes, but his screams said he was in pain after he dropped his sword to the street. She wanted to run away faster than she had ever run before, but she was frozen to the spot where she stood. She could hear boots pounding down the alley, but they didn't compare to the pounding of her heart. She knew the guardsmen had heard Maypes as well. They would be coming to his rescue and unknowingly to their death. She knew none of them would survive an encounter with the shadows. She saw one shadow scale the wall next to Sharletae and was gone. She heard a commotion behind them, and she was sure she could hear the men dying. She wanted to turn and see what had happened to those men who had been running toward them only seconds before, but she couldn't take her eyes off Maypes and his shadow captor.

"We have kept our word," Sorram said quietly.

It took a few seconds for the words to register to Trentos. "Sorram, is that you?" he asked as he released a breath he didn't remember holding.

"Yes," Sorram answered. "Did you expect someone else? We promised you that we would not hunt the guardsmen long as we remained camped here at the city. Well, we have been gone for two whole days and don't intend to return," he explained.

"Yes, you kept your word," Trentos agreed as he slid his sword back into its scabbard. He wasn't about to explain the irony of the boy's statement. If they hadn't returned, he and the girls would most likely be dead and they wouldn't be having this conversation. "My eyes must be playing tricks on me in this darkness. I didn't recognize you two. I thought my worst nightmares had come alive or something. How did— no, never mind." He decided it might be best if he didn't know. These two addled his brains too often to suit him.

"Sorry you ladies had to see that, but it had to be done. Please watch your step, it may be slippery," Sorram apologized as he got closer. "I told Taurwin not to use that hammer. Look how messy it is, Taurwin. Taurwin, you have pieces of the man's head everywhere," Sorram complained. "Garnet will kill us both if we can't get these clothes fairly clean before we return."

Trentos could see the "hammer" tucked into Taurwin's belt and thought it looked more like a sawed-off sledge than a hammer. Then he remembered the sound he had heard and the spray he had felt earlier. The thought of what had happened was enough to make him break out into a sweat. He didn't want to think about what was sprayed all over him right now, but he couldn't stop himself either. The repulsion of it made his stomach want to turn itself inside out.

"That's all right, boys. We will be careful," Sharletae promised with as much composure as she could manage.

"You can't imagine how glad I am to see you. I was nearly scared to death," she added in a shaky voice.

"Sorry about that. I know we can be frightening at times. You don't have to worry. We will be going soon," Sorram apologized in a sad tone. "We will try not to bother you again," he promised as he began to step back into the shadows.

Sharletae could hear the sadness in his voice and see it in his posture. He hung his head and slumped, his shoulders in his shame. It nearly broke her heart to realize the boys thought she was complaining about them. Well, they did scare the bejeebees out of her, but that was before she realized what or who the shadows were.

"That's not what I meant. You are always welcome. No matter how far you have to travel, you will always have a friend and a bed here. I mean it. Both of you have been good to us, and someday we will return the favor if we can," she explained as she stepped forward to cup Sorram's chin in her hand before he could slip away. She could have sworn the boy's eyes were wet when she lifted his chin up to look in his glowing yellow eyes. The dim light from the mouth of the alley had to be playing tricks on her eyes, but she was sure Sorram was crying. Well, maybe not crying, but that was the beginnings of tears if she ever saw them.

"Really?" Taurwin said doubtfully in his gravelly voice.

"Hawkuas! We should tell them about Hawkuas." Rossea spoke up in a trembling voice. She had a hard time getting a grip on herself even after she realized who it was.

"What about him?" Sorram asked as he stepped away from Sharletae and joined Taurwin with Maypes.

"Some guards tried to grab Rossea, but Hawkuas stopped them. He was beaten and taken away. Rossea said she was sure he had killed at least one guard, maybe two. He will see the gallows for it if she is right. You told him to protect the women with his life and he did. To be honest, I thought he was too lazy to do it, but there it is. He deserves better than a hangman's noose for his efforts," Trentos told them. For reasons he didn't understand, he felt relieved. It was as if he actually thought these two could do something about it. Then again, after what he had just witnessed, maybe they could.

"Was he taken to the prison?" Sorram asked as he scratched his head in thought.

"I am sure of it," Rossea replied. The man had risked his life and taken a beating for her. If Sorram and Taurwin could help him, she would—she already owed them so much. What could she or the other girls ever do for them?

"We hadn't planned on hunting the prison guards. He will need to leave the city if what you say is true. Have a couple of your best horses, one to ride and one for supplies. If he requires healing, he will be very hungry and tired, but he will not be able to take the time to hunt. So he will need . . ." Sorram was telling them after a little thought.

"Sorram, Sorram," Trentos interrupted. "We will take care of it. You just worry about what you need to do," he said. He knew time would be essential. They needed to free him. He and Sharletae could see to the rest.

"Yes. I suppose you are right. When do you think they will hang him? Will they wait until the end of the month?" Sorram asked as he rubbed his bloody hand along his chin without thinking.

"I don't know. Killing a guard is very serious. They may expedite matters because of it. They could hang him in the morning, but most likely he will see a questioner first," Trentos answered. He wanted to look away but couldn't. He was mesmerized by Sorram's bloody hand. He could swear it had claws, long deadly claws.

"Too much to do and so little time. I don't like to think about assaulting the prison in this full moon. There is too much light. It is so hard to stay in the shadows. I saw you look up. You must have seen our shadows, didn't you? This will be very risky and most likely sloppy, but we will see what we can do," Sorram promised without hesitation.

"If you don't mind my asking, what do you intend to do with him?" Trentos asked as he pointed at Maypes who was now sniveling.

"We are going to execute him but only after we have a little talk with him. It shouldn't take very long. I don't think he will be able to hold back for very long. He should tell us everything we want to know," Sorram answered matter-of-factly.

"Sorry I asked," Trentos replied. He never liked Maypes, but he didn't have a stomach for torture either.

"Dang it. Why did you have to talk about torturing already? Now look, he has soiled himself," Taurwin complained. Then Maypes's body went limp as he passed out at hearing his pending fate.

"I said nothing of torture. You did," Sorram corrected him. "Besides, I don't have to carry him. You do." He snickered. "Sorry to be rude, but we really do have to be going now."

"I know. You two will be missed," Trentos said as he thought about shaking their hands but thought better of it.

"You two behave," Sharletae said and kissed both boys on the cheek. She wished she could see their faces better. There had to be a way to . . . a way to . . . to what, . . . pay them back? . . . make them happy? What could she possibly do for these two? They had done so much for her and the girls. It was now her turn to wipe the dampness from her eyes.

Rossea didn't say anything, but she hugged each boy in turn but opted to kiss him on the lips instead. They were not boys in her mind no matter what anyone said. They deserved better and hoped one day she would be there when they came to collect. Then she stepped back with Trentos and Sharletae and watched in disbelief as Taurwin effortlessly tossed Maypes over his shoulder. Then he slipped into the shadows at the base of the building's wall. She could have sworn she saw him leap up to the window of the next floor. He continued on leaping from window to window until he pulled himself over the ledge of the roof with Maypes still over his shoulder.

"Damn, I wouldn't have believed that if I hadn't seen it myself," Trentos mumbled. That feat was nearly as impressive as the effect the boys had on Sharletae. He knew her story, and he had thought her heart had been turned to stone years ago. It wasn't that she was mean or necessarily cold, just emotionally dead. He had seen her laugh, but her heart wasn't in it. She could laugh on cue to a joke, but to him she never looked as if she laughed on the inside. The same could be said about the rest of her emotions. She became upset, but he had yet to witness her become angry. She had never even given him any sign that she would cry. For the first time, he saw her in a new light with a new respect. He decided that she was truly a good woman through and through.

"That is a lot of deadweight to carry when you are climbing. I will have to admit that, but he still lacks grace," Sorram said. Then he followed his brother up the wall. He didn't use the windowsills as handholds as his brother had though. He scrambled up the wall as easily as a cat would a tree.

"I think I need a drink," Trentos declared while he was still staring in awe at the rooftop where the boys vanished.

"After we get things ready for Hawkuas, the drinks are on me," Sharletae declared as she continued to wipe the dampness from her eyes. She would not cry. There was nothing in this life that would make her cry again. She would not allow it. She waited for Trentos to lead on, but the man just stood there looking at her with a satisfied look, which caused her to wonder what he was thinking.

The last thing Hawkuas could remember was the guards beating and kicking him. He had lost consciousness from the beating, but he was sure he had killed at least two of the bastards before they had taken him down. He only hoped he had given Rossea the time she needed to make her escape. There was no more he could do for her now. First, he would have to get his senses back, and then he would be able to figure out what they had done with him. They should have taken him to the prison until they took him to the gallows, but Hawkuas didn't think he was in prison. He had been there before for drunkenness or brawling more times than he wanted to remember, and this wasn't prison.

He was outside somewhere. He could smell fresh air occasionally, and wood smoke. He could have sworn he was being carried over someone's shoulder, but that didn't make sense either. He was a big man. It would have taken more than one guard to carry him. He was sure of that. His one eye was swollen shut, and the other must be hallucinating. Several times, he thought he was flying through the air. Then other times, he thought he recognized the slate of a roof. He couldn't be dead already. He hurt too much to be dead. He had to be hallucinating.

"Taurwin, Taurwin, stop. I think he is awake," Sorram said. "Set him down and I will heal him."

"Sorram . . . Taurwin . . . did they get you too?" a confused Hawkuas asked as he tried to look in the direction of Sorram's voice.

"We heard you did well against the guards," Sorram told Hawkuas. "That roof over there is flat enough," he told Taurwin. "There will be horses waiting for you in the stable behind the store. You should go south and leave the empire. They may look for you when they notice you are missing," he instructed Hawkuas.

Hawkuas felt himself being laid down on a cold hard, inclined surface, which made no sense at all. He was injured; they should let him lie down in a flat soft bed so he could get some rest. The wind was blowing, and it felt cold. It felt as if he had ice water running through his veins, but as long as he was cold, he wouldn't feel all his injuries. He remembered receiving both a broken arm and a broken leg before he passed out, but he didn't feel them now. The only thing he could feel was the ice in his veins; that was starting to worry him, but the sensation didn't last long.

As the cold faded, he became aware of where he was and began to remember in more detail what had happened to him. "Where am I? How did I get here? Sorram, Taurwin, what's going on? I remember being in prison and then . . .

no, never mind, I don't want to know. Just tell me how to get off this roof," he told the two grinning fools. He couldn't see what they found so amusing.

"We have to move. It took to much magic healing you. There could be a mage close and he may come to investigate what he felt. Taurwin will have to carry you a little while longer. He will take you to the stables behind the store. There will be horses waiting for you there. Take this and head south and out of the empire. I doubt if anyone will follow you or look for you, but better safe than sorry," Sorram said before he leapt from the roof to the next and was lost into the darkness.

"Is he serious?" Hawkuas asked Taurwin. He didn't get any answer, but Taurwin did scoop him up off the roof and threw him over his shoulder. Hawkuas let out a brief grunt as Taurwin leapt over the alley to the adjacent building. It was too dark for Hawkuas to be able to see much of the ground, but it was enough for him. He decided to close his eyes and hold on for dear life. After all, what else was there to do? With one hand clutching the back of Taurwin's cloak and the other grasping the oversized purse Sorram had given him, they made their way quickly from roof to roof. Hawkuas was tired and hungry by the time Taurwin set him on the ground between the stable and the house where Trentos, Sharletae, and Rossea were waiting with the rest of the girls. There was a two-horse team hitched to a wagon, and it was being filled with supplies.

Trentos heard them arrive before he saw them. Actually, he heard Hawkuas, not Taurwin. It was Hawkuas's grunt and grumbling that had alerted him to their presence. He turned to the sound of Hawkuas's grunt and saw Taurwin trying to get Hawkuas to stand on his feet. He rushed over to give Taurwin a hand and asked, "Is he all right?"

"I am fine, but my legs have gone to sleep. It seems like he has been carrying me for hours. I mean no insult, Taurwin, but you are not the most comfortable means of transportation I have ever been on," Hawkuas responded with a chuckle. "I need a couple minutes to get my shi—stuff together, is all. Trentos, would you help me walk it off?" he asked. He wasn't about to use profanity in front of the women, at least not while Taurwin was present. He had seen what that could earn a man before, and he wanted no part of that.

"What is going on?" Taurwin asked as he pointed at the wagon.

"That's Sharletae's doin'. She has a plan. Don't worry, it is a good one," Trentos assured him as he put Hawkuas's arm over his shoulder and began to help him walk around the stables. "Where is Sorram? He isn't in any trouble, is he?" he asked worriedly. If seeing Taurwin without his brother wasn't enough to alarm him, hearing Taurwin's panting was. The boy had good reason to be winded, but it was not something that you saw every day. Trentos had never seen it, and that was after witnessing the boy do things that wasn't even possible. Carrying Hawkuas alone would fit that category. Well, maybe he was overreacting.

"We had to separate. There is too much to do. We didn't want to be here long. I have to go," Taurwin said in his ruff voice in between gulps of air.

"He is okay then?" Sharletae asked when she was close enough to look into Taurwin's eyes. She didn't think he would lie about something like that, but she wanted to be sure. She couldn't help but worry about why he wasn't here with Taurwin. They were almost always seen together. She could hear Taurwin's heavy breathing and knew the boy was winded. "Taurwin, are you okay? I haven't ever seen you winded like this," she probed. It was understandable, but still worrisome.

"Hawkuas is heavy. I have to go. Sorram will need me," Taurwin stated, then he leapt to the roof of the stable and disappeared over to the other side.

It wasn't the answer she had hoped for, but Taurwin was never the talkative one in the first place. "All right, Hawkuas, it is time you be on your way. Rossea knows the plan, she can tell you about it on the road. You need to put on your new clothes and be on your way," Sharletae ordered, but she never took her eyes off the rooftop where Taurwin disappeared.

"They will be fine. If they can get him out of prison and here in one piece, then they will be able to get themselves out of here in one piece as well," Trentos assured her. He felt as if he should have gone with Taurwin to help, but what could he have done? He wouldn't have been able to keep up, let alone help. Besides, his place was here now. His job was to look after Sharletae and the girls as the boys had asked him to do.

"I know, but it still doesn't help," Sharletae replied. One day she would pay them back somehow. How many times would she make that promise to herself before she would actually be capable of fulfilling it?

* * *

"How long do you plan to push on like this?" Lord Hoovar questioned but continued without waiting for an answer. "I am too old for this, and some of your people are too young. We need to stop and rest. Sleeping in a wagon bed while it is moving isn't enough. Look, half of us can barely stand as it is. Even the livestock have begun to stumble around. It is only a matter of time before someone has an accident or you start losing animals. You will lose time if a couple of the pack mules or, even worse, a couple of the horse teams come up lame," he added.

He had said it all before, and they had heard it all before too. "Besides, I don't think I can listen to any more of Corney's stories when it is my turn to ride in the wagon. The least you can do is let me ride somewhere quiet. With a wagon load of children perhaps," he joked to ease the tension he felt around him. He was rewarded with smiles around the group of men gathered, and he knew his joke had accomplished its goal.

"You are right. I have to agree with everything you said, but I think we can go for one more day, maybe two. We have only been on the road for three days as it is, and I promised we would go as far as we could, as fast as we could. We all did," Daven explained. He wanted to stop as badly as everyone else did but all of them had already promised. A promise he almost wished he could take back. It would help if he knew what danger Sorram and Taurwin were so worried about. Surely, the city guard never came this far from the city.

"I suppose we could let you ride with some of the children though. If we could get some of them to agree to ride with you, that is. Then again, as loud as you snore, we could use that to motivate the children to behave. The ones who get into trouble have to ride with you," he teased with a chuckle. "I think we better start keeping an eye out for some place to set up camp for at least one day to rest though. Are we all in agreement?" he asked, and everyone nodded their head in agreement.

"What in the Sam hill has gotten into old man Bakur? I haven't seen him run like that in . . . in . . . well, never," Daven said as he noticed the old man half running half hobbling up the road toward them. "We better wait a minute and see what he says. It must be important," he added.

"Lord Hoovar, Daven," Bakur began but had to pause to catch his breath. "I'm get'n' too old for this shit. You two had better come and see this. Bring your mage too." he suggested between breaths.

"What is it? Is it trouble?" Lord Hoovar asked as he studied the road to the west with scrutiny.

"I don't know. I was trying to do a little hunting when I came across it. A man should have fresh meat, ya know," Bakur replied as he panted.

"Come across what?" Daven asked impatiently.

"I was get'n' to it. I came across a group of city guardsmen and they're in bad shape. They said they had been attacked and left for dead four days ago. They need a healer and some fresh supplies," Bakur exclaimed.

"City guardsmen, way out here, they have no jurisdiction out here. Are you sure it wasn't an army patrol or something?" Lord Hoovar questioned.

"They are city guardsmen, I am sure of it, and someone gave them a serious beat down too. I don't think there is a single one of them that couldn't use healing and a hot meal. They are in a camp about a league or two from here where the forest narrows down to the road," Bakur explained once he caught his breath.

"I think we better stop here and check it out before we take the families any closer," Lord Hoovar advised.

"Normally I would agree. Hell, I would normally agree to anything that would stop us for a day's rest, but there isn't much in terms of grazing here. The road opens up on the other side of the narrow, and if I remember it, right there should be a small stream and grazing there. If we are going to stop, it might as well be there," Bakur told them.

"Are we that far already? Damn, we have been making good time," Daven exclaimed. "We camped there one night on our way to Pua Dar, right?"

"If it is the place I am thinking of. Remember, the boys were all nervous about going through the narrow. They wouldn't let us go until they checked the forest for thieves. They said it was a good place for an ambush. Do you remember?" Bakur added with a frown.

"Yeah, they were worried about archers hidden in the edge of the forest. They said we would be sitting ducks in the middle of the road," Daven replied. "What about the guardsmen? Are they archers?" Daven asked. It was too much of a coincidence for him to be comfortable.

"Don't be ridiculous. Sometimes I think you are paranoid," Hoovar interjected at the absurd insinuation.

"I wouldn't say paranoid, but he is overly cautious sometimes," Bakur teased with a grin. "No one will have to worry about these guardsmen. They are a threat to no one in the shape they are in now. I would wager in a couple more days, half of them would starve to death. Moreover, if it makes you feel better, I didn't see a single bow in camp. Besides, I sort of told them I would return with some help. I thought we could put them on the wagons until we get them where we intend to set up camp. Once there, Corney and the apprentices could heal them. Once they are healed and fed, they could return to the city on their own. These could be good people. Not all of the guardsmen were bad. Trentos treated us right, remember?" he added thoughtfully.

"You are right. I may be getting paranoid. Does anyone have anything to add? No. Well, is everyone in agreement to Bakur's plan then?" Daven asked and saw that they did. He wondered when he had started acting paranoid. He knew the answer, but he couldn't blame the boys this time. It wasn't their fault. They had good reason to be overly careful. It must have rubbed off on all of them to one degree or another, and he hoped those two were being overly cautious at whatever they were doing now. Wherever they were. "Let's go and save some guardsmen from starvation," he declared with a grin.

Daven had thought that Bakur was exaggerating when he said the guardsmen could die of starvation, but the man hadn't. They were in as bad a shape as he had said they were too. Sahharras had to heal every one of them at least once. Corney evidently couldn't heal a common cold, or at least that was what the mage had claimed. Daven had thought that all magi could heal, but according to the old mage, that wasn't true.

"Just because you watch a blacksmith and understand what he does doesn't mean you can do it yourself," Corney had explained to him. "Healing isn't something to fool around with. If you have the knack for it, you will always be wanted around though." He had a grin for his skilled apprentice.

"Sergeant, what is the city guard doing way out here?" Hoovar questioned. This had better be good, or he would be notifying the local army regiment.

"We were sent out to hunt bison. It was decided that we would replace those hunters that had been hunting the bison after they left the city," the sergeant replied.

"Actually, we hadn't left the city yet. Or they hadn't rather," Daven corrected with a frown.

"Huh? What do you mean?" the sergeant asked as he turned to study the man.

It was obvious the man had no idea who he was talking about or to now. "You told Bakur that you and your men were ambushed four nights ago," Hoovar pointed out.

"Yeah, four nights ago, it is as I said. You can ask any of the men," the sergeant replied defensively.

"That is my point. These people were the ones who had supplied the city with the bison meat and yet you are here in front of them. You were attacked one full day before we even left the city," Hoovar explained. If the attack had happened the day before or two days at the most, it would have been different. They could have traveled on horse fast enough to be this much farther ahead of them, maybe. The farmers had been moving along steadily despite the livestock.

"Are you calling me a liar?" the sergeant challenged as he puffed out his chest.

"No, I am telling you that you were misinformed. You and your men clearly left before these people, who were the ones hunting the bison. If you were listening to what I was saying instead of acting a fool, you would have already figured that out on your own," Hoovar replied calmly as he shook his head.

"Now you call me a fool," the sergeant challenged again as he squared up to Hoovar.

Hoovar's patience was starting to wear thin with the neanderthal. He saw a few men stroking those pungi stick these people valued so much and knew he wasn't alone. "I would have thought you have been beaten down enough for this week," Hoovar replied calmly, but he did think "illumini" and square up with the fool. The eyes on his weapons began to glow brightly in the setting sun, and he knew it had its effect on the man. "I meant no insult, but if you are looking for a fight, let's be done with it. I will not have you behaving this way with one of my people. Come on, if you want to fight, here I am," Hoovar challenged with a glare.

The sergeant came to his senses rather quickly. "S-s-sorry, m'lord, it has been a trying week. I haven't shown proper respect and gratitude toward those who have come to our aid. I humbly ask your forgiveness," the sergeant begged.

"There is nothing to forgive. I remember how one's blood tends to run hot after a defeat in battle. Try to remember that the next time. Some lords are not as forgiving or as patient," Hoovar warned him. "You need to eat and rest after healing. You should go and do both, and we will talk in the morning."

"Yes, m'lord, and thank you," the sergeant replied.

Hoovar watched the man as he walked off and waited until he was out of earshot before he asked, "What do you think, Daven?"

"Something is not right about his story. Not only did they leave before we did, but he claims they were ordered to hunt bison. We know there are some bison in the forests but the main herd is on the plains to the northeast. That is where Sorram and Taurwin took all of theirs. Why would they hunt here? On the other hand, they could have been headed somewhere else to hunt, but where in the world was they headed? We are already farther away from the city than the boys traveled to hunt. Then what did they plan to hunt the bison with, their swords? I don't believe that. Unless they planned on using the magi they lost to do the killing for them," Daven answered.

Hoovar listened patiently and decided he had underestimated the Daven fellow yet again. He was quick-witted indeed. Actually, the more he learned about these "farmers," the more he respected them. They knew things he wouldn't have expected a farmer to know. A lot of it was common sense, really, but they were farmers. He could be wrong, but half of these people were more intelligent than the lord of the city and the overlord put together were. Then again, that wasn't saying much.

"Thommaus, do you have anything to add?" he asked finally.

"Either the man is lying or he doesn't know what their real orders were," Thommaus stated as he frowned in the direction of the guardsmen.

"I assume you have something to support that statement besides a hunch," Hoovar replied.

"Yes, sir, I scouted around to see if I could find the tracks of their attackers. I thought it might be a good idea to know how many thieves it takes to kill three magi, put down thirty guardsmen, and abduct their commander. I didn't find a single track or any sign besides what the guardsmen left behind, but what I did find is disturbing. The guardsmen had two camps, one on each side of the road. They had foliage and brush stacked around both camps to make them hard to detect from the road as well. If they were going to hunt buffalo, they had expected them to walk right down the center of the road. If you believe that I am a monkey's uncle," Thommaus concluded.

"Well, that would explain a thing or two. Maureas, did you know he was a monkey's uncle?" Hoovar joked. A good commander did his best to keep spirits up among his men. He may not be a commander anymore, but he would need these people. If he wanted them to look to him instead of those two strange boys, he had better start playing his part. "Sahharras, did you learn anything today?" he asked.

"Corney showed me a couple new weaves, but most of the injuries I was able to heal with weaves in which I was familiar. I didn't realize how tiring healing could be on the healer. I fell asleep several times before I was able to heal all of them," Sahharras answered honestly.

"That isn't what he was talking about, Sahharras," Corney corrected as he laughed.

"I don't understand the question then," Sahharras answered with a frown.

"I watched over her all day even while she slept. She is my apprentice after all. She did well, better than I could have, actually. I hate admitting that. Anyway, what he meant was what did you learn from the rest of the men? A healer should always listen to the patients, not only to help diagnose what ails them but what bothers them as well. You will find some talk more freely around a healer because they trust the one who had just healed their broken arm. Others will talk just because magic frightens them. Please allow me to demonstrate. Thommaus is correct—there were two camps. The men are not sure what their orders were either. They were told they were to hunt bison, but they knew they were being led in the wrong direction, which didn't bother them.

They had heard the stories of those who had tried to hunt the great beasts before them. They figured they wouldn't find any and return to the city. Four nights ago, someone crept into one camp killed the magi there and made off with some loot. Then the perpetrators hit the other camp, but one of the men woke to the call of nature and surprised two of the perpetrators. A fight broke out and the guardsmen lost. The first camp was woken up by the commotion in the second camp and came to the rescue, or so they thought. They were intercepted by the perpetrators and beaten down as soundly as those in the other camp had been. They believe they were attacked by superior numbers, but if you listen closely, you realize the men talk about men with two distinctly different fighting styles.

"The physical descriptions are vague at best, but the perpetrators wore the hoods of their cloaks up to conceal their identity as they fought, which shouldn't have been necessary in the darkness, and beat every one of the guardsmen. The description of one of their attackers was a man of slight build who was quick as a viper and moved through the night like a phantom. Every man that fought this first man thought he had fought a phantom as well because no one even came close to laying a finger on this man. The second man had been described as a man with girth like a blacksmith and strong as a Minotaur. This fellow fought different from the first. He was more direct and less evasive. There were at least two men who thought they had at least landed a blow but said it was as if the man was made of stone. There was one fellow who had four broken ribs but claimed he was hit only once by this brute. He didn't think he was hit by any weapon, and he claims to have been hit by a fist. If that isn't enough to make your head swim, hear what I left out. The loot the bandits made off with wasn't gold or anything a thief would normally be after, nor did they actually steal anything for that matter. The bandits took all of their long bows and arrows. Then they burned them in the fire of the second camp. More than one of the men believes magic was used because of how fast and thoroughly the weapons were consumed by the flames. Of course, some of the men believe they were attacked by some sort of specter and there are a few other irrational theories. However, I believe that for most of them, that is how they believe the events unfolded. See, apprentice, when you become more accustomed to your weaves, you will be able to listen to their conversations while you administer your healing. For now, you were right to concentrate on your weaves and them alone. It would be a shame to lose a patient just because you are trying to listen to gossip. You did do very well today if I have forgotten to mention that before now," Corney explained and grinned like an overproud father.

"Interesting indeed," Hoovar said after a moment of thought. "I wish Sorram and Taurwin were here so we could ask them a few questions. I feel they may be able to shed some light on the events of that night," he added as Daven's words repeated themselves in his head: *Remember, the boys were all nervous about going through the narrow. They wouldn't let us go until they checked the forest for thieves. They said it was a good place for an ambush.*

"Corney, did any of the men say when their captain came up missing?" Thommaus inquired.

"None of them know. Nor have they been able to find his body," Corney answered.

"Sorram and Taurwin couldn't have anything to do with this. They were with us four days ago," Maureas pointed out. "They couldn't be in two places at once."

"Three days ago actually. Depending on how late it was when the attacks happened, they could have. That would have given them almost a day and a half to travel from here to the city. They would have had to change horses a few times, but it could be done. I have seen messengers cover that much distance in the same amount of time but on good horses, and the change of horses is planned ahead of schedule," Hoovar corrected.

"That may be true, but I don't know if those two can ride a horse," Daven told Hoovar. "At least I have never seen them ride one." He knew they couldn't ride. Daven had seen the two boys get close to a horse before, and it wasn't pretty. Those two cause all kinds of disturbances walking around in the city during the daytime. You would have thought the horse had stepped on a snake the way it acted sometimes. Even the horses that had been around them for a while wouldn't go near them. It was strange, but that was the way of it. He wasn't about to tell Hoovar any of it though. Of course, he wasn't about to tell the man that he was sure the two boys could outrun a horse either. It wasn't that he didn't trust Hoovar, but Sorram and Taurwin's secrets were another matter.

"Somehow that doesn't surprise me. I am starting to believe nothing you could tell me about them would surprise me at this point," Hoovar joked, but no one laughed. He wondered if they were holding something back from him. Of course, they were. Those two boys were heroes to them. They would defend and protect them no matter what the situation was. Then again, they may have been justified in attacking the guardsmen if what he suspected was true.

*   *   *

The lord of the city was not having a pleasant morning. He was afraid for the first time in his life, and he didn't even know who or what he was afraid of yet. He had listened to this morning's dull reports while he waited for the general of the guards to give his. However, the man never arrived for his report. The general's first lieutenant had asked for an audience instead, which he granted, of course. He would know why the general had kept him waiting and why he had sent his underling in his stead. The man would find himself in the lower cells if he found the excuses deficient.

"M'lord, I regret having to be the bearer of bad news," the lieutenant began cautiously.

"Your general sends you in his stead because he failed to do the simple task I set for him. He may find himself on his way to the gallows instead of the lower cells and you in his place. If it is so," the lord of the city threatened. He couldn't believe the gall of the man to send him his errand boy to deliver more news of failure.

"I am afraid the general was unable to attend you this morning because he is dead," the lieutenant informed him. *If that wasn't a good reason, the lord of the city would what, hang a corpse?* he thought to himself. The thought nearly made him laugh. He struggled to focus before he ended up hanging in the general's place.

"Dead! How did that happen?" the lord of the city asked as he bolted to his feet. This was bad news.

"No one knows for sure, at least that is what is in the reports. The reports say his head was found on a pike, same as the other two that had been found yesterday morning," answered the lieutenant nervously.

"What? I ordered that courtyard to be watched, the guards around my palace doubled, and someone still got past all of the guards and placed another head in my personal garden. Were my orders ignored? What do I have to do to secure my palace?" he demanded in a rant. Yesterday he had awakened and stepped out on his balcony, which overviews his private garden as he did every morning, but that morning there were two heads on pikes looking up at him. One he recognized as the guardsman with an ear missing. He had known the man since the man was a boy. The man had been his nephew. The only son to his sister and now he was dead. His nephew went by the name of Maypes to hide his relationship with the lord of the city. He had set Maypes to the task of punishing those who had stolen from the city coffers at the Arena. Sure, what they had done was legal, but it was still stealing as far as he was concerned. He wanted them to pay for their deception. Evidently, Maypes had been unsuccessful in his attempt to disperse justice as he was ordered.

The other head was too bloated and disfigured for him to recognize, but he did know the name once it was revealed to him. That man had been sent on a special assignment as well. He had been sent with archers to take back what rightfully belonged to the city in the first place, but evidently, he had failed to do his duty as badly as his counterpart had. Now, the general of the guard was dead as well. "I thought I had ordered a guard posted on my chambers and my private garden," he repeated.

"Yes, and there was a guard in place," the lieutenant confirmed nervously.

"Well, did they question any of the perpetrators? Never mind, I will go and watch the questioning myself. I will know who is behind this and I will enjoy watching them squirm while the questioner applies his trade. You are dismissed," he ordered as he adjusted his sword belt. It would be comforting to see the questioner apply his trade to at least some of the perpetrators.

"The questioner is dead," the lieutenant informed him abruptly.

"What? When did this happen? How did it happen?" he demanded as he stormed off the dais toward the lieutenant.

"He was killed the night before last. He was murdered in the lower chambers of the dungeon where he applies his trade. You would have been notified earlier, but I believe with all of the events of late, it was probably considered of little consequence," explained the lieutenant.

"Of little consequence? What else have I not been told?" the lord of the city demanded.

The lieutenant hesitated and began to pace before he began. "I do not know how much you have been told. Therefore, I will start from the beginning and tell you all that I am aware of at this point in time. Two nights ago, a prisoner was brought to the prison and turned over to the questioner for his special treatments. The man was already beaten badly and unconscious. He was therefore unable to give his name at the time of incarceration. It was assumed that the questioner would record all and any information the man gave during his interrogation. When a guard went to offer the questioner relief, which is standard practice during long sessions of questioning, he found the questioner dead. Judging by the corpse, he had been tortured and dismembered before he died. The prisoner was not to be found. I should add that no one but a select few prison guards is allowed in that part of the prison, especially during the questioner's private sessions with prisoners. Nor was there any record of anyone else coming or going from the prison that night. There were no visitors or any other prisoners brought in. We were unable to retrieve the name of the missing prisoner or the list of his crimes because the guardsmen who brought the prisoner in for the session were murdered that same night along with twenty-two other city guardsmen. One of the two heads found in your garden that morning belonged in this group. The other head belonged to a captain who was on a special assignment outside the city. I don't have any knowledge, record of the orders, or what the special assignment entailed, I am afraid. The other man with the missing ear was recently raised to captain, but I don't know of any reason for him to be singled out either. The bodies of both men haven't been discovered at this point in time. The rest of the guardsmen have had their throats torn out or their heads smashed. There were also seven guards reported missing, but one of those turned out to have fallen and broke his ankle. He has seen a healer and will report for duty in a few days. Then last night—"

"What was that? Their heads were smashed. What do you mean?" the lord of the city asked.

"It appears they have been hit with something hard enough to crush their helms and smash their heads. I went to one of the scenes to see for myself, and the description is accurate. It was quite revolting, to be honest. There were bits of the man's skull splattered across an area ten to twelve paces lengthwise, and his helm had been smashed nearly flat," he replied as he shook his head to rid himself of the vision. He had to see for himself, but he wished now that he hadn't. Sometimes ignorance is bliss.

"How is that even possible?" the lord of the city asked in disbelief.

"I do not know. My first thoughts were of magic, but every mage commanded to investigate the scene reports no magic was used," he explained.

"Can we trust the magi to tell us what they know?" he questioned.

"In this matter, I believe we can. They have lost some amongst their ranks as well. I don't know for sure how many total, but we have discovered the bodies of nine magi the first night. They may be missing more. They are elusive on the subject. I don't think they would admit to losing any of their numbers if we hadn't found the bodies first," he informed the lord of the city and then paused before he continued.

"I do believe that sums up the events that we know of for that night, which brings me to the events of last night. There were guards inside and out of every gate leading to your private garden and to your personal quarters. There was also a guard placed every thirty paces in the hall and stairs leading to the tower where you slept last night. We lost forty-three men and another eight are missing, but we didn't lose a single man in the palace except the general. I personally handpicked every man assigned to the palace last night and will do the same again today. However, none of them reported seeing anything out of the ordinary until dawn when your private garden was searched. I don't know how anyone got into it without being seen by at least one guard. It is as if the perpetrators had wings because they didn't go through the gates. Tonight I will double the guards in the garden and triple the guards on the walls. Whoever it is has to be a skilled climber. I have also asked the magi for their assistance in the matter, and they have agreed to patrol the palace walls alongside the guardsmen. Whoever is responsible will not slip through again. You have my word on it," he promised.

"I will have more than that if you are wrong, Lieutenant," the lord of the city threatened.

TENSIONS

"Good morning, Sergeant," Lord Hoovar greeted when the man approached. "Would you like something to eat? You will have to help yourself. They don't wait on anyone around here, but I have not seen them send anyone away from their tables yet. I could almost get used to this kind of informality. I don't know why, but it is comforting for some reason." None of these people treated him as a lord. It wasn't that they showed him disrespect, but they didn't scrape and bow every time he looked either. They treated him . . . Well, they treated him the same as Corney and Thommaus did.

"I would appreciate that greatly. I don't know why, but I am starving," the sergeant replied.

"It must have been your first experience being healed then. After you have been healed, it seems like you have a hole in your stomach and you will get tired easily for a few days. At least I always did. You get used to it after a few times and just deal with it. We plan to rest here at least a day or two while we try to replenish supplies. Well actually, we just need the rest. You and your men are welcome to stay with us until then. Besides I would like to try and figure out what had happened to you. I wouldn't want to encounter a horde of thieves on my journey home. Nor do I necessarily want to have to deal with them when I get there. If I have to, I will ask the army to send a few patrols through to hunt your attackers down," Hoovar explained as he studied the man.

"That is kind of you to offer, but we need to return to the city and report the attack as soon as possible," the sergeant replied.

"Suit yourself," was all Hoovar said and turned his attention back to his breakfast.

"M'lord, if you don't mind. Could I ask a couple of questions of you?" one of the guardsmen asked once he sat down beside Lord Hoovar.

"I don't see why I would. What is it you want to know?" Hoovar replied to the young guard.

"Well, a few of us were talking last night and, well, . . . Well, are all these people your retainers?" the young guard asked.

"No, not retainers, but they do farm my lands to the north or they will, I should say. What's bothering you, son? Go ahead and spit it out. If you haven't noticed, we don't put much stock in formalities around here," Hoovar assured the man.

"I have noticed, otherwise I would never have approached you. The thing is this. Why don't you have any guards? Even minor lords have at least a couple of retainers to watch their backs, so to speak. After the events a couple nights ago, don't you think you should consider increasing the size of your security force? You have been most generous toward us and I would hate to leave you so lightly defended.

Shouldn't you take some of us with you until you can get home where you will be safe?" the young guard proposed.

"Are you applying for the job?" Hoovar asked with a grin. He hadn't had the need of a formal guard since his retirement and hadn't even thought twice about not having one.

"Yes, I would be honored to serve such a generous master," he confirmed. He had never seen nor heard of a lord who treated his people as . . . as, well, maybe not equal, but at least in a friendly manner. He could be mistaken, but there was something different about this man.

"What is your name, son?" Hoovar inquired. He really shouldn't even consider such foolishness.

"Markus, but everyone calls me Mark," he answered. Maybe he could secure a real job, one where he could actually be proud of having for a change.

"Okay, Mark, what qualifications do you have?" Lord Hoovar probed.

"Well, I have been a guardsman for two years almost. I know how to use a sword and a long bow, but that is about it," Mark admitted. He knew no lord would want to hire him with his little experience, but he didn't want to go back to being a city guard anymore. It had put food in his belly and coin in his pocket. He had even taken pride in what he was doing at one time, but not any longer. He knew they were not hunting bison no matter what the sergeant said. They had been lying in wait to ambush someone. It may have even been these people. That isn't what he signed up for, and neither had the other men.

"That is a good start. I happen to be in the market for a new personal guard, the last one I had left that position for a pretty face. Now he has new responsibilities," Hoovar informed him. He saw that had put a smile on Mark's face.

"Really? I mean, I am sorry to hear that. It is hard to find loyal men nowadays," Mark consoled with excitement.

"What do you think, Thommaus? Do you think you could train him to replace you?" Hoovar teased.

"If he still wants the job after hearing a few of Corney's stories or spends a few nights listening to your snoring. If he can survive that, I will teach him the rest," Thommaus joked and slapped his knee as he laughed. After he was done laughing, he wiped his eyes and continued. "You know it is funny you should bring up security. I have been talking to Daven on the road, and something was bothering him. Now it bothers me. You know those farmers who vanished off the western quadrant?" Thommaus inquired and knew he had struck a nerve when his boss winced. "They are here. Daven is one of them, it seems. He told me that he planned to go back to the farm he left a year earlier."

"But that doesn't make any sense. Why in the hell did they leave in the first place? It couldn't have been the high taxes," Hoovar griped. He had heard Daven say he wanted to return to his farm, but Hoovar hadn't made the time to ask the man why he left his farm in the first place. He hadn't realized that the rest of his disappearing farmers were here either.

"Well, actually it was. I couldn't afford the taxes and the farm was confiscated, or at least I thought it was. We were so thrilled to find a place to take up farming again that we never questioned where we would be doing it. It wasn't until we were already on the road and Thommaus was describing our destination that we realized that we were essentially going home," Daven spoke up after hearing part of the conversation.

"How is that possible? I haven't even collected taxes from anyone in the outlying parts of the estate since I took over management of it. I didn't send anyone either," Hoovar protested.

"I don't know, but I believe someone hustled all of the people in the outer lands of the estate, but why evict them? They were receiving all of their coin for nothing. Once everyone is evicted, no more coin. What is worse is they are still out there somewhere. The perpetrators had been mounted and appeared to be in matching armor according to Daven and the rest of those who had been evicted. The pungi sticks are formidable weapons, but not against someone on horseback. They would be nearly defenseless against trained cavalry. I think you should consider hiring more than one personal guard. Then they could patrol the outskirts of the estate and offer some protection to those who work for you," Thommaus concluded.

"I'm not sure if I can afford what you suggest," Hoovar protested.

"We will be paying taxes. It would be a small investment to ensure we are able to continue paying taxes," Daven reminded Hoovar.

"I suppose you are right, but I think you may be safer if you armed yourselves. Even a patrol can't be everywhere at the same time," Hoovar pointed out.

"That is true. I have been thinking about that too. Daven's boy could start making weapons for them if we were to set him up a forge and if you would allow them to arm themselves. The only problem lies in authority. With proper weapons, they could defend themselves and the patrol could police the countryside and act on your authority. For example, if they captured a thief, they could turn him over to the patrol for justice. If I am not mistaken, they wouldn't legally have authority to do much more than defend themselves no matter what you decreed," Thommaus added after a little thought.

"We don't know how to use a sword. We would be lucky if we didn't stab ourselves with them," Daven objected.

"No, Thommaus is right," Hoovar argued. "More than half of the group has more skill than most army trainers. I have seen it." The shock on Daven's face almost made Hoovar laugh aloud. "The pungi sticks Sorram and Taurwin have taught you are not so different from a short sword or a dirk. If your boy could make two light, short swords for each of you, even a man on a horse wouldn't be safe. Of course, it would be better if some of you started practicing regularly with the long bow. It would help your hunting and your defense. There may be some minor problems with legalities, but I am sure there is no law prohibiting peasants from being armed outside of city walls. It just isn't done because of the expense. Most farmers can't afford to have a decent weapon made. Then again, most nonmilitary people don't have the opportunity to train on any weapons either," he explained.

"I could teach them the long bow. I can even show them how to make their own. I can fletch arrows as well. The army's fletchers produce better arrows, but mine are sufficient," Mark offered.

"You will do no such thing. Why are you wasting the lord's time? You have a duty to the city. You can't just abandon your post. I will see you hang first," the sergeant threatened as he returned with a plate piled high with sliced venison.

"When my year is up, I am free to go if I choose to do so, and if the lord Hoovar will have me, I will go. There is no honor in the city guard anymore. I did not enlist to harass honest citizens. I wanted to help people, not hurt them. You have—" Mark ranted as he stood defiantly until a backhand from the sergeant stopped him.

"That is enough. I suggest you shut your mouth before I shut it permanently, private," the sergeant bellowed and prepared to strike him again.

"What is he doing in camp?" came a rough growling voice.

"Taurwin, Sorram, you are back. It is good to see you again. We were just discussing security and the possibility of arming everyone with swords," Daven told them. "It seems the discussion got a little out of hand." He scowled at the sergeant.

"What is he doing here?" Sorram repeated with a growl.

"It is a long story. Please sit and let me fill you in on what has happened since your departure. Everyone, sit and calm yourselves," Hoovar insisted. He would not have this escalate. He had let the sergeant provoke him once already. He wasn't about to let the man do it again.

"I think it is time he and his men left," Sorram stated coldly. "He is not to be trusted. He is like a rabid animal. He is sick and should be dealt with when there is time." Sorram coldly stared at the sergeant.

"I don't have to take this from a boy too young to need even a razor. I demand the right to teach him some manners. He may be one of yours, Lord Hoovar, but he should know when and who to show respect. Allow me to put the youngling over my knee and I will teach him to sing a different tune," the sergeant challenged.

"I will not tell you again, sergeant. Sit down before I let you try and put that boy over your knee," Hoovar scolded while the eyes of the serpents on the hilts of his weapons began to glow blood red. He waited until the sergeant had taken his seat before he continued.

"That is better. I don't suppose either one of you two would like to tell me what you were up to while you were gone." He waited, but he couldn't even get them to take their glares off the stubborn sergeant. "Somehow I didn't think so. Sorram, Taurwin, I would like you to meet—" he began.

"We know who he is. We know more than we did the last time we met. The description of him was clear," Sorram said cryptically.

"Fine, be that way if you want. Sergeant, these are the two hunters who have been killing all of those bison. Do you still want to try to put one of them over your knee? I didn't think so, besides it would be no way to show your gratitude toward them. All of the meats you have eaten since you have been in our company including the meat you are eating were from the stores of meat we packed. These two boys have provided it all. The rest of the camp cleaned and butchered their kills, but they were the ones responsible for the harvest of the animals. Well, except for the two rabbits old man Bakur provided," Hoovar informed the sergeant.

"For some reason, I just lost my appetite then," the sergeant growled as he threw what he had been eating to the ground, but he hadn't seen Sylvy and Sahharras approaching. His plate and its contents accidentally splashed onto Sylvy.

"Hey, this is one of my best dresses," Sylvy scolded.

"Watch where you are going, you filthy—" The sergeant never finished what he was saying. He didn't have time to finish. He didn't have time to protect himself or even blink. He was snapped up by the throat and held suspended in the air. He clawed at the hand and tried to pry the fingers back that held him so he could breathe, but they were immovable as stone. Slowly the hand began to close tighter and tighter. He knew he didn't have much time. He had to pull his sword, but he couldn't feel his arms any longer. He fumbled for the hilt but found nothing. It was that boy who held him, the one with the strange voice. He could hear someone yelling, but he didn't know who it was or why he or she was yelling. It was getting dark already. He couldn't see. He had to get . . . had to . . .

"Taurwin! Put him down. Taurwin!" Sahharras yelled at him. Then she smacked him on the back of the head to get his attention. "Taurwin! I said put him down!" She waited then smacked him again. "I mean it, put him down! Now, damn it!" She let out a sigh of relief as Taurwin tossed the man down like a ragdoll and then stood over him.

She tried to push Taurwin to the side, but he didn't budge. "Listen to me, Taurwin. I didn't heal this man so you could kill him, and I am too tired to heal him just because you lost your temper. He didn't hurt Sylvy or me and I don't care what he says. Taurwin, are you listening to me? Stop it. He didn't do anything you have to kill him for." She wasn't sure what Taurwin was waiting for, but he wasn't killing the man anymore. The man would be bruised and sore but would not require healing, but Taurwin was not moving away from the man either. He stood there staring down at the unconscious sergeant and waited.

Then the sergeant finally shook his head and opened his eyes. When the man finally realized what had happened and who it was standing over him, his eyes bugged out, and what blood there was left in his face vanished.

"No . . . no . . . help me . . . ," the sergeant pleaded as he tried to scramble away.

Taurwin slowly reached down and yanked him up by his collar. He held the man barely an inch from his face. Then Taurwin showed all of his teeth before saying, "Behave, or die. Your choice." Then he dropped the man back to the ground. Taurwin then turned to Sorram and said, "I go or he will die."

"I will catch up soon as I see if there is any hunting to be done," Sorram told his brother. Then he turned to Daven and asked, "How are supplies?" as if nothing out of the ordinary had occurred.

"Is he always like that?" Mark asked. "He is so intense. I thought he was going to kill you for sure, Sergeant," he added nervously.

"No, he isn't always like that. He is a good boy," Sahharras said defensively.

"If Taurwin was going to kill him, he would be dead, not that I blame him. Taurwin only wanted to get his attention in a way the piece of . . . so he would understand," Sorram informed him.

"I am still here. Don't talk about me like that when I am right here," the sergeant complained.

"It isn't polite to behave like that and you know it. You should apologize right now," Sahharras scolded.

"There were two camps. Two camps with the captain in charge of one. Who was in charge of the other? Two of them had to know what their orders were and it sure wasn't bison they were hunting," Sorram explained.

"Are you calling me a liar, boy?" challenged the sergeant.

"Yes, I am calling you a liar, and if I could think of the words, I would call you worse," Sorram said calmly. "If I were you, I would take my hand off the hilt of that sword. It would do you no good. I am not my brother. I would kill you before you were able to draw it."

"That is enough posturing and bickering. I have heard enough," Hoovar interrupted. "Sergeant, as soon as you and your men are well and able to travel, I suggest you be on your way. Until then, all of you are welcome to our fire and share our bread. Do you understand, Sorram? You tell your brother I expect him to act a little more civil next time he comes to camp," Hoovar ordered.

Sorram stared at Hoovar for a moment before he turned away and said, "It will be as you wish. As long as he is in camp, he is welcome. The rest are welcome any time." Then he turned to Daven and asked again, "Do you need any fresh meat?"

"Yes please," Daven replied. "Two deer will be sufficient." Then almost as an afterthought, he said, "We do appreciate your concerns, Sorram, but we already knew he was lying, but we have no proof. Don't tell me how you already knew, okay? I don't want to know." He patted the boy reassuringly on the shoulder.

Sorram turned and took two or three steps but stopped and returned to stand in front of Mark. "It is a shame you want to quit the city guard. They need good men like you who want to serve and protect the people, but it would be an honor to have you. It would be a good thing if Lord Hoovar could find a couple dozen like you. If you return to the city and decide they need you more, it is understandable, but if not, bring some friends with you," Sorram suggested with a grin as he held out his hand. He shook Mark's hand and then trotted off into the woods to find Taurwin.

"I do believe you just got your first recommendation," Hoovar joked at Sorram's surprising statement. "I bet you didn't expect that because I sure as hell didn't. I tell you, what if you decide to come back with ten men including yourself? Good men, mind you. I will hire them all for a small patrol. If you don't want the job, I would appreciate it if you kept an eye out for someone who would be suitable." Hoovar became more serious.

"You have a deal," Mark agreed as he held out his hand.

The rest of the day was uneventful. The livestock was herded to and from the small stream while the others rested or practiced with their weapons. The guardsmen were very impressed with the skill the farmers showed. The sergeant mostly kept to himself and talked to no one. The fresh meat was a relief, and everyone ate their fill. Hazeel and Fredriech had gone to fetch their instruments for a little music.

"Did I ever tell you how the city Pua Dar received its name?" Corney asked Sahharras.

"I hope this story is appropriate. There are children present," Hoovar told his old friend.

"Of course, it is appropriate. It is a history lesson," Corney assured a doubtful Hoovar. "Oh, Sorram, Taurwin, it is good to see you. Come, you would like this story. Come and sit."

"We will take the night watch," Sorram stated coldly.

"That is fine. Just remember not to go near the livestock," Daven reminded him. "You two should sit for a while and relax a little. It would do you both some good. Hazeel and Fredriech will play their instruments in a while."

"For a little while," Sorram agreed and sat beside Sahharras, and Taurwin sat beside Sylvy.

"You know, history is very important. It is best to learn from others' mistakes, but it isn't always easy to learn from their mistakes. I wonder why that is. It seems we humans are prone to reliving our forefathers' mistakes. We have the same useless wars, kill, and prey on each other. It is rather sad actually now that I think about it," Corney rambled. "I wonder what mistakes we are making right now that will be repeated in the future. I should write the—"

"Corney, you were about to tell everyone how Pua Dar got its name," Hoovar said and shook his head. "Sometimes, Corney, I don't know about you."

"Oh yes, that is a good story. Haven't I told that one before? Sometimes I do ramble on so I can't remember what I have said already. Do you remember—" Corney rambled some more.

"Are you going to tell us a story about Pua Dar or not?" Hoovar grumbled.

"Yes, I was just getting to that. You see, there was a small kingdom with its capital north of where Pua Dar is now, and it was ravaged by wars. The larger neighboring kingdoms were always fighting over the smaller kingdom. They fought each other nearly as much as they did with the army of that kingdom. Out of this chaos came a crafty general who changed the way wars are fought forever. The crafty general—" Corney was saying.

"Pua Dar, Corney, you were telling us about Pua Dar. Not some long-forgotten general," Hoovar scolded with a frown.

"Well, I was getting to that. Okay, let's see. First, *Dar* means 'village' or 'city' in a dead language spoken by a forgotten people. Piqua Dar actually started as a village to a primitive tribe of nomads. The village was called Piqua then and Dar for city. They lived off the bison herds so they did move around some, but the bulk of their people lived in the Piqua village along the river. One year, the wars in the northern kingdom were so horrible that the entire capital city was destroyed and the people fled to the south. The primitive nomads helped their neighbors from the north, but when the people were strong enough, they retook their kingdom. They didn't rebuild the capital city but instead built a massive fortress for their new emperor. They still needed a capital city, but the emperor didn't want all of the bureaucrats bothering him. He wanted them close but not that close. Therefore, he took the village from the nomads and built his capital city in its place. Then he placed his bureaucrats there. It is said once that the bureaucrats took over the *i* and the *q* was dropped from the name. Does anyone know why? I will tell you why. Once the bureaucrats had taken over, everyone knew there was no IQ in Piqua anymore and it has been known as Pua ever since," Corney finished and began to laugh and didn't stop until he had to wipe tears from his eyes. He had everyone laughing—well, almost everyone. Sorram and Taurwin didn't laugh, but they did smile. The sergeant didn't smile or laugh. He got up and left the area grumbling as he left. Both of the boys eyeballed him as he left, but they didn't say anything.

*   *   *

"What have you heard?" Sharletae inquired with anticipation.

"Too much," Trentos replied. "I think things will return to normal soon. Well, sort of. Let's have some tea, and I will tell everyone what has been happening." He led the women to the large kitchen where a large pot sat on the stove. He started for the pot, but Sharletae stopped him.

"Sit down and start talking. I will pour the tea if that will get you talking a little faster. We have been cooped up in this house for days now. I for one want to get out and about. I need to check on the rest of their businesses," Sharletae told him.

"Okay, it stands like this. The night Hawkuas was arrested, there was a number of guards killed and a handful of magi. There was also a prisoner reported missing, but they didn't have a name or description of the prisoner. There were several prison guards along with some of the city guards missing the same night. None of them has been found, and it is assumed they are dead. No, I forgot they did find one of the city guards, but he was injured off duty. He supposedly fell and broke his ankle before he reported for duty and has been off duty through all of it," Trentos told her.

"That must have been the luckiest fall he ever had," Sharletae joked as she poured the tea.

"Yeah, you only know the half of it. He has retired. He never will return to work. He left the city soon as he could travel. Someone said he went to visit his family and spoil his grandchildren. I bet you will never guess who it was," Trentos teased. He could tell that by the look she gave him that she wasn't in the mood for guessing games. "Right, it was Sergeant Avary, the guardsman that had arrested Sylvy.

You remember how Garnet talked about the man. She had said that she was in debt to the man. Well, the way I figure it, Sorram and Taurwin have paid in full. Anyway, the only other thing I found out about that night was that there were two heads found in the morning stuck on pikes in the lord of the city's private garden. The next night, the guard was placed on alert and the lord of the city slept in the tower for his protection. More magi and guards were found dead, including some guards in the barracks. They had their throats ripped out while they slept. Then there were more missing, and they are now assumed dead as well. There was another head found on a pike. It was in the same garden as the other two had been found in, but this time it was the commanding general of the city guard himself. The third night, there was only a couple of guards found dead and only one missing, but the lord of the city was missing. His head was discovered in the square stuck on a pike. They haven't found his body yet nor has any more guardsmen been killed or been lost. No one knows for sure who or even what was responsible. The guard doesn't have any idea what to do either. The magi shut themselves in rooms located at the overlord's palace after losing members the second night. The overlord has sent for the army. The army has agreed to send a full banner to keep the peace until this is over, but I will bet my last coin it was over when the lord of the city had his head put on that pike," Trentos assured Sharletae.

"A whole banner . . . that is a lot of men. You are sure it is over?" Sharletae said and sat rubbing her chin.

"I know that look. What are you thinking, woman?" Trentos asked with a grin.

"I am thinking the girls are going to be busy and so are the taverns. We had better get ready. I bet those men would pay for many things they have been missing. Come on, we got work to do," Sharletae said with a smile as she pulled him from his chair.

"Why do you women always find work for us men?" Trentos complained.

"Because then you are too tired for the other," Sharletae teased and they both laughed.

*　　*　　*

"Lord Hoovar, your healer has informed me that my men and I are ready for travel. Therefore, we will be leaving you and your people this morning," the sergeant informed him as he ran his fingers through his hair.

"I am glad to hear you have been given a clean bill of health. You should take extra rations just in case. I am not saying she doesn't know what she is doing, but she is young. That healing can make a man awful hungry as you have learned," Hoovar replied politely.

"I thank you for your hospitality, Lord Hoovar," the sergeant said formally and then spat on the ground.

"It was our pleasure having you," Lord Hoovar lied with civility. He knew he should be insulted by the man spitting on the ground after saying his name, but he wasn't going to be provoked, not again. He didn't know why the sergeant wouldn't let it go.

"We will leave soon as the men have finished their meal and are assembled," the sergeant elaborated.

"That will be fine. I believe we will move on as well. There is little left for the livestock to graze on here," Hoovar told him. *There, the moron should understand we would be moving away from him as fast as he moves away from us. Maybe he will knock off with the constant posturing.*

"We will have to travel as fast as we can. It is important that I report in as soon as possible," added the sergeant.

"Yes, I am sure it is important. Be safe in your travels," Lord Hoovar agreed. *This is ridiculous. How much chitchat did the man want to do before he left?*

"I am glad you agree. Therefore you will not object to my commandeering some of your animals and wagons for the journey," the sergeant said.

"Commandeering? Are you kidding? You realize that it isn't even funny," Hoovar protested.

"We will take only what is needed," the sergeant assured him.

"Are you even listening to what you are saying?" Hoovar asked in disbelief. The man wasn't right in the head.

"I think what I said is quite clear. We need the animals to speed our journey, and instead of taking all of your horses and saddle, I will fit all the men into a couple of wagons. I am doing you a favor. I could use one saddlehorse or two for a scouting though. The two tied to the back of that wagon would do nicely. Then the scout would have a remount. It will not hurt a few farmers to walk," the sergeant concluded.

"Those two horses! Really, you want those two! Are you shit'n' me? You are mad! Do you have any bloody idea who those horses belong to?" Lord Hoovar shouted back. He took a breath to calm himself then another. It wasn't working. He closed his eyes and counted to ten while breathing deeply. That didn't help any either.

"The answer is no. You will not take those horses or any horses for that matter. You will not commandeer any horses or beasts of burden. I will not allow you to commandeer as much as a dog or cart. You will march back to the city. Good day to you and I wish you well," Hoovar explained. He managed to do it calmly despite the rage he felt. The two horses the fool had picked out belonged to Sylvy and Sahharras, both of which had been gifts from the two boys. If Taurwin had left the man unconscious for soiling one of Sylvy's dresses, could you imagine what the boy would do to him for taking the little girl's horse? Sylvy loved that horse. She was always over there brushing and talking to it. On top of that, the man wanted to take the horse from the person who had healed him and his men free of charge. She could have charged enough to buy her own horse for that much healing.

"You must have misunderstood me. I wasn't asking for permission. That is how commandeering works. I am seizing what we need, and that is all there is to it. There is no need for you to become upset. This is how it will be. We will need two wagons with supplies and rations. I will take those two horses, and we will be on our way. Good day to you," the sergeant sneered.

"What horses is he talking about?" asked Sorram as he trotted up to the crowd gathering around to bid farewell and good riddance to the guardsmen.

"Don't worry about it, Sorram, I am handling it," Hoovar assured him.

"I am taking those two horses and two wagons and teams for our journey back to the city," the sergeant stated without even the slightest hesitation.

Sorram wanted to tell the sergeant that Sylvy would beat him senseless and Sahharras would refuse to heal him if he tried to take those two horses, but he couldn't. He couldn't stop laughing to get a word out. The image of Sylvy thumping the man all over camp kept him laughing hysterically no matter how hard he tried to stop.

Lord Hoovar thought Sorram would tear the man limb from limb for that bold statement, but he was surprised when the boy began to laugh. It was then that everyone gathered began to laugh at the man. It was so hard to figure out those two boys. He never seemed to know what they were going to do even when it seemed obvious. Hoovar watched the man's face turn beet red and knew he was about to blow a gasket. "On what authority do you act, Sergeant?" he inquired as he put all his effort in not joining the crowd and laughing at the fool.

"The lord of the city, of course. You know that much, don't you?" was the answer the sergeant gave.

"Where are your orders then?" Hoovar probed. He knew the man didn't have any written orders. He had asked to see them before. "It doesn't matter if you claim that you lost them or that your captain had them. The fact remains that you don't have any orders. If you somehow produced orders stating that the lord of the city ordered the seizure of two wagons with teams and the horses of a little girl and a healer, I would hang you for forgery and attempted theft. If you order your men to seize the said property, I will hang you for theft. If you lay one hand on either of those two horses and try to seize them yourself, I may let Sorram and Taurwin deal with you. I remind you of who you are. You are a sergeant of the city guard. You are not in the city. If the lord of the

something to him, but he couldn't remember what it was. What could that sound mean, or why did it make him think that? Then he couldn't concentrate for hours after he heard it. He would keep hearing the voice over and over again in his head for hours. It was as if . . . as if he should recognize the voice, but it was hard enough to remember what the boy said instead of what he sounded like.

". . . that is why you will never catch your horse," Sorram explained with a frown. He was sure the man wasn't paying attention to him.

"What was that? I apologize. I was thinking of something else. You know, Taurwin, I knew someone once who sounded exactly like you," Hoovar told the boys with a scratch of his head.

"Really, who was that?" Sorram inquired as he stared at Hoovar in disbelief.

"I . . . I can't remember, to be honest," Hoovar answered. "That was what I was thinking about. I was trying to remember who it was, but I came up blank." He scratched his head some more. He was rewarded with that nightmarish smile from both boys.

"You should be careful. You almost sounded like Corney just then," Sorram joked as he nudged Taurwin in the side.

Hoovar couldn't help but smile that time. He knew they were right. He was worried about his old friend, but who was to say whether or not it was he who was losing his wits instead. He was getting too old. Sometimes . . . "Wait, why can't I catch my horse again?" he asked before he became distracted again.

"Because you are with us, horses, cows, and chickens they all act the same when we are near. Dogs don't seem to care for me very much either, but for Taurwin, it is cats. Now, does that make any sense at all? I can understand why animals we hunt fear us but a dog. I couldn't pet a dog as the others in camp do, even if my life depended on it. Can you believe that?" Sorram explained. "We could circle around and herd your horse back toward you. That is, if you wish us to," he offered with a grin.

"Whatever, I just need my horse. Do whatever it takes," Hoovar agreed out of frustration. To Hoovar's surprise, the boys took off in opposite directions, neither of which was in the direction of his horse. Then they were gone in an instant. "Shit," he cursed and spat on the ground.

"What is the matter, Lord Hoovar?" Daven asked as he walked up from behind the man. Daven knew what had happened but didn't want to point out the obvious.

"Something has spooked my horse. The boys have convinced me they could herd it toward me, but I think I may have been had. They were going the wrong directions. I am afraid I will have to figure it out for myself. I just don't understand what got into the animal. It is normally steady as anyone could ask for," Hoovar answered as he scratched his head.

"Don't be so quick to dismiss what those two tell you. If they said they would herd it back, then they will. Just take a minute or two and wait and see," Daven advised. He heard Lord Hoovar sigh and knew the man thought it was a waste of time, but the man did wait. Hoovar wasn't going to wait very long though.

Hoovar stepped toward the horse, but Daven caught his sleeve and said, "Do it for me." Daven was sure the boys would come through. He was about to let go of Hoovar's sleeve when the horse suddenly reared and charged toward them. The horse stopped beside Hoovar and continued to prance and tremble until Hoovar calmed the horse.

Once the horse had calmed down, Hoovar mounted it quickly. "I guess I didn't need them after all. Now I have to go see where they ran off to," Hoovar grumbled. He had turned his horse in time to see the two boys emerge from some thin brush in the direction the horse had been. "There they are. A little too late, but at least I know where they are," he added triumphantly.

"You still don't get it, do you? You aren't going to be able to ride that horse beside them. The horse will not go near them at least until it gets used to them. Didn't they tell you? I thought I had mentioned it before, actually," Daven said as he ran his fingers nervously through his hair. He did not feel comfortable talking about Sorram and Taurwin's peculiarities and suspected he never would.

"I can hardly believe it. I have never . . . I have only met one person to have that kind of effect on animals in all of my long years. There was a reason for it in his case," Hoovar replied as faint, long-forgotten memories returned to him.

"Well, now you know three," Daven said with a smile. "Who was the other person?" Daven asked curiously. He couldn't believe there was someone out there with something in common with Sorram and Taurwin. He wondered if it could have been a distant relative or something. Then he chastised himself for the foolish thought that the way an animal acted toward you could be hereditary.

"He was . . . Well, it doesn't matter who it was. Let's just say I doubt if those two have much in common with him," Hoovar replied hesitantly. He knew why the emperor was that way, but he wasn't about to tell anyone except on his deathbed and that wasn't going to happen anytime soon. "What are they doing now?" he grumbled. "Come on, we are burning daylight!" he called to them. He let out a sigh once they reluctantly started forward, but the closer they become, the more his horse wanted to prance. It became so agitated he had a hard time controlling the animal.

"All right, I give in. You two stay where you are," he told the boys. "I guess that is their 'I told you so' faces." He pointed out to Daven who was grinning like a Cheshire cat. "And now I see yours. How close can I get to them?" he asked with a sigh of resignation.

"It depends on how used to being around them the animal is, and how well trained the animal is can make a difference too. My best guess is about as far as they are now, but if you were to tie your horse with a couple of the others, it might help. Let's say you tied it up to the back of the wagon with Sahharras and Sylvy's horses until he becomes more accustomed to them. Neither of their horses will let the boys touch them, but they will let the boys as close as five or ten paces without too much trouble," Daven advised. "Then you could ride in the wagon. Of course, it may be simpler if you simply let the boys run alongside us at a distance. You should remember they scare the rest of the animals as well. I don't know how many times I have had to remind them to steer clear of the herds," he added quickly.

Hoovar eventually gave in and agreed to let the boys travel at a distance, but they had to keep it within fifty paces. This was only the beginning of a long day, and Hoovar knew it. Throughout the morning, the boys tested the limits of the agreement. Sorram went so far as to argue the length of a pace. He wanted to count a pace as the length of ground he could cover with one step at a run. Hoovar had to resort to demonstrating the length of a single pace. Of course, Sorram had to demonstrate his one pace. Sorram's pace turned out to be more like ten or better, which was unacceptable, of course. Then the boy had all the children jumping around seeing if anyone could "outpace" him. Taurwin was the winner of that contest. By noon, the boys had lost interest in jumping all the way and turned to sparring.

This wasn't as bad because it made it easier for Hoovar to keep tabs on them. The problem was that it didn't last long either. The two boys were out of challengers too rather quickly. That left them sparring with each other, which would not have been too bad, but they didn't pay any attention to where their sparring took them. They would be too close to the column and spook one animal or another. Then they would fall behind or disappear into some brush. Hoovar was constantly riding around trying to monitor them. He couldn't take his eyes off them for a second or they would be gone. They never went far and always came back after he called to them, but they were wearing him out. Then after some coaxing from the boys and those in the column, he regrettably agreed to spar with them. He moved as fast as he ever had, but he wasn't even in the same league with either one of them.

Sorram was unnaturally fast. Maybe the fastest Hoovar had ever seen. If that boy ever armed himself with a couple of swords, he would be nearly as deadly as the plague. Then there was Taurwin. That boy wasn't as nearly as fast as Sorram, but his strength was just as inhumane. By the time Hoovar gave up trying to best either one, he was worn out and sore from head to toe. The fact that he couldn't beat them wasn't what bothered him. There were a number of men out there who could best him and he accepted it. What did bother him was the fact that he never even came close to scoring on them, not once. He felt as adequate as a child would if he sparred with a blade master. By the time they stopped for the night, he was too stiff and sore to move. He reluctantly had to ask Sahharras for healing before he ate dinner. Then he ate until he thought he would burst and decided to go to bed early.

That should have been the end of a long day, but it wasn't. "I want you to bed down close to me tonight so you can't sneak off and cause any mischief. Is that understood?" he commanded the boys.

"We normally don't stay in the camp at night," Sorram told him.

Hoovar didn't want to hear any of their excuses. He was tired and irritable. They needed sleep, or they would be whining when it was time to get up in the morning. All young men seemed to think they could go on forever once the sun had set but never wanted to get moving when the sun rose in the morning. He could vaguely remember doing the same many years ago. "As soon as you are done eating, wash up. I don't want to hear any whining either. You two should be tired enough after all that horseplay today," he added.

"Well . . . actually . . . we don't generally let them stay in camp at night," Daven whispered. "Come and I will explain where we can be more private." He quietly motioned for Hoovar to follow him.

Hoovar grumbled about it, but what other choice did he have? He followed Daven to hear what the man had to say.

When they were a good distance from the rest of the camp, he stopped and asked, "Okay, what is it this time? Do they actually snore louder than I do or something?" Hoovar joked with a chuckle. If he had been in a better mood, that joke would have had him splitting at the sides. He did feel better though. He would even feel better once he closed his eyes.

"Oh no, they don't snore. They never snore because they don't sleep. I only know of one time that one of them wasn't conscious. It was only a couple of hours, and he said it was only because he had been injured. They don't sleep, and they have a hard time sitting still doing nothing. Therefore, they normally leave camp at night so the rest of the camp can get some sleep. Usually they are off hunting or they handle guard duty," Daven explained.

"You can't expect me to believe—" Hoovar didn't have to finish what he was saying. The look on Daven's face said it all. He was serious as he had been about the strange behavior of the animals around the two boys. "I have seen their bedrolls and their tent. Who sleeps in them if it isn't the boys?" Hoovar inquired. He had seen the boys' bedroll being set out the night before and it being packed away again in the morning. He had thought the boys had gotten up before him and no more about it. That is, until now.

"My wife or one of the other women does that. Not everyone here knows the extent of the boys' uniqueness. One of the women will mess up the bedroll in the middle of the night so it appears they have slept in it. The women tell me it is to make them appear normal or at least a little," Daven confessed as he poked at a dirt mound with his boot.

"Please tell me you are joking. They have to sleep, or I should say I have to sleep. I can't stay awake all night to keep those two out of trouble," Hoovar pleaded. Then he tried to get a grip on himself. This was not the place for begging. He would survive. He would adapt and overcome. It was what he always did.

"What is it exactly you want to keep them from doing?" Daven inquired. He still wasn't sure how to act around a "lord," and he didn't think most lords put up with too many questions.

"I am trying to keep them from sneaking off and murdering that sergeant of the city guard," Hoovar confessed. "I was told they will keep to their word, but when I asked for them to promise not to harm the man, they flat refused. The only thing I could get them to agree to was to stay at my side until tomorrow night. I figured the man would be too far away for them to bother with by then," he explained. There was no way they would be able to find the man by then.

"Why bother? They were right. There was something wrong with that man. He was lying about the hunting of the bison and who knows what else," Daven argued and spat at the ground.

"Yes, he was lying, but since when is that a capital crime? A wife asks her husband, 'Do you like my new dress?' He lies and he will hang. Listen to yourself, man," Hoovar exclaimed.

"I didn't mean to suggest we should hang the man for lying. I was trying to point out the fact that he was guilty of something even if we are not sure what it was. They were going to ambush someone. It could have been us," Daven argued.

"You know better than that. If they kill the man, it is the same as murder. Then it would fall on my shoulders to see them hang. Let's face it, I would be dead before I could ever get a rope around their necks. The only way I could do it is if I got them to promise to hang themselves. Thommaus and I together couldn't handle one of them, let alone two. Therefore the only thing I can do is keep them from committing the crime in the first place," Hoovar explained. It was too dark here to see Daven's face clearly, but Hoovar was sure that the talk of hanging those two had shaken the man badly.

Daven had seen the scars around the necks of the two boys firsthand, but he had never thought about how they had gotten there. Who had done it to them and why were two questions he didn't even want to contemplate. Would they have hung themselves? How do you go about convincing someone to hang himself or herself? The questions themselves sent chills down his spine. "I suppose you are right, but that still doesn't change the fact that there are a lot of folks in camp that need their sleep," he agreed. He would agree to almost anything in order to change the subject.

That was how Hoovar found himself sleeping out of the camp away from everyone else if that was what you would classify what he was doing as sleeping. The two boys only stopped sparring long enough to wake him because they had become hungry again. Four times, they woke him during the night so he could escort them to the large pot of stew so they could eat. He had never seen anything of the like in all his years. Then he felt as if he had been thinking that all too often of late. He couldn't stop thinking that he knew the answers somehow but couldn't remember or didn't want to remember. Either way, he didn't like this feeling and had no idea what to do about it.

By the time Hoovar had his bedroll packed and was ready to leave the next morning, there were some herds already on the move. He couldn't believe it. How could he be this late? He had been up every couple of hours. How could he have not noticed everyone else getting ready to leave? He was exhausted and couldn't wait until this evening when he would let the boys leave his sight.

The day went as well as the day before had. Hoovar figured they must have covered approximately twenty leagues a day and the guards should have covered the same. That meant the guardsmen should be approximately eighty leagues in the opposite direction. "You two have kept your word. After you finish your dinner, you are free to go hunting. I believe two deer would be adequate to replenish supplies," he informed Sorram and Taurwin as they finally sat down to eat again. He had expected them to be happy, but they didn't look happy. Instead, Sorram started pouring the stew down his throat while Taurwin brought him more. The boy didn't even bother chewing.

"I thought I had told you not to eat like that," Garnet scolded Sorram as she frowned and tapped her foot.

"Sorry, but I am in a hurry and I will need my strength tonight," Sorram apologized in between bowls.

"Why are you in such a hurry, and why do you think you will need 'your strength' tonight? The way I understand it, you two shouldn't have any trouble hunting down a couple of deer," Hoovar questioned as he studied the boy. He waited for an answer that never came. "I will expect both of you back in the morning. You do understand that, don't you? You can't take a week's journey to go after the sergeant," he informed them.

"Be back in the morning with two deer. We got it," Sorram replied between bowls.

"You are not going after the sergeant," Hoovar commanded. He waited for a response, but the boys had gone stone-cold. Their eyes had the look of a predator fixed on its prey. Could he have underestimated their inhumane abilities? No, there was no way they could cover that much ground before daylight. Then without warning, Sorram stood up and started trotting toward the edge of camp. Hoovar decided to go with him.

"I don't know why you hate the man so, but you are not the law. If you kill the man, you would be guilty of murder. You will hang for it. Do you understand what I am saying?" Hoovar lectured as he ran beside Sorram. Then at the edge of camp, Sorram left him behind in a trail of dust. *God almighty, could that boy run.* Hoovar was left there gaping at the boy as he disappeared into the growing shadows.

"He is something else, ain't he," Daven told Hoovar to break the silence. "I have seen him run like that twice before, and it still amazes me."

"How long can he keep that pace?" Hoovar asked as he rubbed his jaw.

"I don't know. I don't even know if that is the fastest he can run," Daven admitted. "You don't really plan on hanging him if he kills the sergeant, do you?" He looked into Hoovar's eyes.

Hoovar looked back into Daven's eyes and replied, "I hadn't, but if he gets caught, that is the law." He wouldn't look away first or bend on this. Too often people believed that bending the law was okay or looking the other way didn't hurt, but that is a slippery slope. You do it once, and there was no way to know when it will stop. He wouldn't break the law again, not like before. How many were paying the price now for his bending the rules for the "better good"?

He was relieved when Daven finally looked away. "Come on, I for one need to get some rest," he declared with a sigh of relief or regret. He couldn't decide which.

Hoovar wasn't surprised to see that Taurwin had left the camp while he had been occupied with Sorram's hasty departure. There wasn't anything else he could do for now. He would have to get some rest and see what tomorrow brings. Damn it, that boy had better be back in the morning.

The next morning, Hoovar woke up as the sun started to peek over the horizon and he wished he could simply roll over and go back to sleep. Instead, he dragged himself over to the fire for some breakfast. To his surprise, Sorram was there ahead of him. He sat down opposite the boy and studied him. Sorram was filthy, but that didn't make him a murderer. He had sweat stains under his arms and between his legs. It was obvious the boy had run hard. The question was, how far had he run?

"Did you get him?" Hoovar asked and waited for a response. He didn't expect one and wasn't disappointed. Sorram barely looked up from the stew he was nursing. Hoovar thought the boy's cheeks looked sunken in as if he had been starving for days. That was when he noticed that not only was the boy's cheeks sunken in, but the rest of the boy's clothes seemed to hang off him too. Hoovar wasn't positive, but he would have guessed the boy had lost ten to fifteen stones since the night before. How was that possible? Why did he even bother asking himself stupid questions like that anymore? The boy must have at least tried to reach the sergeant to murder him and was back this morning. Hoovar would never trust the boys. He couldn't trust murderers and nor did he want them around. How was he to get them to leave though? Half of these people worshipped them. If the boys left, how many of these farmers would follow?

Hoovar didn't have any trouble keeping an eye on Sorram for the rest of the day. Every time Hoovar looked for him, the boy was found moping along at the end of the long column. The boy didn't spar or trot off in the woods all day. Hoovar almost sympathized with the boy. It was obvious the boy had put enormous effort into finding the sergeant and was paying the price now. Exhaustion was expressed in every movement and motion the boy made, and there was no relief for him. He couldn't get close to the horses let alone ride one. He may have been able to sneak onto the back of one of the wagons, but Hoovar doubted it.

TRAFFIC

Hoovar was surprised by the boy's recovery as the night came on. Then by the next morning, the boy appeared to have put most of the weight that he had lost only a day before back on. He saw Sorram running and sparring as he had two days before. He also saw that it had an impact on the pace set by the farmers as well. They were traveling at a brisk pace that wasn't there yesterday. Hoovar was delighted over their progress for the next couple of days, but the morning before they were to turn to the north, there appeared to be trouble on the road ahead. A large dust cloud hovered above the road on the horizon. It indicated that a large party was on the road and traveling with haste. Of course, he couldn't tell who was causing it, and this had the farmers worried. They didn't generally trust anything or anyone they didn't know. They wanted to leave the road and travel across the land, and Hoovar knew this for what it was—a serious mistake. And he didn't have any reservations about how he felt about it. For once, they actually listened to him without any protest. Well, maybe there was just a little argument. There is always a first time for everything, he thought. Then he waited for the other shoe to drop.

Hoovar told them that they should continue until they could see who it was on the road with them. Then they could decide the proper action to take. He reminded them that if it were part of the army on the move, they would have to give the right away to them. They were to herd the livestock off the road as far as possible until the army passed. They may even be able to do a little trading if there was time, but he would have to ask the commanding officer first. Then again, if it was a group of civvies like them, they wouldn't have to give up right away, but they should try to stay to one side of the road. Hoovar felt it was only common sense to remember that everyone has as much right to the road as anyone else did. Excluding for the army, of course. It only made sense to make an exception in that case. He doubted that the dust cloud was created by the army anyway. There wasn't any reason for them to be on the move this far into the interior of the empire. At least not the kind of numbers it would take to cause that much dust to be kicked up anyway. There were always small patrols looking for bandits and such, but he would guess, whoever it was, the number was close to a thousand or more. It was more likely to be someone herding a large herd of livestock to somewhere. The only time that large of a number of troops were on the move was to prepare for an invasion or something of that nature. He wasn't worried, and he would know soon enough. Unless he was wrong, he figured he would know by dusk.

He wasn't wrong about when he would know, but he was wrong about who it would be. It was the army on the move, and he was anxious to see if he could learn why they were here of all places. He rode ahead of the rest who had left the road, and he hoped to discover who was in command. He was accompanied by Corney, Sahharras, and Thommaus. They stopped short of the marching column and waited for a representative to come forth. He watched until finally a corporal with an escort of ten men rode out to meet him.

"Good evening, Corporal. Allow me to introduce Lord Hoovar and battle mage Cornelius Stone," Thommaus greeted.

"Good even—Lord Hoovar, the Lord Hoovar? Of course, it is none other! My apologies, it is my honor to be in your presence. I will ride back and notify General Basserus of your presence immediately," the corporal replied nervously as he dry washed his hands. Then he rode away with his escort faster than he had come.

"It never ceases to amaze me how much effect the mention of your name has on some people," Thommaus teased with a grin. "There for a minute I thought he was going to swallow his tongue." He chuckled.

It didn't take long before another escort was on its way. Hoovar waited patiently while he tried to remember if he knew a General Basserus. He couldn't remember any, but then again it had been more than a few years since he wore the armor himself. He knew there could have been more than a few changes since his departure from command.

When the corporal finally returned with his commander, he dismounted and knelt as he said, "Lord Hoovar, please allow me to introduce General Basserus. General Basserus, this is the famed Lord Hoovar."

"Get up, man, and stop that before you hit your head on a rock or something. I am a retired general, not the emperor himself. I don't require or desire all that nonsense," Hoovar scolded in disgust. Then he continued. "General Basserus, my people have started to set up camp, and there will be fresh home-cooked food shortly. If you wish, it would please me greatly if you joined me for dinner. We could discuss what trouble has you traveling double time with what appears a full banner through the interior of the empire, if it doesn't break any confidentiality, of course. I wouldn't want to pry, but I don't like the thought of being caught off guard by bandits dangerous enough to require the attention of a full banner," Hoovar added as an invitation as politely as he could manage while probing for information.

"They always said you were no-nonsense and straight-to-the-point kind of commander. I regret I never had the opportunity to serve under you directly," General Basserus replied with a grin. "I suppose I could spare a few minutes to enjoy your hospitality, but I am afraid it may not be much more than that, Lord Hoovar." He extended his hand in greeting. "You are obviously headed toward your estates, but if you don't mind my asking, where are you returning home from?" he asked curiously.

"Pua Dar," Hoovar answered as he reached out and shook the general's hand. "I had a meeting with the overlord and other business there," he added as an explanation.

"Pua Dar, was there any trouble there when you left?" Basserus asked eagerly.

"No, no trouble at all, at least none that I am aware of," Hoovar answered. "What is going on? Or can you answer that?" he probed again and watched the general to see if he could detect any lies.

"I am not so sure. I am told some sort of uprising, but something doesn't feel right about it," Basserus answered and he watched to see Hoovar's reaction.

"Uprising? You must be joking. There hasn't been an uprising since the empire has been formed, well, not in the interior like that. There are always little skirmishes with resistance fighters of some sort when new lands are acquired, but nothing I would consider an uprising," Hoovar exclaimed as he scratched his head. Well, at least he couldn't remember any.

"All I know is the lord of the city has been murdered and the overlord is scared shitless. I mean, he is very concerned. He asked for the western army for assistance. I have been sent with a full banner of foot, three squads of cavalry, three ranks of bowmen, two ranks of pikemen, and two fists of magi to answer his call for aid. If the report is accurate, he has lost over a hundred guardsmen and a couple dozen magi. The report also said that the lord of the city wasn't only murdered but also beheaded. They found his head on a pike in the city square. His body still hasn't been recovered as far as I know. I would have said it was the work of an assassin, at least that part sounds like the work of an assassin, but I have never heard of assassins working in such a large scale before. I have read the strategies the empire employed with its assassins. I believe those texts were outdated though. What do you think? Could it be assassins sent to send a message for some wrongdoing?" Basserus inquired as he followed Hoovar's lead and dismounted.

Hoovar led them back to camp as he thought over what he had heard and asked a few questions. Then he hobbled his horse and then checked it twice while he thought about his response. "If it was the lord of the city who was murdered, I would guess an assassin was the culprit. Then I would suggest you look at whoever had the most to gain from his death, but assassins don't normally kill so many. Nor do they kill targets like lowly guardsmen. There must be something else going on. I don't think the overlord will be much help to you when you get there either. Judging by my dealings with him, he is less than competent. That is one thing about the military. The incompetent don't live long to ruin other men's lives," Hoovar explained as he led Basserus to the fire where the others had gathered for dinner. "Have you seen any sign of bandits or thieves on the road ahead of us?" he asked and everyone turned their attention on Basserus.

"No, the scouts have not reported anything of the sort. How about you? Have you seen any?" Basserus inquired.

"We haven't seen any thieves, but not many thieves will try to rob a group as large as this," he added. "We did come across a party of city guard who had been sent out to hunt bison. They claimed to have been ambushed by thieves, but I haven't been able to decide what exactly did happen to them. Their story doesn't quite add up, if you know what I mean," he informed the general as he sat down and motioned for the general to join him.

"What do your scouts say happened?" Basserus asked with a grin.

"Scouts? Are you forgetting that I am retired?" Hoovar answered with a chuckle.

"I was just checking. My scouts seem to be a little confused. They reported someone has been keeping an eye on us since noon, but they have yet to produce any proof. There is even a rumor that there are spirits watching our every move," Basserus admitted and shook his head. "Can you believe some of the superstitious garbage some men will believe?" he added.

"That is interesting," Hoovar replied. He suspected the scouts were talking about Sorram and Taurwin, of course, but he wasn't sure what he intended to do with them. "There is a man here I would like you to meet. He is a very competent man. If your men would like to do some trading, this is the man for them to see," Hoovar explained as he looked around to locate Daven.

"Daven, Daven, come here, I would like you to meet General Basserus," he called to Daven when he saw him striding up to the fire with his wife and son.

"It is my pleasure, General Basserus," Daven said and stuck out his hand in greeting.

"Hoovar said you are the man to see if any of the men wish to trade. Since he gave you a recommendation, I think we may set up camp on the other side of the road if Hoovar has no objections, that is," Basserus said and shook Daven's hand.

"I don't know what your men may need, but we have plenty. We were well stocked when we left the city and we haven't been gone long," Daven explained. "They should feel free to trade with all here. We are simple farmers though, not merchants. If it isn't against protocol, do you mind if I ask what brings the army here? There isn't trouble or thieves afoot, are there?" he asked nervously. He never knew the proper etiquette for addressing people of rank.

"Speaking of trouble, have you seen Sorram or Taurwin?" Hoovar asked Daven after making his decision. "I would like you to meet these two as well. They are your mysterious scouts, I have no doubt. To answer your earlier question, they didn't believe or like the sergeant's story. They wouldn't say much more than that." That wasn't the complete truth, but it wasn't a complete lie either.

"No, I haven't seen them in a while. Do you want me to send Sylvy for them?" Daven asked as he frowned. He suspected those two would want to avoid this many strangers, especially since they were military.

Hoovar knew instantly Daven didn't like what he was suggesting. "Yes, please do. They may be able to find some fresh meat for the general and his men," he told Daven. "You see, they are not scouts but uncommonly gifted hunters I have stumbled upon," he explained to Basserus.

"Fresh roasted meat does sound nice. You remember how difficult it is for the hunters to get any game while the army is on the move, don't you? I swear the sound of boots marching will scare off every animal for leagues. They will have to be very good hunters to be able to get enough game so every man with me can have a bite," Basserus said. There was no way they could, and he knew it.

"Have Sylvy tell them I require twenty nice deer as soon as possible," Hoovar told Daven and watched him go with a shake of his head in disapproval.

"You don't really expect your hunters to produce twenty deer, do you?" Basserus said in disbelief.

"Surely you have heard of the bison harvests by now. Well, these are the two who had done the hunting," Hoovar boasted. Then he realized that he was doing just that— boasting. It was only a couple of days ago he was trying to figure out how to get them to leave and now he was . . . he was . . . what, proud of them? Maybe they were not as bad as he thought. It wasn't as if they caused trouble constantly. They had behaved fine the last couple of days. Even if they did want to kill the sergeant, could he blame them? The thought had crossed his mind once or twice. No, it was one thing to think it out of anger but something else to try to act on those thoughts. Then again, they were young and still had hot blood in them. They may settle down as they get older. Maybe if they were old enough to marry, that would settle them down.

"Yes, as a matter of fact, I have received some of the cured meat with our last supply shipment," Basserus admitted. "The textbooks always said you were the luckiest man alive when it came to battle. That luck must have gone with you when you retired. They must be very valuable indeed. They wouldn't happen to be interested in a military career, would they? I could use someone with that kind of woodcraft," Basserus replied as he scratched his beard.

"I don't think so. Besides, they can be difficult to handle. I suppose that may be an understatement. You see, from what I hear, they have grown up in the wild and I half believe it. They don't have much regard for authority. Then again come to think of it, I am not sure they understand authority or the law," Hoovar admitted to him. He saw the look of disapproval in Basserus's eyes. "They can hunt like nothing I have ever seen though," he added but wasn't sure why he even cared whether Basserus approved.

"I guess we will see soon enough," Basserus replied and was silent.

Hoovar knew he hadn't handled it well but decided to let it go instead of making things worse. It didn't take long before the deer started arriving. There were four deer delivered before the first hour had passed, but neither Sorram nor Taurwin entered camp. Hoovar didn't even notice Sylvy trotting out of the camp and beyond the tree line to meet with them. The only thing he saw was Sylvy telling her father that Sorram and Taurwin had brought four deer and that they had left for some more. Daven had Sylvy lead him and some of the soldiers to where the boys had laid the deer carcasses.

"They didn't even bother to field-dress them," one of the soldiers complained.

"That one is missing a hind quarter," complained another soldier.

"They do the hunting, we do the cleaning," Daven replied calmly.

"They need to eat too," Sylvy scolded as if that should make sense to them.

"Come on, we better get busy before they bring more back," Daven commanded. Sylvy's statement made sense to Daven when he first heard it. They would need to eat and it was unlikely they would come into camp with so many strangers about, but then he began to think about it. They would not have time to cook the meat while they hunted. He knew the boys had claimed they had eaten uncooked meat before, but he just didn't think they . . . there was just no way . . . Daven finally decided to concentrate on the task in front of him. He would clean the deer and not think about what those two did or didn't do.

The smell of fresh roasted meat permeated the valley as venison cooked over fires on both sides of the road. The soldiers mingled freely with the farmers and bartered for what they could. Some of the soldiers danced to the music of

Hazeel and Fredriech while others sat and feasted with good company. Hoovar tried to pry more details about what was going on in the world while Basserus tried to get a better feel for the situation he was marching toward in Pua Dar. Hoovar warned him about the surly sergeant he had met on the road, but there was little he knew about any strife in the city itself. Hoovar never did get the opportunity to introduce Basserus to Sorram or Taurwin. The two boys didn't come into the camp to give him a chance to do it. He was disappointed but not sure why he should care. Why should he care whether Basserus met them? He had no reason to try to impress the man. He had sworn to himself when he took the lordship position that he would never be caught up in politics the way most lords did. Yet here he was doing exactly that, and he felt dirty for it.

"I have to admit I had my doubts, but your hunters did produce like you said they would," Basserus told Hoovar. He would love to get his hands on a couple like them. The reports from his scouts said the hunters had somehow gotten into camp with all twenty deer without being seen, not a single glimpse even. Those hunters would be very valuable assets indeed. No wonder Hoovar decided not to produce them. He wouldn't risk losing them to someone else. Not that he blamed the man. He would have done the same. He would have to remember that Lord Hoovar, retired or not, was still retaining highly skilled men under his employment.

The next morning, both groups were up early to continue their travels. The army took to the road first, but Basserus never stopped looking for those hunters. He had his scouts out all night to locate the whereabouts of Hoovar's two miracle hunters. He thought they would have camped close, but he must have been wrong. The scouts never did find them, and he never had his chance to try to hire them away from Hoovar. He wasn't used to being disappointed, but evidently, they were very good. Some of his scouts expressed the theory that the hunters didn't camp at all. They said there had been someone toying with them all night. He wanted to disregard the theory, but it was his most skilled scouts who thought it. The younger less experienced scouts didn't think the mysterious hunters even existed. He almost believed it was because only his best scouts could tell there was anyone there at all, but that was nonsense. No one was that good. He had enough scouts out that night that a field mouse should have had trouble not being noticed. Then again, someone had delivered the deer. He was starting to get a headache just thinking about it. Well, there was nothing to do but go on about his business for now.

Hoovar didn't understand it, but he felt a little sad to see the army leaving him behind. He knew that part of his life was over by choice, but it didn't help. It was the one thing he had been able to do well, and he knew it. Hoovar let out a sigh, turned away from his past, and looked toward his future. The camp was busy with people scrambling this way and that to prepare for the day's travel. He saw Sorram and Taurwin run from the cover of the trees on the far side of the camp. Hoovar decided he would walk over and talk to them. He would like to know why they never made an appearance so he could introduce them to Basserus. He didn't know why it bothered him, but it did. He was used to giving orders to soldiers and the orders being followed. He knew things were different with civilians, but wanting to introduce them to someone was a small request. They should have been happy to oblige. When he got to where he had last seen the boys, they were gone again. He looked around and couldn't see them, but he did see that all the herds were on the road and some of the wagons. He looked back the way he had come, and the camp was now empty. He decided he would talk with them later. He walked to where his horse was hobbled to mount up to leave.

Hoovar saw Sylvy leading her horse and decided to ride over and ask her if she knew what those two boys were doing today. By the time he had saddled his horse and caught back up to her, she was juggling three of those flames while leading her horse.

"Whoa, should you be doing that unsupervised, young lady?" he asked while trying not to sound too alarmed. He saw one of the balls flicker. He watched her frown, and then the ball came back to life as if she frowned it back into existence. The whole scene would have been adorable if it hadn't frightened him something fierce. There was something seriously wrong with a little girl being able to juggle fire like that if anyone asked him.

"Corney said I need to spend more time practicing. He also said I should try practicing while I am doing something else at the same time. So I am trying to practice while I walk my horse," Sylvy answered as she scowled at one of the flames that flickered in and out.

"Most people ride their horse instead of walk with it," Hoovar teased. His dig caused one of the flames to disappear completely, and the look she gave him for it made him wish he hadn't said it.

"Taurwin and Sorram said I need to get more exercise and practice more while we travel. They said riding too much has made me soft and lazy. I was trying to get some exercise while I spent time with my horse and practice my magic for Corney. Later today, I am supposed to start my lessons on the old tongue, whatever that means. I swear there ain't enough time in the day for all of this. I wish I didn't have to sleep like Sorram and Taurwin. Then I would have plenty of time," Sylvy complained. She smiled at the flame as it came back to life and then she added another.

"Talking about Sorram and Taurwin, you wouldn't happen to know what they are doing today or where they went," Hoovar inquired as he tried to look into the trees. It was preferable to watching a little girl wield dangerous magic balls of fire. He had no idea what he had said wrong this time, but all four of the flames flickered and went out. He suspected she was about to let him know.

"They are exercising also. They may have mentioned that they need to be better fit if m'lord wishes to request twenty deer very often. If m'lord wishes it, he could ride out to find them. They planned to run laps around us today so they could keep an eye out for trouble and still get more exercise. It probably wouldn't hurt m'lord to at least thank them for their efforts to please him," she scolded while emphasizing the *m'lord* before she picked up her pace and left him behind.

Hoovar knew he could have matched her pace but decided not to do so. Part of him wanted to, but the other part was relieved she had left him behind. There was something wrong with her. Since when did little girls practice with weapons and magic instead of dolls? He never had any children of his own, but surely, things hadn't changed that much since he was a child. He had half a mind to lecture her about her tone with him; after all, he was an elder, not to mention being a lord. If she wasn't . . . Then Hoovar thought about her words again.

These people never call him m'lord. None of them does it. Well, Daven did sometimes, Hoovar admitted. Not that it bothered him, but why did she keep calling him m'lord as she had? His retainers at his manor house never gave him attitude. Not even the first maid would dare give him attitude, nor would the head accountant. He wasn't like the other foolish lords. He treated his people well, and he deserved better treatment in return. If someone was to ask . . . ask . . . What were their names? He didn't remember their names. No, it wasn't that he had forgotten their names. He didn't know their names. Some of those people at his manor had served him for years, and he had never even asked their names. The little girl was right. He had become the very thing he disliked—a foolish, pompous lord, someone who didn't pay attention to those who were beneath them and took their service for granite. He just didn't want to admit that he had been given lip by a little girl, and worse, she was right in doing so. He would have to go and talk with Sorram and Taurwin.

Sahharras had been relieved when she saw the general Basserus take to the road with his army. He hadn't recognized her from the one time he was at the tower to see Krotus's progress on the new elite soldiers, but she had recognized him. She had avoided the general as much as possible after she had recognized him, but Lord Hoovar had asked multiple times for her to find Sorram and Taurwin so he could introduce them. She acted as if she had no idea how to find them, not that the boys would have been foolish enough to come if she had called to them. The general would have surely recognized them, but he never had the chance.

MEET THE NEIGHBORS

They were only days away from the farm he had left nearly a year before, and Daven could hardly stand it any longer. He couldn't sleep, eat, or think straight. Only a few more days, he told himself repeatedly. He would be home with time to spare before the spring planting would have to be done. There were barns that would need built as well as new houses. There may even be enough time to allow construction of a corral or two for the animals before the planting would demand all of his attention.

Sorram and Taurwin had even offered to help him with the farm. Of course, they didn't seem to know anything about farming, but an extra good strong back or two couldn't hurt. Of course, he wasn't sure if Jerhod would be able to help much this year. It looks like he will have more work than he can handle of his own this year. Once he has a forge set up, he would be busy repairing tools or making short swords for anyone who wanted one. Hoovar had agreed to pay for those at a cost though, but how could you complain about that.

Garnet was looking forward to returning to a real home. Living in a tent wasn't what women dreamed of evidently.

That comment forced a snicker out of Daven. This may be the best year they have had yet. Jerhod had more than a job. He had a career, and a good one at that. They had purchased plenty of fine seed and some livestock as well. Sorram and Taurwin seemed excited about learning how to farm, and Sylvy was doing well with her studies, so she had been told. Corney said she should have enough strength by the spring planting to heal the crops. She didn't know how you heal a plant, but supposedly, it "promotes a fine harvest." Sylvy had tried to explain about using spirit, water, mineral, and a touch of fire for warmth in early seasons; but it didn't make any sense to her. Garnet wasn't sure if Sylvy should be learning any magic that contained fire at her age. She had said as much to Corney, but he had assured her that Sylvy was fine. He had even gone as far as suggesting that Sylvy use her horse to ride to some of the other farms to help them as well. She had heard that Sahharras and Corney would be around to visit each farm also.

Even Lord Hoovar had made promises to visit the farms more regularly. Now that was a surprise. Not only did he promise to make regular visits, but he has also started calling everyone by their names. He almost knew everyone's names now, and if he didn't, he apologized profusely. That wasn't the only changes the man had made either. She noticed that he no longer held himself apart from everyone else when the camp was being set up or torn down. He would walk around and offer a hand to anyone who looked to be in the need of one. She didn't know what had made him start doing these things, but they were working for him. She hadn't heard anyone grumble about lords being too good to get their hands dirty in days. Some have actually started calling him lord and turning his offers down as if he really was too good for it. She thought she had even seen Sorram and Taurwin give him looks of approval occasionally. Then again, she thought she had seen them look at him as if they wanted to kill him when no one was looking, but that was probably just her imagination. The best part was that most people had quit coming to Daven with their problems. She may be able to reclaim her husband yet.

Hoovar hadn't been pleased with Sorram or Taurwin the day he rode out to interrupt their exercising to thank them. He had really intended to thank them, but somehow they had taken control of the conversation. First, they had plain flat refused to discuss why they had disregarded his summons the night before, but they had no problem reminding him that respect is earned, not demanded. Sorram had told him just that while stroking the snakehead hilt that looked over Hoovar's shoulder. Hoovar knew why Sorram had done it that way, and he hated having to be told something he already knew by a boy. It seemed that every time he was alone with them they were reminding him one thing or another. It was "the people need a strong leader," "they will need a fair ruler," or "will need a diligent protector." It never stopped with them. He was putting more effort into this lordship bullshit than he ever intended, and he was still being badgered by a couple of boys too young to need the use of a razor. He was starting to wish he had sent them away when he thought they were murderers. What made him even angrier was the fact that they were right and he knew it. At least the rest of the people were starting to come around and believe in him. Hoovar would guess that at least half of them now brought their problems and concerns to him instead of

Daven, which should make Daven and his wife deliriously happy. Some even started calling him m'lord on their own free will while others have started turning down his offers of assistance of menial chores. Garnet never refused his offer to drive their wagon for a spell though. Then again, maybe he owed her a little extra for how her husband had helped put and hold the group together.

Hoovar wasn't going to complain, at least not after this morning. This morning for the first time since he had been with the group, someone brought Hoovar his breakfast as they did for Sorram and Taurwin. He thought he might have even caught a look of surprise and approval from the boys. They still didn't exactly warm up to him, but they seemed to be a little distant to everyone—well, everyone except Sylvy and Sahharras. He knew that some of that was because of the way the domesticated animals acted around them. The animals were not as afraid of the boys as they had been when they had started their journey home, but not even Sylvy's horse would let either Sorram or Taurwin touch it. They could at least run alongside the stream of people and animals as long as they stayed a few paces away from them.

Today, they had stayed even with the Hyzer wagon and watched Sahharras and Sylvy's lessons with Corney on the bench beside him while he drove it. Hoovar wasn't sure why they were so fascinated by the lessons. Corney had told him that he didn't sense any ability in either boy. Hoovar decided it didn't matter; nothing was going to spoil his day. Things were going too well for something trivial like that to bother him. Hoovar saw Thommaus riding back from the front and decided that no matter what Thommaus said, it didn't matter. It was going to be fine.

"There is a coach approaching from the north, and it appears to be in a hurry. Should I instruct everyone to the shoulder to let it pass?" Thommaus asked as he reined in his horse.

"Is it a single coach, or does it have outriders?" Hoovar asked as he tried to look ahead to see for himself.

"I didn't see any forerunners or any sigils, but there appear to be almost a dozen armed men on horse behind it. It is hard to tell at this distance, but it will be on us soon," Thommaus explained quickly.

"Without foreriders or sigils, we have to assume it is a simple coach with the same rights to the road as we. Remind everyone to make room for it, but we are not stopping unless the coach requires aid," Hoovar ordered. There it was again, that look of approval. He didn't imagine it. Why would they think that his answer was significant? It will be fine, he told himself once again. He went back to driving the wagon, and he noticed that the boys went back to watching Corney's lessons.

Daven was at the lead of the mass of farmers and their herds when Thommaus found him and told him that they were to move everyone to one side of the road to make room for the upcoming coach. Daven was riding Sylvy's horse today as he had for the last several days, and he was beginning to enjoy riding the fine animal. It wasn't that he had never ridden before, but there was a difference between riding a plowhorse and riding this animal, which the boys had purchased for Sylvy. At first he had been rather upset about the frivolous waste of money such as this animal represented, but now he was even considering buying one for himself. He wouldn't buy an animal quite as fine as hers, but something better to ride than the team that pulled his wagon at least; after all, it wasn't as if he couldn't afford it, unlike before.

It was times like this that made him appreciate the fine animal. He would be able to make his way up and down the column with ease as he informed everyone what to do, and he would be able to hop off at any point to offer a hand. Once he dismounted and let the reins hang, the horse would stand and wait for his return. It would not move until someone picked up the reins once again. How had someone trained the animal to do that? He had no idea, but it was very useful. If he tried to do that with one of the horses that pulled his wagon, there would be no telling where the animal would wander off to while grazing. Sylvy's horse allowed him to ride up and down the milling mass of farmers and their livestock to give hand to anyone who needed it without looking for a place to tie his horse or taking the time to hobble the horse. The animal's usefulness still amazed him, and he would need it now. It was easy to inform everyone to move to the side of the road, but it was another thing to actually get everyone and their herds to thin out into a long column instead of a milling mass of animals and people. He hadn't noticed just how disorganized they were, until he had witnessed the uniformity and precision of the army as it marched. He knew it was like comparing apples and oranges—well, maybe it was more like comparing apples to . . . to . . . a pitchfork, but he still wouldn't mind at least a little less chaos.

Daven's thoughts were cut off at the sound of a rumbling coach and the crack of a whip. His head spun around to see that the coach was already upon them, and the fool driver was using his whip to try to clear his way. The driver's whip had sent some sheep clamoring to get out of the way, but not to the side of the road. He saw the family trying desperately to gain control of the flock and herd them back to the side of the road. Then he saw the father of the family as his face twisted in pain when the whip struck at the man's back. He could clearly see where the whip had cut the man's clothing to bite at his flesh. The man continued trying to herd his flock while the driver struck him repeatedly until he finally fell to the ground in a twitching and withering ball. Then the driver turned his attention to the herd and had them scattering in all directions in no time.

It was then that Daven spotted the young boy and girl still struggling to round up some of their animals while their mother screamed at them to run. He spurred the horse into flight toward the scattering flock and the oncoming coach. He reached the children before the driver did and leaped from the horse to cover the children as he pushed them to the ground. By the time he was up again, the coach had gone past to seek out new victims. Daven took only a second to check on the children before trying to get back to his horse. He mounted as fast as he could and decided after seeing the looks on one of the guards that stopped to stare him down that maybe he would leave well enough alone. The rear guard sneered at him as he stroked the hilt of his sword and then rode off with a laugh. Daven watched in disgust as the coach picked up speed and headed toward the next herd and new victims of their cruelty. He knew that what comes around goes around. He decided that it would be a pleasure to be there when the driver got his just deserts. He felt his chest tighten as he wondered where Sorram or Taurwin were. Maybe he would get his chance and decided that he didn't really want to be there when the driver met those two. He almost felt sorry for the man and felt dirty for not trying to warn him at the same time.

Bakur was a simple man with simple needs. He had left his farm with what he could carry on his back, and he was returning to it the same way. Well, all except the small chest that rode with Sorram and Taurwin's chests in the back of the Hyzers' wagon. Even with that, he refused to buy a horse or team. He just didn't need them. He would return to his small farm, plant his garden, and hunt rabbits and squirrels. Only this time he would not have to worry about having a bad year. He would be able to use his winnings to smooth out any rough times, and there should be more than ample gold to do that. He did have to admit he did like his new clothes. He hadn't wasted any money on fancy clothes, but he did treat himself to several practical outfits. He figured those clothes should last him quite some time if he took care of them. He saw Daven ride past while instructing everyone to move the herds to one side of the road. He decided he had better give a helping hand or they wouldn't get the herds moved until it was time to set camp for the night.

Bakur was helping the families that were the closest to him try to herd the livestock when he saw the coach and heard the coachman working his whip at the front of the column. What he saw made him furious. Without thinking, he set off in the direction of the coach. He didn't know what he intended to do about it, but the man would at least hear a few choice words. By the time he had reached the coach, pandemonium had broken out. There was sheep, cattle, and a few hogs scattering in every direction. He was about to shout at the driver, but he realized he had gotten too close and the driver was about to strike him with the whip next. He saw the cruel man sneer and draw his arm back to send the lash at him. Bakur turned his back to the whip and covered his face to protect his eyes, but he never felt the whip's bite. He was hesitant to look back to see what the man was waiting for, but then he heard the man grunt and curse. Bakur turned his head to see Sorram reeling in the whip and take it by the handle.

"There are others who will need your help. We will handle this," Sorram said to Bakur then he turned back toward the driver.

Bakur didn't want to be in his way, so he scrambled to remove himself from danger. He hadn't taken his first step when he heard the crack of the whip and the coach driver scream. Then the sound of the whip repeated again and again. He wasn't sure which sound was worse—the constant crack of the whip, the man's screams, or the screams of the frightened horse team. He had his answer when he heard the most bloodcurdling howl he could have imagined. That sound was enough to make one lose his mind, he thought, as he grabbed first one child and then another that had been working a nearby herd while he was trying to find somewhere else to be. He didn't know how many times he heard the crack of that whip, but it was hard for him not to wince every time he heard it sound and he prayed it wouldn't be accompanied by another howl. By the time he had the two children to the side of the road, he didn't hear the cries of the man anymore. All he could hear was the constant cracking of the whip. The lashes were coming so fast now it seemed to be more than just one whip was being used. The last sound he heard before he covered his ears was another god-awful howl. The howl was half wolf howling at the moon and something else, something much worse and more frightening than the one before. The howl was so loud that he could swear that he felt it as it vibrated through him.

*   *   *

Thommaus saw the chaos the coachman was causing from the back of his horse and spurred his horse back in the opposite direction to notify Hoovar. Hoovar would have authority to put an end to the man's foolishness. He rode as fast as he ever had even though it was but a short distance.

Thommaus hadn't been gone long before he came riding back, and Hoovar knew there must be trouble at the front of their little procession. He had seen that look of worry before, and it didn't come without reason. "What is it, Thommaus?" Hoovar asked.

"The coachman is using his whip on anything and anyone who is in reach to clear the road. I think you might want to mount up and come forward to put a stop to it," Thommaus replied.

Thommaus's news set Hoovar's blood to a boil the instant the words had left the man's lips. These were his people, and any attack on them was the same as an attack on him himself. "I wish someone would give that ass a lesson on proper manners," he grumbled without thinking. He heard Sahharras groan, but when he looked at her to see what the matter was, all he could tell was that she was horrified.

"I will be there in a minute," he said as he casually passed Corney the reins to hop off the wagon and fetch his horse that was tied to the back of the wagon.

Thommaus didn't catch everything Hoovar had mumbled, but there was no mistaking Sahharras's groan. He knew instantly what she was looking at as soon as he saw it. She was watching Taurwin, and he had quickened his pace. He didn't know why it had made her groan like that, but when he looked over at Sorram, the boy was picking up his pace as well. It wasn't as if the boy had taken off at a sprint though. He hardly looked to be running at all actually, but the boy's long graceful strides were beginning to eat up the distance. Then he saw Taurwin following a little ways behind, and he appeared to be running for all he was worth. "You had better hurry or you may be too late," Thommaus urged as he realized that the boys were speeding up the road toward the coach.

Hoovar's gaze followed Thommaus's eyes, and he cursed as soon as he saw what Thommaus was looking at. He was sure it was the same thing that had caused Sahharras to groan. He saw Sorram and Taurwin running up the road toward where the carriage was. He was sure he was going to regret his words as he remembered the old expression "Watch what you wish for" that he had learned to be true so many years ago.

"Go!" was all Hoovar said as he scrambled for his horse. By the time he was mounted and urging the horse for more speed as if someone's life deepened on it, he had lost sight of Sorram and Taurwin. He had no idea what those two were going to do, but he suspected it wasn't going to be very diplomatic. He ran his horse as fast as it could, and he knew it wasn't going to be fast enough.

Thommaus turned his horse once again as soon as he heard Hoovar's command. His horse charged after the two boys, but he still wasn't going to catch them. They would reach the coach before him with time to spare, and it dawned on him that he had no idea what he was supposed to do when he got there. He wasn't sure whether he was supposed to help the boys or stop them from . . . He didn't even know what they were planning to do in the first place. He hated chaos. There should have been a plan because without one, someone always suffered. He continued riding as he watched the events unfold, which he could not control or influence. He saw that Sorram would reach the coach first, but Taurwin wasn't far behind. It was frustrating to realize that somehow he had gotten so far behind. It appeared that Taurwin was headed straight for the teams drawing the coach while Sorram angled off to the side. Then Sorram leaped the last of the distance with unnatural speed to snag the end of the whip out of the air before it could strike an old man. He then gave a yank on the whip, which dislodged the driver from the seat of the coach, and the man tumbled on to the road. He thought Sorram must have said something to the old man and the old man made a dash for the side of the road. He couldn't hear what had been said, but the horses were dancing around nervously and raising all kinds of racket. Once the driver was pulled from his seat, the horses began to bolt straight for Taurwin. He saw Taurwin stop to raise his head in what could only be described as a howl, which stopped the horses in their flight.

Those horses were dancing around looking for somewhere else to go when he witnessed Taurwin leap an impossible distance to strike the lead horse in the head with . . . with his fist and the horse went down like a boned fish. If Thommaus didn't know any better, he would have sworn he heard the skull of the horse being crushed even at this distance. The only good to come from Taurwin's strike was the fact that the coach wasn't going anywhere now. The other horses appeared frightened out of their wits, but there was nowhere for them to go with the lead horse laid out unconscious on the road. The constant cracking of the whip and the screams of the driver drew his attention back to Sorram who was now using the whip to flog the driver. Thommaus saw the personal guards trying to make their way around the coach through the swarming mass of panicked livestock. Thommaus was close now, but he would still be too late to intervene. Thommaus thought Sorram would have to flee soon or they would cut him down, but he was wrong again.

Taurwin landed in between the guards and Sorram to intervene. Thommaus didn't see him jump there, but that had to have been what the boy had done. He must have jumped from the front of the horse teams to the other side of Sorram. How far was that? Twenty paces? That cannot be right. It wasn't possible. That didn't matter; if Taurwin could just slow the guards down, he could get there in time to lend a hand because he was closing the remaining distance quickly. He saw Taurwin raise his head and he heard another howl, but this time it seemed worse. It was so loud it hurt. His horse must have thought the same because it reared up and he had to fight to control it. He eventually lost the battle for his seat, and he was thrown to the road where he landed hard. He was still rolling on the road and trying to get to his feet when he heard Hoovar's horse whinny a little distance away. By the time he got back to his feet, he saw that his horse was headed for the tree line alongside the road and Hoovar was still trying to calm his own mount. He turned back around in time to see another runaway horse headed straight for him. He dived to the side, but he was too late. The pain that shot up from his ankle told him he wouldn't be going far until someone came for him or Sahharras healed him. The pains shooting up from his ruined ankle were nearly unbearable as he tried to crawl out of harm's way. He had to get farther away before another horse or any other livestock for that matter trampled him and left him for dead. He didn't even notice the gnarly old hands trying to pull him to his feet at first. Thommaus was grateful though when the old man Bakur and another man whose name he couldn't remember but swore he would learn it when there was time started carrying him off to safety.

Hoovar was disgusted with himself. He had taken too much time to retrieve his horse and now all he could do was ride like a mad man to arrive too late. He was catching up to Thommaus slowly, but he couldn't tell what exactly was going on up ahead. He could see glimpses through the scattering livestock but not enough to know what was going on or what had made that ungodly howl. Just thinking about the sound of it made shivers run down his spine. Then it came once again, and this time it was enough to make his bowels want to turn to water. Then his mount began to dance and buck. He witnessed Thommaus lose his mount while he struggled to control his own. Hoovar could see better now that most of the livestock had thinned out and ran off to god knows where, but what he did see didn't give him a warm fuzzy feeling by no means. He saw Thommaus knocked down and nearly trampled by a fleeing horse. It had to belong to one of the mounted personal guards with the coach who were now getting to their feet to face off with Taurwin. For the first time, Hoovar recognized the sound of the whip that Sorram was working like . . . like . . . he had never seen anything like it previously. The boy had that whip sounding as it struck the driver time after time. *Crack, crack, crack*, without any pause, it sounded. He noticed that the coachman wasn't even moving any longer. The man was a bloody mess and curled into a ball. Hoovar wasn't even sure if the man was conscious by this point. He wasn't too concerned with him though. He had never heard of someone being whipped to death in a few minutes, but the way Sorram was wielding that thing, this could be the first. There was always a first time for everything, but he was more concerned about Taurwin for now.

The boy had foolishly squared off in front of the guards as if he meant to prevent them from stopping Sorram from whipping the stupid driver to his death. The boy didn't even have any weapons in his hands. He still had the pungi sticks tucked into his belt as the closest guard drew his sword. Hoovar urged his horse forward, but the animal continued to fight him. He wondered if he could run the rest of the distance if he dismounted. It wasn't that far now, but he wanted to keep the advantage of being mounted. Two men were carrying Thommaus to safety as he rode past his longtime friend and employee.

Hoovar winced as he watched the guard prepare to thrust his blade into Taurwin's belly. Why didn't Taurwin move, get out of there, or something? He saw the guard thrust and miss his target. Hoovar was as shocked as the man holding the sword as he watched Taurwin box step to the outside of the man's thrust to catch him by the elbow with one hand while Taurwin's other hand grasped the sword hilt. Then it appeared that Taurwin took a deep step while working the man's arm like . . . like a whip. The man went rolling with such force that he knocked down several of his comrades to the ground as he rolled into them. That caused the remaining guards to pause for a brief moment before stepping toward the boy. The boy had been unarmed and had taken out nearly half of their number, and they merely paused—morons. Now, the boy had a sword. It was now that Hoovar recalled those sparring sessions with Sorram and Taurwin. Hoovar had wanted to save Taurwin from the guards, but now he decided he would have to save the guards from Taurwin.

Hoovar watched and continued to struggle to control his horse as Taurwin stepped back and drove the sword into the cobblestoned road as if it were paved with butter. That made more than one man among the guards miss his step, Hoovar noticed. Hoovar continued to force his horse forward slowly while Taurwin slowly drew his pungi sticks and stepped forward to face his adversaries. The guardsman closest to Taurwin stepped forward hesitantly as he prepared to engage Taurwin. The guard's first cut was aimed at Taurwin's head, but Taurwin easily knocked the blade up with his pungi sticks. He stepped in underneath the man's blade. Hoovar could have sworn Taurwin had placed one leg in behind the guard before he turned to give the man a devastating blow with his elbow to the midriff. The blow lifted the guard up into the air off his feet and sent him tumbling into the next closest guard. Then to Hoovar's amazement, he saw Taurwin tuck the pungi sticks back under his belt before engaging the next guardsman. There were only three men left on their feet, but some of the other men were starting to get back to their feet when the closest man lunged for Taurwin. Taurwin stepped to the outside of the man's thrust with unnatural speed. Hoovar thought one hand went to the sword hilt while the other arm, with the palm up, slid under the man's chin and lifted this man into the air. The man was then thrown forcefully to the road as Taurwin then turned his palm to the road and brought his arm down. The guard knocked the remaining standing guard down and two who were nearly to their feet. Then with the man's sword in hand, Taurwin did backward handsprings back to where he had driven the first sword into the paving stones. Hoovar couldn't tell when the boy had picked up the other sword or who it had belonged to, but he watched as Taurwin added two more swords to the first driven into the paving stones of the road. Hoovar didn't know how long it lasted, but he knew it wasn't long. The guards had decided to rush Taurwin as they got to their feet, but it hadn't been a good idea, obviously. The guards would get up and rush Taurwin and Taurwin would throw them into each other and then backflip to add a new sword or two to the collection driven into the road. Taurwin continued to pummel the guards one at a time until Taurwin was left to stand over them as they lay in fear with their swords driven into the road on the other side of their victor. There were no more guards able to get to his feet. Sahharras would have to administer to every one of them before they would be able to go on their way. Hoovar realized he was no longer moving with his mouth agape when a voice shouted from the coach.

"This is an outrage! You have attacked my men and me in broad daylight, in front of all of these witnesses no less. The overlord will hear of this, you mark my words. I will see justice done, Hoovar. You are not above the law. Despite whatever you may believe," the voice boomed.

Hoovar knew that voice and now understood why the coach driver had acted as he had. He looked at the bloody mass lying on the street and almost felt sorry for the man.

"That will be enough, Sorram. You may stop now," he said calmly, and to his surprise, the crack of the whip stopped instantly. He half expected the boy to continue, but he didn't.

"At ease," he decided to add and gave both Sorram and Taurwin a downward hand motion. He nearly laughed as they both sat down and studied him with confused looks. He had only meant for them to calm down, but this would work too. "You may come out and discuss this man-to-man if you wish, Roaran. If your father is with you, he may come out as well. If you don't wish to discuss matters, that is fine with me. I am well within the law. You should at least have a look at your men," Hoovar advised as he dismounted. He knew he hadn't broken any major law at least. He was obligated to notify the coach driver's master of any punishment of this sort prior to administration of said punishment, but only out of courtesy. Of course, he hadn't actually given any sentence against the man. It may be questionable whether Sorram and Taurwin were following his commands or not, but the bottom line was that the coachman had struck first. Yes, it was thin, but he didn't think that anything could be made of this incident.

Hoovar waited patiently as the door to the coach opened slowly and Roaran Pizolla II stepped out of the coach. He hadn't remembered the boy being so big. Roaran II was over two paces tall, well filled out, and quite muscular. Hoovar thought the boy, young man, could be considered rather handsome if it wasn't for that oversized bucket head of his, but what did he know about looks anyway. The boy's father, Lord Roaran Pizolla, on the other hand, looked the same as Hoovar remembered. He was above average height, thin framed, and had a full head of thick black hair. He too may have been considered dashing at one time or another if he could control those weasel looks or at least try to look you in the eye just occasionally. Hoovar hated trying to talk with the man. He had the feeling that Roaran looked down at him or thought little of him at least, every time he had talked to the man in the past. Hoovar had gone out of his way to pay social visits to their estates when he had first accepted lordship over the neighboring province, but he stopped after a few unpleasant encounters.

Roaran Junior strutted over to Hoovar and looked down at him. "What is the meaning of this? Why did your men attack us without cause?" he asked as his face turned redder and redder. "This is an outrage!" he spat out in a rant.

"Your man was whipping everything in sight, including women and children. He has scattered livestock from here to the end of the empire. My men were merely defending themselves, their families, and their livelihood," Hoovar answered more calmly than he felt. "It was your man who had drawn first blood, not mine," he added. He didn't believe much of that mattered legally, but it was all true somewhat anyway.

"We will not be treated this way and you should know that by now. You are not the commanding general any longer and have no right to block the road. Our man was attempting to clear the road as instructed so we may pass unhindered. We have important business in Pua Dar, and this little fit you have thrown will not stop us," Roaran Junior shouted as he poked Hoovar in the chest with his finger.

Hoovar thought he heard a low growl, and when he looked to locate its source, he saw that both Sorram and Taurwin were no longer sitting on the road. They were standing in a fighting stance if he had ever seen one while

Roaran's men were still trying to get some of their comrades to their feet. He signaled the boys to calm down with his hands, and they went down to one knee. They didn't sit on the road as they had before, but he would settle for that. Despite the fact that they still looked as if they were ready to pounce.

"I'm talking to you. Don't you ignore me, old man!" Roaran shouted as he poked at Hoovar again.

Hoovar felt the heat. It started in his chest and coursed out through his veins until he thought he would burst into flames. He took a deep cleansing breath and was shocked at all the odors that he could smell in the air. He could smell the rotten sweat coming from Roaran, distinguish two distinct musks of the boys, the smell of livestock and manure that came with them, and the coppery scent of blood. He closed his eyes, only to open them to a world that had become so brightly colored it burned his eyes and they began to water. He could hear Roaran but not make out his words. He felt the man's constant poking, and as he began to turn toward the man, he took a step back and his left hand caught Roaran by the back of the hand. He held on to Roaran's hand from thumb to pinky and began to twist as he continued to step away. Hoovar's right hand went to his sword hilt while his left turned Roaran's world upside down. Hoovar watched Roaran's face twist in pain and fear as he began to fold up and fall to the road. The look the neanderthal gave Hoovar as he looked up at the blade against his neck was priceless, however. Hoovar could hear that all-too familiar growling, but then he realized it was coming from him this time. He didn't understand what was happening to him or why, but the knowing look he got from the two boys told him that they understood. For a brief moment, he thought he felt as if he had some sort of connection with them. It was as if he could sense their thoughts and feelings in his head, but that was complete nonsense. Hoovar cleared his throat and released his hold on the arm he held twisted in an unnatural position. However, he didn't sheathe his sword. That he held out in the sun as he examined it. The snakes appeared to slither and strike out in rage toward Roaran, and he wondered if he would ever get used to that. He gave the blade a twirl and sheathed it with a flashy maneuver he didn't remember learning, practicing, or ever seeing before today. Well, at least he didn't remember it.

"I think I have heard enough from you. If I were you, I would refrain from poking me ever again. You may call me Lord Hoovar, not old man," Hoovar informed Roaran. He was surprised how calm his voice sounded. He didn't . . . but he did feel calm. He actually felt cool as winter springwater. How could that be unless he had just imagined all of it? The bright colors were gone, along with all the smells. Great, now he was definitely losing his mind. How much time had passed? Was everyone looking at him? Was he going to start rambling on like Corney?

"You shouldn't have done that, Hoovar. He is my boy after all," Lord Pizolla declared with a frown as he crossed his arms over his chest.

Hoovar had forgotten about the pompous fool until he had spoken up. "I shouldn't have to. He is your boy after all. But if you are unwilling to rein him in and call him to account for his actions, I will do what is necessary," Hoovar replied as he stared defiantly. "I suggest you see to your men and your spoiled child and be on your way. My patience wear thin." He turned his back on the fool and began to walk away.

"Don't turn your back on me. When my business is done in Pua Dar, I will deal with you. You mark my words, I will," Pizolla threatened with hostility.

Hoovar paused for a second but decided the man wasn't worth it. He did, however, stop to see what Sorram and Taurwin were doing. He decided it might not be a good idea to leave them there because they kept eyeballing the Pizollas as if they were a piece of fresh meat, and they did look hungry. He signaled them to come along and was relieved when they obeyed.

Daven had been anxious to check on his family, but there was so much to be done. Herds had scattered in every direction, and there was no telling how far they had gone. He would have to round up some of the men to organize their efforts if they wanted to gather all the animals before it became dark. His family would have to wait. Once again, what needed to be done outweighed what he desired. Well, that is how life was now, wasn't it, but it didn't turn out the way he had expected this time. By the time Daven found Thommaus to tell him what he thought needed to be done, Thommaus was already gathering men and women together to bring order out of the chaos. He found that his son was among the men and his wife was with the women. It was Hoovar's idea to use Sorram and Taurwin to herd the animals together. He had suggested that the boys could quickly run out past the fleeing animals and circle around. It was his opinion that the animals would be frightened by them as usual and would turn back around. As the boys circled around and around in tighter circles, all they would have to do is gather the frightened animals and separate those into their appropriate flocks or herds. Daven had to admit that it did actually sound logical and should work. The boys were eager to get away anyway.

Evidently, he had missed the tongue-lashing Sylvy had given them over the death of the lead horse of the coach. He wished he had been there to see it though. From what he was told, it was quite comical to see a little girl call them down. He was even happier when Hoovar's plan did actually work.

* * *

Sahharras had feared for the worst when she saw Sorram and Taurwin run off to deal with the coach driver. She wasn't worried that they could be hurt, but she had seen their justice before. She knew they meant well, but their justice was a little heavy-handed. She figured it was because of the heavy-handed punishments they received at the tower. She just knew the boys were going to kill the man, but they hadn't. The only thing they had killed was a horse, and Taurwin swore that was an accident. Of course, Sylvy still scolded him until her mother finally came and dragged her away. Sahharras believed him. He had only wanted to knock it unconscious and had overestimated the horse's resilience. What he believed would knock the horse out had accidently crushed the poor animal's skull. By the time she had waded through all the chaos to offer healing to any in the need, the horse was already dead. There was no healing death, or so she was told.

DECEPTIONS

He couldn't decide whether he had arrived in the capital city too late or not. He had come here to find Sahharras, but she was already gone. What made matters worse was the fact that he couldn't sense her "shield" any longer. The way he had woven the shield was the reason for its deterioration, but the beacon hidden in the threads was more important to him than the effectiveness of the shield itself. Of course, no one else would be able to sense it because it took a small weave of spirit, water, with a touch of fire to detect the stupid thing. At least he hoped no one had noticed any of the irregularities in the weave. Then again, if they had, he would not be free to search for her either. Someone would have been around to ask him questions about it. There were just too many things out of his control. He had to regain control or all would be lost.

The incident at the tower had been a stroke of luck as well as the sentence of death by hanging. It could have been death by beheading or burning at the stake, and he doubted if Sorram or Taurwin could have survived either of those sentences, but hanging was another story. They should have survived that without even breaking a sweat. He took care of the burial detail himself so no one would have the opportunity to notice any shallow breathing that may occur when the subjects were cut down from the gallows. Well, that and the fact that he needed to know where to go to make sure they did escape. He was surprised how well that part of his ad-libbed plan had worked out.

Even Sahharras's part of the plan had turned out relatively simple—well, until now anyway. She had been sentenced to a life of slavery, and he hastily volunteered to weave the flows for her shield personally. Actually, he had demanded the right to take a hand in her punishment since she had essentially been the one responsible for his experiments when they had gotten out of control in the first place. She was the trainer in control, he had explained. The trainer and attack dog alike are guilty if they attack the wrong target, he had told the council of the magi, and it had worked brilliantly. He had woven that signal into her shield so he would be able to find her anywhere on this hemisphere. Once he left the tower and relocated her, he was sure she would lead him right to the boys. The best part was that no one appeared to suspect anything and it was working. Then before he had even left the tower, he felt her signal weakening. It wasn't moving away. It was just deteriorating. It wasn't supposed to do that unless she tried to cut away her shield with her spirit. He hadn't taught her how to do that yet, but he couldn't think of what else it could be. Of course, he hadn't told her not to attempt to cut it away either. Actually, he hadn't told her any of his plans. Why would he have? You don't explain to the pawn why you have sacrificed it or explain to the foot soldier why he has to march forward.

He had to get out of the tower before he lost his ability to relocate her. His plan for getting himself out of the tower was a little problematic. He had been restricted to the tower for decades for speaking against the emperor, but the emperor had also ordered, "No harm shall come to Krotus due to his intimate ties to the emperor." That was his key to his freedom. The others had broken their bond with the emperor through suicide, and he would use this same tool to gain his freedom. After he was done with Sahharras's shield, he buried "the subjects of his experiments" and began to mope around the tower like a spoiled child that had his favorite toy taken away. He quit eating from the kitchens and sustained himself on that vile concoction he had invented for the boys. It had all the nourishment a body needed, but he had to admit it did taste horrible. Well, he didn't have to eat much of it. He only had to eat enough to keep from starving to death. He did want to lose weight to give the appearance that he was starving though.

Within a week, he had been summoned to the council of the magi to answer some questions to an inquiry. He failed to present himself to the consul, which forced the guards to come to his rooms to retrieve him. What they found wasn't what they had expected though. They found him hanging from the rafters in an attempted suicide. Of course, healers were able to heal his injuries easily. It had still been risky. If he had hung himself too soon, it would have been another story. He wasn't like the boys. He was still humane despite the emperor's bond. Of course, if he had waited too long, they wouldn't have taken the attempt seriously.

The result wasn't what he had hoped for, but he wasn't going to complain about his luck either. After a rather long and insufferable inquiry, he was assigned to a crew of magi to recatalog the archives in the main vault. This put him in arm's reach of some of the most valuable mystic artifacts known to man, including the Elven Book of Magic and the Dwarven Hammer of Thordain. Those fools didn't even know what they were, but Krotus knew. Then again, he had the advantage of being around when the emperor had stolen them and ordered the things locked away forever. Actually, both items were supposed to be destroyed, but no one could figure out how to accomplish the task so the emperor had to settle for locking them in the world's most secure location. It was everything Krotus could do to hide his excitement about his new assignment. He wouldn't have been able to if he only knew how to work either one of them though. Then again, if he knew how to use them, he may not have to hide his excitement.

Either one could have the solution to get him out of the tower, but he was going to have to continue as he was unless he came up with a more effective plan. By the third week, it took a group of magi to see that he ate on a regular basis. It was about then that he felt the weakening of Sahharras's beacon. He had to step it up before it was too late. Three more suicide attempts later before he finally received the assignment he had been waiting for all along. He was to accompany a recruiting party to scour the countryside for new apprentices throughout the interior of the empire. It was a bullshit assignment. The guild of the magi never recruited in this manner. No, it hadn't recruited from the interior since . . . since . . . it was a small kingdom fighting for its very survival. He had barely been a boy then. That didn't matter now. What mattered was he was sent out of the tower, and his chaperones sure had been surprised.

It had been too easy. He volunteered for the cooking detail. He had claimed to have a knack for it. It wasn't a lie, exactly. If you had lived as long as he had and spent most of those years in army camps, you learned a thing or two about cooking in the rough. There were all kinds of tricks and wild herbs to make the army rations taste better. He had also learned through his experiments with the boys about poisons and hiding them in food.

Both boys had grown rather stubborn about taking poisons toward the end. Well, he couldn't blame them though. From what he witnessed, the majority of them were rather painful even if the boys could survive the strongest doses of the most powerful poisons. He had even forced them to drink some solutions that he couldn't figure out how to use as a poison. Those had to be kept in glass and glass only. Any food would be destroyed by the solution. Hell, the one liquid he tried to mix with some food ate through the plate and the serving ware. Well, he never did understand a lick of alchemy. Those in his group must not have either because not a single one of them noticed the trace amounts of the almond-scented additive he mixed in with the dessert he had prepared for them.

None of them woke in the morning either. That left him to burial detail once again, and by the end of the day, he believed he was getting somewhat proficient with that stupid shovel. The ironic part was that he buried these morons in the same mass grave that had held his expired experiments. He was relieved to see that those experiments were not present when he started adding the corpses to the ground in the remote section of the forest. Well, it wasn't much of a forest, but it would have to do. He didn't have time to go to the north into the Simol hills so he could hide the bodies in a major forest, now did he. This little forest would have to do. He had to be on his way.

His current problem was he couldn't detect Sahharras anywhere, and when he checked with the prison, she was no longer there. Someone had actually bought her. He couldn't believe it. He had thought listing her occupation as a tower-trained herbalist was a brilliant idea. He didn't believe anyone would be crazy enough to buy her. If he had listed her as a simple herbalist, it would have been different. There is always a demand for anyone in the field of medicine whether it is midwife or just a hedge doctor. A slave owner would have snagged her up in a heartbeat, but a tower-trained herbalist should have been different. Any slave owner should have feared her shield deteriorating or her somehow escaping something he couldn't see or understand.

The good news was at least he hadn't arrived too early either. There had to be a full banner of regular army stationed at the city, complete with support archers, cavalry, and pike, in response to a series of murders and assassinations. If the rumors could be believed, nearly half of the guardsmen and magi in the city had been systematically exterminated along with the lord of the city and the general of the city guard.

If he had arrived during that little ruckus, his name might have been added to that list, if those who were responsible were whom he suspected. The death of the lord of the city and the general was a fact that he had confirmed, but the rest of it may have been an exaggeration. He couldn't confirm the number of guardsmen or magi that had been slaughtered, if there had been any at all. The boys had been trained to be assassins. They were to be the best. If they had killed any of the guards at all, it was rather sloppy work for them. Well, it wasn't as if their training had been completed. Actually, their training had hardly begun. He hadn't even started working on domesticating them yet. They were barely housebroken as far as he was concerned. Then again, that may be a little unfair. It wasn't as if they were allowed out of their cage to relieve themselves. Sahharras had finally taught them to use chamberpots, but they still soiled themselves too frequently. On the other hand, most of those mistakes were due to the fact that they were not conscious at the time. The problem was that they stank something awful when they had an accident. Every time they had the slightest mishap, his neighbors living in his wing screamed bloody murder. He was forced to order the beating of both boys more times than he could count. He knew it wasn't their fault, but he wasn't about to give in to their demands that he end his experiments because of the smell of a little feces. Those demands had planted the seeds for his current plan though.

He may not have been allowed to teach them much in way of domestication, but they did receive the most intensive weapons and combat training he had access to at the tower. He had even recruited a few specialists to teach a couple of skills. He was sure they could survive nearly any encounter short of the emperor by now. Well, a Minotaur or an elf can be very dangerous, but how likely was it that they would run into either one of those? They weren't likely to be fighting any dwarves or centaurs in the near future either. Then again, that will not matter once they reach maturity. Once they reach maturity, they would only have the emperor himself to fear on this plane, and if he wasn't mistaken, it would be the emperor who would be in fear.

None of that will matter if he didn't find them. He would have to make sure they hated the empire and therefore the emperor. He had made sure that all of their tests and tortures had been "in the name of the emperor" or "for the empire." It was always one bullshit saying or another. They had to hate it so they could fulfill their destiny.

* * *

Hoover was pleased to see that the Pizollas were finally departing. He thought he would be able to relax a little, but then he remembered the surly sergeant. He wondered if the sergeant made it to Pua Dar. He would have to remember to keep an eye on those two for a few days to make sure they didn't run off to cause any trouble. Then again, they didn't act as if they wanted to kill the Pizollas. If he didn't know better, he would have guessed that they didn't care one way or another about the Pizollas. He would just have to keep an eye on them anyway just to be sure; besides, he would hate to miss any of their antics. The show Taurwin put on defeating the guards was impressive, but when Sylvy scolded him for accidentally killing that horse, Hoovar thought he might explode. He had to walk away before he did too. It had to be the funniest scene he had witnessed in years. That was before the Pizolla guardsmen demanded Taurwin return their swords. The looks on their faces was priceless as Taurwin obliged by walking over to where the blades were driven down into the paving stones of the road. Then he effortlessly snapped every blade off in the stones and handed them over. The guardsmen stood there, mouths agape as they looked from what remained of their blades and back at Taurwin who grinned back at them in defiance. Hoovar wasn't surprised when not one guard complained about having only half of a blade returned to him.

It wasn't until the coach had been cleared of the dead lead horse and had prepared for departure before Garnet saw its passengers. It wasn't the first time she had seen some of these men. She had to find the others who had told similar stories of being evicted from their farms. Not all of them had seen the coaches' passengers because everyone had been preoccupied with more important concerns like collecting their livestock together but those who had left no doubt in her mind. Those who had evicted them off their farm and those who rode in the coach were the same.

* * *

General Basserus had no idea what had happened in Pua Dar before his arrival, and he didn't care either. This had to be the easiest post he had ever been assigned to. The crime rate was nearly nonexistent, and he was sleeping in a palace instead of a command tent. There wasn't a single thing needing his attention, and he relished it. He was staying in the palace built for the lord of the city, and he was enjoying all the comforts that came with it. The head cook was as marvelous as the palace's spacious accommodations. The city offered many benefits he was unaccustomed to as well. He had begun to wonder just how long he would be able to milk out this assignment. The problem was that there wasn't a single reason for the overlord to keep him here. He had to find some way to convince the overlord to appoint him as lord of the city. He really doubted he would be raised because he signed the orders to clean out the sewer drains. He had to find something beneficial to the city and fast. He had to be running out of time.

* * *

Daven had planned on returning to his farm and picking up where he had left off before this ride had begun. However, sometimes things don't work out the way you expect them. Hoovar had argued with him for hours about his return to his farm and had finally won him over. Hoovar wanted him to move his family farther north from their old farm so Jerhod could set up his forge in a more central location. This made sense. He knew it would be beneficial to both Jerhod and the others as well. Having a smith to fix or replace broken tools was invaluable. It was really a one-sided argument since Daven's only reason for wanting to return to his old farm was that it was his old farm.

He had given in reluctantly, but things were starting to come together finally. The new house was finished, and the barn would be done shortly. There was still time to break ground and plant at least one more field. The garden was planted, and there were some sprouts already beginning to show. There were a few potato sprouts as well. It had been a lot of grueling work, but the finish line was in sight now. Well, at least on his farm it was. He would have to help some of the others with the building of their houses next, but at least his was almost done. It wasn't as if there hadn't been problems, of course. Some of the problems were nearly comical now that he looked back on them.

The first problem they had was deciding where everyone was to go to farm. Hoovar had insisted on the Hyzer family staying in the center of the new farms. He had also insisted that all of the farms be located in clusters. This didn't go over well with anyone. Daven, along with everyone else, was used to farming in isolation. He explained to Hoovar that you had fewer disagreements with your neighbors if you didn't have any. If you wanted to make your garden a little bigger, you made it bigger. With that many families living in the same area, there was bound to be grazing disputes as well as land disputes, he had explained. Hoovar had won this argument as well, but not as easily. Hoovar had argued that it would be safer if they lived in clusters and came to each other's defense. Hoovar had insisted that it would be safer from thieves and bandits it they stayed closer together. His proposal was very similar to what Daven had already suggested, but there was a difference in what the two men considered a close proximity. Hoovar insisted on locating all the buildings in each cluster so that they could cover each other with a long bow whereas Daven had thought within eyesight would be close enough. Hoovar even pointed out that he was risking losing land that remained undeveloped. There wouldn't be enough of them to develop the entire western quadrant of the province if they stayed as close together as he was suggesting. Of course, he didn't want everyone to live on top of one another either. It had taken several days to hammer out a rough plan as to where everyone was to go.

That had only been the beginning. Then the real work had yet to begin. One of the first things that was built was

Jerhod's forge. The smith from Hoovar's manor house came to assist getting Jerhod set up and started. When he was satisfied, the man returned to his own forge, which served the majority of Hoovar's estate. That was nearly the only thing that went without some sort of hassle, and to Daven's surprise, all too often the problem involved Sorram or Taurwin. Those two had strange notions sometimes. He had figured they would be a true asset when it came time to cut timber for all the new barns and houses. Those who had invested heavily in livestock wanted their barns built first while they continued to live in the conical tents they had brought from Pua Dar. That required lumber in large quantities. Daven sent Sorram and Taurwin with axes to help some of the other men, but it wasn't long before one of the men returned to complain.

Sorram and Taurwin didn't want to cut the trees down. Not because they were lazy but because they didn't want the trees cut down at all. They insisted that it would be a crime to cut down any oak because so much wildlife depended on it for a food source. Spruce and pine were homes to wildlife as well. They said that they should only cut the trees that were already dead. You name the species of tree and they had a reason to save it. Daven had to go and get them so the other men could cut the trees down. If he didn't know better, he thought they were going to cry over it. Then he had the brilliant idea to let them clear the fields. That would give them something useful to do and they could do that without being supervised, or so he thought.

It didn't take them long before Jerhod came to ask him to prohibit Taurwin or Sorram from ever touching a hoe or shovel again. They were breaking them faster than he could repair them. Daven had never really worked with the boys before this. He had heard how hard and tireless they worked. He assumed that they would be an asset to have around, but it hadn't worked out that way. He didn't understand how they knew so little about things he took for granted. They had supposedly made those magnificent weapons of Hoovar's but would look at you dumbfounded if you suggested to fix their own shovel or hoe. They could hunt any animal and kill it but not cut down a tree. They did have to pray over every animal but still save a tree. Who ever heard of such a thing? Everything Daven tried to get the two boys to do ended in disaster for one reason or another. He was reluctant to ask them to do much more than carry something or run errands for the other men.

Then he remembered their work with the stonemasons. He didn't know exactly what they had done for the masons, but he knew it would be nice to have some cut stone for foundations for at least some of the buildings. Daven wished he had thought of this before because he hit pay dirt with this idea. They didn't break any tools, and they could cut more stone than he thought possible in a day. He thought that they might have cut enough stone already to build a couple of small icehouses. He wasn't about to stop them until he thought they had enough to make a small one for each cluster of farms. Those could be very valuable indeed. They even produced their own mortar. Daven hadn't even known it was possible to produce your own. Hell, he didn't have any idea where they cut the stone from for that matter. Nevertheless, he had planned to use mud and straw for mortar before they delivered their first wagon of mortar. Mud and straw was what everyone used—well, anyone who couldn't justify the expense of purchasing mortar, that is. Filling the gaps between stone or wood every year was going to be a thing of the past and good riddance. That would be one less thing to have to worry about every year.

* * *

Sahharras and Sylvy didn't go with the others to the farms. They stayed with Corney and Hoovar and continued their training. Sahharras hated being separated from Sorram and Taurwin once again, but they were not exactly children anymore. They didn't need her to wipe their tears away. They could take care of themselves. She still worried about what kind of trouble they may cause, but she figured Daven could handle it. He seemed competent and a fair man. Besides, she was supposed to keep Sylvy company, but Sahharras was starting to think she got a raw deal. Sylvy was a handful and so stubborn. Corney wasn't much help either. He was knowledgeable when it came to magic. He would answer any question if you could keep his mind on track long enough to get an answer, but he encouraged Sylvy to learn things Sahharras wasn't sure Sylvy was ready for. The tower would never have allowed Sylvy to practice a fraction of the weaves he had her doing. Then again, the same could be said of her own instructions. She was learning enchantments and wards she had never heard of or read about in any of the books at the tower. She had to admit there were a few she really looked forward to trying to put to use.

The thing that surprised her most about her lessons was how much she had to learn about how things were made. It seemed that all the enchantments varied on what materials were used to make the item—the size, the shape of the item, and what processes were used in the construction of the item. You used different weaves to strengthen wood then metal, and it altered slightly from metal to metal, the same as oak varied from pine or walnut. The weave would very slightly again if the wood was cured. Whether it was cured by sun or over a fire could change the results as well.

Wards were not as bad unless you were trying to use multiple wards. There was one set of flows to ward crops from varmints and another set to ward against harmful insects, but to ward against both the ward used the flows in a completely different arrangement. Evidently, it was possible to ward livestock from predators but then not even the farmer would be able to approach them when it was time to butcher. It had something to do with intent, she had been told. Of course, you didn't actually ward the living plant or animal but the area where it lived. You warded the field and not the plant itself. The same was done for the livestock, but you did heal the livestock for parasites. Then you could produce a weave to ward off parasites from the barn as well.

Then the weave for an icehouse was a simple configuration repeated throughout the structure and held in place by a simple square knot, but the proportions of the flows varied. The proportion of the wall thickness and the volume of the house's interior were the key, but the materials used and roof construction played a part as well. You had to mathematically calculate the proportionality to your weave, which you had no positive way to measure. Some of it was mathematics, but a lot of it appeared to be guesswork or at least past experience. It wasn't as if you could use one cup of water, two cups of spirit, tied to three gallons of air. It was more like one flow of water about the thickness of your pinky finger, two flows of spirit the size of your thumb braded together. Then take three flows of air half the thickness of your wrist coiled around those braded flows tightly and tied with a flow of fire in a knot that was so complicated it took her half a dozen tries to get it right. Then a precious gem would be tied to that with the simple square knot of spirit to allow it to collect all the heat energy from the icehouse. If you could master the previous knot and get the proportions of your flows correct, the rest was a walk in the park. Then if you didn't get the proportions correct, your icehouse would be no more than a cool house, or even worse, freeze anything that entered it almost instantly. All of it together though was enough to give you a throbbing headache. To make matters worse, while she was stuck studying mathematics, architecture, and metallurgy, Sylvy was riding around on her horse with a gardener for an escort helping the plants grow in the farmer's private gardens. Somehow, it just didn't seem right.

Corney had promised that they would be joining her soon though. It takes more strength than Sylvy had developed so far to cover a field. Sylvy would have to walk up and down every row of the field while applying her weave because she didn't have the strength to reach more than a few paces. Well, maybe she could go every other row, but that would still take forever. Corney said he planned to let Sylvy link with him to do a whole field at a time while she was to take care of the various livestock. That almost didn't seem fair either. She would be stuck weaving the parasites from the livestock, which she hadn't done yet, but did sound disgusting while they tended the fields. She said as much to Corney too, but he reminded her that she was the only one able to do it so it was her job. Then he told her that sometimes a field isn't very pleasant either, "depending how recently it had been fertilized if you know what I mean." She did know what he meant. His humor did help a little, but she still wasn't happy. Then again, she would get to visit with Sorram and Taurwin so maybe it would not be so bad.

* * *

Daven was tired as he had ever been. He suspected he wasn't alone judging by some of the haggard looks on the men around him. The only two who didn't look like they had been through the grinder were Sorram and Taurwin, of course. After the barns and houses in his cluster had been finished, they moved north to work on the farm buildings located there. By now, every farm had their seed planted, and everyone was concentrating on the construction of the buildings whether it was barn or house. They originally planned to have them all done before winter set in, but he wasn't sure if that was realistic now. There was just too much to be done, and fall harvest would consume all of their time too soon. The only time he stopped working was when he was asleep or he was eating.

He did stop to visit with Sylvy for a little while a couple of days ago when she had been at one of the farms he was working. However, she had already finished whatever it is she did to their vegetable gardens and was exhausted herself. She had actually fallen asleep while she was telling him all that she had been doing. Her escort scooped her up and said he would see that she got her rest. Then by the time Daven stopped working for the night, she had moved on to the next farm. Well, at least he knew Garnet would get to see her next. It didn't seem right to have one so young work until he or she collapsed from exhaustion like that. It didn't look like she was doing anything when he watched her doing it, but it must have worn her out. He had heard Sahharras scold Sylvy for doing that very thing. Using magic until you were that tired was dangerous, he had heard her lecture. Then why was she doing it? Then he realized it was the same reason they all did. It was because it needed to be done. He supposed that whatever it was she did was no worse than cleaning out a barn to fertilize a field. Well, maybe more pleasant than that, he thought as he passed out on his bedroll.

* * *

"Daven, . . . Daven, . . . Wake up, Daven," Sorram urged as he attempted to shake the man awake.

"Just leave them over there, I will butcher them in the morning," Daven replied in his slumber.

"We didn't hunt. You didn't tell us to hunt," Sorram complained as he tried to shake Daven awake again. "Quit fool'n' around, this is important," he added after a little thought.

"What? Sorram, what is going on? Why are you here? I thought you two were supposed to be cutting stones for the next farm," Daven replied once he came to his senses. He rubbed his eyes and tried to get them to focus, but it was too dark for him to make much out.

"There may be danger. We have come across tracks of men on horseback. We came to warn you. We didn't know if we should kill them or not," Sorram explained quickly.

"Men on horseback . . . Why would you want to kill them? I don't see why you would think there is any danger, they could just be traveling through. No need to worry, now let me get some sleep," Daven stammered in his stupor.

"We have met one of them before. One of the men was on the coach. You remember the big man. He is one of them, and they are not just passing through. They have been riding around. We saw the tracks. They stick to paths less traveled and game trails. I don't think they want to be discovered. They must be up to no good," Sorram explained as he continued to shake Daven's shoulder. "I didn't say I wanted to kill them. I said I didn't know if we should kill them," he added as if that would make more sense.

Daven had to think for a moment to try to understand what he was being told despite his sleep calling to him and he wanted to obey. Why couldn't those two make more sense for once? Why would Sorram care if a coachman were riding around on a horse for that matter? No, that isn't what he said. The big man from the coach was riding around with other men. Riding around and trying to stay hidden. They were sneaking around, but to do what? They must be hunting something. What would they be hunting here? They were looking for . . . prey . . . Why here? Unless the hunting . . . or the prey was easier here . . . They must be hunting easier prey.

That thought woke Daven up. What would be easier prey than a little girl with a gardener as an escort would be? "Oh shit! I need a horse," Daven declared as he bolted from his blanket. It wasn't the coachman. It was Roaran or his father, and they weren't hunting game. They were hunting trouble.

*   *   *

Hoovar was as happy as he had been the day he finally returned to his manor house. He had missed the oversized bed, but he couldn't stand being cooped up for very long. Well, there was that, and the piles of papers and the books he still had to finish. He had been gone for nearly a year, and the paperwork hadn't stopped in his absence, damn it anyway. Nor would it stop during his absence this time, but he didn't care. He was entitled to a couple of days for holiday. Besides, he wanted to see that Markus and his men started their training right away.

Once he escorted them to Thommaus, they could start straight away. Not that what Thommaus was doing was unimportant because the farmers would need their barns and houses. Nevertheless, ever since he had been told that Roaran was the one who had evicted his people in the first place, he had a sour stomach. He didn't believe for a minute that whatever this was about was over already. He didn't know when, but there would be trouble eventually.

Markus and his men were a pleasant surprise, and their timing couldn't have been better. Corney and Sahharras were preparing to depart to do their thing to the fields or whatever Corney had planned for her to do. Hoovar had been worried about letting them go by themselves, but Corney had insisted that they could handle it themselves. Now, he had an excuse to accompany them and make sure Corney didn't get Sahharras lost in the wilderness. The only thing that was afoul was the news Markus brought with him. It wasn't really news. The man had only mentioned it—well actually, Hoovar had overheard Markus talking about it to the others that had come with him. Unless Hoovar misunderstood what he overheard, the surly sergeant never made it back to Pua Dar. He had disappeared one night to never be seen again. Hoovar didn't ask what night it was because it didn't matter. Even if it was the night Sorram went after the man, that still wasn't proof. Besides, that would have been impossible. At least that is what he told himself.

* * *

If Daven had thought he was tired before, he was wrong. Now he was tired, and his backside was killing him. If he never rode a horse again, it would be too soon. After Sorram woke him up, he roused the other men from his cluster of farms. They saddled some horses to return to their homes. He had to convince Sorram and Taurwin to go north and warn those to the north while they went south to warn the rest. He told the boys to tell the others "to not let a moment go by without a bow within an arm's reach," and the boys promised that they would. Then he had to explain to them that the boys had done right by not killing the men and shouldn't unless attacked by them. It was questionable whether or not they understood that they were not allowed to kill the men unless it was in self-defense. He couldn't get them to make any promises, but he couldn't waste any more time repeating himself to them either.

* * *

Thommaus thought they were making good progress despite not having Sorram and Taurwin at their disposal like Daven and his group had, although the boys had been delivering some cut stones to his work sites and, more importantly, they had delivered an ample supply of mortar ready to mix. He didn't know where they got it, but he was more than grateful for it. The limestone was well cut, and with the mortar, the foundations on these buildings would outlast their owners and quite possibly the owner's grandchildren. There was the possibility that some of the structures themselves would out last the owners. Now, if the boys cut enough stone so they could make a few icehouses. He knew Corney would be more than happy to take care of the magic ward part. He had seen Sylvy the day before working something on the gardens. She looked tired, but damn if that wasn't the best-looking garden he had ever seen when she was done. She had told him she had all the farms done except the last cluster to the south. After she was done with them, she was to wait there and rest until Sahharras and Corney joined her. Then they would return so she and Corney could do the fields and pastures while Sahharras looked after any livestock.

The news Daven and Garnet brought from the northern settlements was disturbing, but he was sure that Daven and his wife were overreacting. Even if Sorram and Taurwin were right about one of the Pizollas being in the area, it didn't mean there was any danger. Thommaus did instruct everyone to keep their weapons close to hand before he left with Daven and Garnet to warn the last farm to the south. It was better to be safe than sorry. He had also offered to ride on without the Hyzers. That would have allowed them and their mounts some overdue rest, but there was no dissuading them from accompanying him. While Thommaus rode, he tried to calm them down and assure them that Sylvy would be safe. He also pointed out that she was hardly defenseless. He had sparred with her once or twice himself. He knew she was merciless with those pungi sticks of hers, not to mention that she was a mage apprentice. He pointed that out too, but it did no good and the tension was contagious. He found himself riding faster and faster the farther they went. He had to force himself to slow down occasionally and dismount to walk his horse. Daven and Garnet never said a word, but they would dismount and join him every time but he knew they didn't like it. He knew it was a bad practice to ride a horse too hard because once the horse was played out, you were done. You could make good time if you paced your horse and walked him a little every now and then. Then if you needed him, he would be there for you. He had seen men ride their mounts too hard to get to the battle, only to have the animal die before they arrived if they arrived at all. Those men usually didn't live long enough to learn from their mistakes.

* * *

Hoovar saw the black smoke and knew it wasn't from a cook fire. He had seen building fires before, but not on his estates. Everyone knew how dangerous fire was and handled it with care to prevent such catastrophes. Armies used fire all the time as a weapon to destroy and to frighten, but there wasn't any war here. He would know what caused the fire soon enough because it was where they were going anyway. He only hoped none of his people was hurt. He could see the worry in Sahharras's and Corney's eyes too. Well, how could he blame them? Sylvy was supposed to be there waiting for them. He didn't know who else was there, but they probably knew them as well. "If no one has any objections, we will double-time it until we arrive," Hoovar declared as he picked up his pace.

*   *   *

Thommaus wasn't sure if the Hyzers' horses would make it to the farm if they rode them any harder. However, once they saw the smoke on the horizon, he knew time was a luxury they didn't have. The people at the farm would need help controlling the fire to keep it from the other buildings or, even worse, spread to the forest. Then there would be some with injuries from fighting the fire to attend to as soon as possible. How the fire started in the first place worried him more than the existence of the fire. He had seen to the construction of those chimneys himself, and he hadn't seen anything wrong with them. It wasn't as if there would be a chimney fire from lack of cleaning already. They had just been built. However, as they rode closer, he knew it wasn't a chimney fire. He could see that every building was ablaze and there was no one fighting the fires. He couldn't see where everyone had gone, but he would know if what he suspected was true in a few minutes. If he were right, there would be hell to pay.

Hoovar had seen the bodies suspended in the air by the tall poles through his looking glass, but it wasn't the same as being there. Now he could make out their faces and he could recall their names. There wasn't a man among the corpses. Every one of them was that of a woman or a child under the age of twelve or so. He remembered watching some of those children play in the evenings on their journey. He had watched these women go through their forms as Taurwin or Sorram instructed them. He had thought their practice was foolish. Who would do such a thing to women and children? What purpose would a woman have to learn the use of a weapon? Evidently, someone out there would, and this was why those women should have been armed with swords or bows instead of sticks. He had never even seen this kind of barbaric display in all of his years in the military.

"You two cut them down and you two keep a watch for them while they do it. The rest of you are with me. Spread out a little and look for any survivors. Keep your weapons at the ready. I don't know who is responsible for this, but there maybe some of them still hanging around," Hoovar commanded as he drew his sword. He took the lead and started to circle around to the west of the burning buildings. There he saw Thommaus and the Hyzers riding in from the north.

Thommaus's heart sank as he saw the buildings he had worked on just days before set ablaze without anyone doing anything about it, and the lack of people troubled him more than the loss of the buildings. There was always a chance that some of them hid in the forest for safety, but it was unlikely. It was his job to protect these people. No, it was his job to train those who were going to protect them. None of that mattered . . . not when these people were his friends. There was Corvain's wife who made the best shepherd's pie and . . .

"Is that her?" Garnet wailed as she dismounted and ran to where a small body lay.

Hoovar saw Garnet dismount, run to something, kneel down, and begin to cry. The slight rise and fall of the ground prevented him to see what she had found, but he had heard that sound before. It was the sound of a mother who had recently lost her child. There was nothing else like it. He never was able to become accustomed to that sound. All too often, noncombatants are caught in the line of fire in war, but there was no war here. This shouldn't be happening. Whoever the criminal was responsible for this was going to pay with blood. He would see to that personally. He watched as Garnet scooped a small body up in her arms. She started running toward him as she ranted. No, she wasn't carrying the body to him but to Sahharras.

Sahharras quickly seized the elements and began to probe Sylvy for her injuries and they were many, but the worst had to be the burn that covered her right side and back. Sahharras had a hard time seeing her weaves through her tears as she administered her healing powers. She reached out for more and more of the elements to strengthen her weave until her head hurt. She wanted to cry out as the pain began to increase with the increased flows of the elements. She could feel needles of fire piercing her mind. She knew there were no real needles, but that was what they felt like to her. She couldn't control a single ounce more, but it didn't matter. There was nothing she could do to save Sylvy. It was beyond her ability and power. She couldn't hear Sylvy's heartbeat or her breaths. She tried every weave she had used before and started on the new ones Corney had tried to show her. She refused to give up until finally her legs gave way and she slumped to the ground in her exhaustion.

"I'm sorry. I can't. I don't have enough strength," Sahharras sobbed.

Hoovar became angrier as the scene before him unfolded. He gritted his teeth and fought the tears that formed in his eyes. It had been his responsibility to protect his people, and he had failed. This was his fault, and there was nothing he could do to make it right. Sylvy and the rest had died because he and his newly formed rangers were not in place in time. He should have foreseen this and acted sooner. He should . . . No, "shoulda," "woulda," and "coulda" won no battles. Now it was time to move on. It was time to seek out those who were responsible.

Thommaus couldn't watch the tragedy any longer. He turned and was about to command the men to follow him to look for any survivors when he saw Sorram and Taurwin running for all they were worth toward the scene he couldn't bear to look at any longer. They covered the distance faster than any horse could. He realized that not even their inhuman speed had helped them get there in time. He stopped to watch them as they approached. They were filthy as he had ever seen. Their clothes were damp and lathered around their necks, armpits, and between their legs. He had seen horses ridden to lather that way, but he had never seen it on a human before this. Once they got closer, he could see the salt stains from dried sweat on them as well. Their hair was wet and greasy looking as if they hadn't bathed in days, but it was the look in their eyes that frightened him. Maybe he was imagining it, but they didn't appear angry or upset. They didn't express any emotion at all. It was as if they had turned off everything inside.

Corney watched his young but skilled apprentice apply weave after weave without success. He judged that she had drawn and used every ounce of strength she could safely. He was about to tell her to stop before she hurt herself when she finally collapsed. He knelt down to comfort her, but the awful smell of unwashed bodies made him look up to see Sorram and Taurwin arrive. They looked as bad as they smelled, but they didn't look angry or sad. They looked . . . looked . . . driven.

"Give her to us," Sorram said as he and Taurwin began to remove their shirts.

"Yes, heal her, Sorram. Heal her like you did Jerhod's hands," Daven pleaded. He didn't bother to try to hide his tears. He had always thought it was unmanly to show weakness, but to outlive a child was something no parent should have to endure. There was no punishment or curse too great for this travesty. If Hoovar didn't do something about this, he would ask Sorram and Taurwin to teach him to fight. Then he would see it done himself.

Markus had been excited about his new employment, but this was more than he had bargained for. Hell, he had only been on the job barely a week and he had found himself in the middle of . . . of . . . Whatever was going on? Who would kill women and children and why? Why? There was no reason that could justify the sick, cruel . . . sick . . . There was nothing to justify what he had seen, no reason. His anger and revulsion at what he had seen was clouding his mind to the point where he couldn't think clearly. He was eager for Hoovar to lead them to who was responsible so he . . . they could dispense justice. It was to be his and his men's responsibility to see these people safe and he had already failed them. Any fear that he felt as they rode up to the slaughter was lost in a sea of anger and thirst for vengeance. He didn't even recognize any of the victims, and he was overcome with the need to see justice carried out for such heinous crimes.

Markus had followed Hoovar's commands as they searched for survivors. He was hoping to find one of the perpetrators. That was when Markus saw the woman as she located a lost loved one. He didn't know if they were survivors or recent arrivals, but he did recognize the little girl once he had gotten a good look at her. It was the little girl . . . the one whose dress was soiled. It was soiled by the sergeant when they had been traveling from Pua Dar. He had met her on the road, and he remembered her as a spirited little thing. The sparkle in her bright blue eyes had been replaced by a dull gray stare. Her dress had nearly been burned off her. He wanted to turn away to hide his tears, but he couldn't. He let his tears flow as freely as her father's were and refused to take the easy way out by turning his back on his new responsibility. Markus didn't even notice the two strange boys' arrival until they had begun to remove their shirts. The large boy was the one who had nearly killed the sergeant. They both had threatened to . . . He was stunned at what he saw. From the neck down, both boys were covered with . . . scars . . . brands . . . old wounds. *What in the . . . ?*

Thommaus had expected to see two well-muscled young men. What he did see was anything but what he expected. He was mesmerized by the countless scars that covered them from their necks down. He had seen plenty of scars on old soldiers to be able to recognize the differences from an arrow puncture wound to the slice from a blade. He could even identify the telltale signs of past floggings and whippings. To see multiple examples of these on the same person was not unheard of before, but nothing to this extent. He couldn't even begin to guess at the number of scars that adorned the skin of each boy. There were even a number of scars, which he had no idea what had caused them. It was the shape of these scars that had him mesmerized. They looked similar to some of the symbols that he had seen in Corney's books.

Corney had no idea what Sorram thought he and Taurwin could do for Sylvy. She was gone, and that was that. It was a hard lesson to accept, one that some magi struggled with all of their lives, but neither one of these two was magi. He began to wonder if it was harder for the average person to learn than for a mage. Sometimes people expected a mage to be able to heal everything, and if you failed, it was because you were not trying hard enough. Where did people get those ideas?

Then they started to remove their shirts. *What the . . . ?* He could see that they were covered with scars, but it was the scars, which appeared to be burned from the inside of their skin, that he was most curious. He recognized them for what they were. He also knew what most of them meant because they were his specialty—warding. These two had been enchanted to advance healing similar to what may be done to an army hospital to promote quicker healing. He could also make out warding against infection, disease, and as hard as he looked, he couldn't make out all of them, but none of this was possible. It was impossible to ward or enchant a living thing, not that he had ever tried. However, he had read books written by those who had. There had been exploration in warding and enchanting living tissue in hopes to eliminate illness and disease. The manuscripts claimed that both warding and enchanting living tissue caused madness or, more often, death. It was written that both were caused by the severe pain as the warding or enchanting began to change the test subjects. Corney had always wondered if the books had it wrong or if those who had conducted the experiments somehow had done it wrong. Now these two were living proof that it was possible. That raised the question of how.

Garnet held out her daughter to Sorram and begged him to save her, but he just laid out his shirt on the ground with Taurwin's. Sorram motioned her to lay her broken and burned daughter upon the shirts and she complied. Then both Sorram and Taurwin knelt over her. They were joined by Sahharras, and at first, it didn't appear that they were doing anything besides praying. Garnet decided to kneel and pray with them. She noticed that the others had followed her lead. No one spoke, and there was an eerie feeling in the air. It was just a slight chill, really, but an unnatural chill. She had noticed this happening when Sahharras had attempted to heal Sylvy but had not thought anything about it until now. She remembered having felt the same thing when Sorram had healed Jerhod's hands.

Sahharras knelt down and tried to calm herself as Sorram probed Sylvy as she had already done. There was nothing left for him to do that she hadn't already tried. "Sorram, you can't heal death," she whispered as she tried to study him. She wasn't sure what he was going to do and wondered if he knew. "She is gone," she added as she tried to comfort him with a squeeze on his shoulder.

"S-s-she's . . . n-not . . . g-g-gone s-s," Sorram stated with a lisp so strong he was hard to understand.

Sahharras knew the sound of his voice was a bad sign for things to come. When Sorram turned his head to look her in the eye, her fears were confirmed. They had gone to such measures to fit in but know everyone here would know just how different Sorram and Taurwin were. Now, they would risk revealing everything for Sylvy. She hoped they did not regret their sacrifice later when they realized they could not save her.

Hoovar had spent more time in his lifetime around magi while they were casting their spells than most people even lived. There was nothing different about the slight cool breeze from any other time when he had witnessed healing. He watched silently as if he would actually be able to see something happen this time, but he knew he was kidding himself. In all his years, he never once saw any of the actual weave or spell a mage cast. Sure, he saw the ball of fire or a wound heal itself in minutes, but he would like to see just for once what Corney saw. Maybe he would be able to understand what the crazy old mage was talking about once in a while. He heard Sahharras's statement and it was an old saying. One he had heard before, and he loathed it. The hatred began to build up in him once again. When he couldn't take kneeling there over the corpse of the "silly Sylvy who prays for the souls of animals," he started to rise so he could lead his men to dispense justice on the fiends who had done this to her.

However, when Sorram turned his head to talk to Sahharras, Hoovar had to stop and stare. The boy's face had changed. His nose was flat and broad while his chin and mouth had jutted out. The boy had the makings of a short muzzle, and to make the image complete, his canine teeth were sticking out. They were sticking out nearly as long as a man's little finger. If Hoovar wasn't mistaken, the teeth were somehow getting longer. Hoovar knelt back down to see if he had imagined it, but the boy had turned back to Sylvy. He couldn't see. Hoovar would have to circle around to the other side of Sylvy just to gawk at the boy.

Daven recognized the cool breeze for what it was and waited for Sorram to work some sort of miracle. Sahharras's words echoed in his ears as well as Sorram's reply. He wanted to scream that Sorram had to be right. She wasn't dead. His little girl was too . . . too stubborn to die, but his thoughts were interrupted as the temperature suddenly plummeted. He looked around to locate the signs of Sorram's magic and was spellbound. The buildings that were ablaze just moments ago now barely smoldered. Then even the smoke was gone. The air had become painful to breathe because of the extreme frigid temperature. He heard others begin to cough, but then their coughs were lost in the winds that stirred up. This was nothing like the healing Sorram had done for Jerhod. The winds had stirred up dust that stung his eyes, but when he looked at Sorram, the dust seemed to disappear around him. Overhead Daven heard the rumble of thunder. He looked up to see clouds forming. Then the clouds began to churn and boil. He could see the rain begin to fall, but not a single drop touched the ground. Those too seemed to disappear. The lightning struck and thunder rolled. Then it struck again and again. Then the lightning strikes started to strike time after time without pause. The noise was deafening. He started to shake and shiver. He didn't know if it was because of the frigid air and strong winds or if it was out of fear. Then he looked at Sylvy's burned body to see if it was working, and to his amazement, Sorram didn't appear to be doing anything at all. He just sat there kneeling over her body. The boy didn't move at all, not even a hair . . .

not even a hair. How the wind wasn't touching the boy . . . but Sahharras was. She was hitting him on the shoulder and shouting at him, but Daven couldn't hear a thing she said.

Markus tried to keep his mind on his job. He wasn't supposed to let himself get caught up in the events. He was a guard—no, he was a ranger, a bringer of the law. He tried to remember that as he looked around. He looked anywhere but at the little girl's corpse. He had to collect himself. Focus on protecting those that remained. The perpetrators could come back or even be watching now. He would protect these people. He swore he would. Then the air became colder than he ever thought possible. He had seen magi work their craft before, but not like this. Part of him wanted to ask if there was something wrong, but he knew better. He forced himself to focus on the forest to the west. The perpetrators could launch a quick attack from there. The sound of the building fires died down and then stopped. He turned and was dumbfounded to see that the fires had gone out completely. He began to walk over to investigate the phenomena, but before he took more than a few steps, he saw frost begin to form on the charred remains of the nearest building. Then the lightning struck. He looked to the sky, and it was as if the Fallen One and the Creator were doing battle straight overhead. Clouds rolled, boiled, and spun. It was all wrong. The lightning was striking so close he could feel his hair on his head rise and fall with it. The smell of ozone was unbelievable. He couldn't hear anything but the thunder from the constant lightning strikes now.

Garnet held her eyes shut and prayed to the Creator for a miracle. She prayed that Sorram was going to deliver that miracle. He wouldn't let Sylvy die. She knew he loved her like a sister and he wouldn't fail. She continued to pray even after the air became so cold it hurt to breathe, but the constant sound of lightning was deafening. She opened her eyes to see if her daughter was any better and was surprised to see fresh blood on her daughter's face. Garnet reached out to wipe the blood from Sylvy's pale face, but a clawed hand caught her arm. The hand didn't hurt her arm, but it held her in a firm grip and slowly pulled her hand away from the blood. She carefully looked to her side to see a creature that had to have been Taurwin only minutes ago that was shaking its disfigured head at her. She had no idea what kind of nightmare she had opened her eyes to, but when she looked at Sorram, she saw he had changed too; at least she was sure it was Sorram. His face didn't look as it had before, but the creature knelt over Sylvy as if praying.

The creature's face looked more like some sort of cat than a human's face, but where its eyes should have been, there were deep pools of blood. The blood formed tears so dark red in color they almost appeared black. The blood tears flowed freely down its cheeks to join the blood that had seeped out of its ears. Then the blood ran down its chin and past two hideous-looking teeth that stuck out of its mouth. The blood was running in a stream down to her daughter by now, but there was so little blood on her. She watched as the blood flowed, but there was never a pool of blood on her. What was he doing to her? What . . . ? Where was the blood? Then she saw that Sylvy's blue eyes were no longer clouded over. They were glassy and wet. Garnet was on the wrong side of Sylvy to see if the healing was working on the hideous burns, and when she looked back to the creatures that knelt over her daughter, they once again resembled Taurwin and

Sorram. They still looked odd, but those two would never have won any beauty contest in the first place. Nevertheless, Sorram still had two long teeth jutting from the upper lip of his mouth.

Sahharras knew Sorram was beyond her control as soon as she saw his face. He had begun to change into his other form. There were too many here not to notice, and there was no way to keep his secret now. All she could do now was watch, hope he could save Sylvy, and not hurt himself in the process. When he started drawing staggering amounts of elements into himself, she feared for him. He drew in too much and too fast. He was going to kill himself if he didn't stop soon, but he didn't. She watched as he drew more and more of the elements into himself. He started a weave she had never seen anything like before in her lessons or in any book, but he didn't release it. She didn't know what he was doing, and she became more frightened as he continued to draw on the elements. Sorram looked brighter than a midsummer sun to her by the time she decided to reach over to shake his shoulder.

"Sorram, you can't hold any more. You will hurt yourself," she exclaimed but then she realized there was something wrong with him. He was bleeding out of his ear and bleeding badly. She didn't know what he had done, but she began to pound on his shoulder as she shouted. "Sorram, stop! You'll die! Please stop!" she screamed frantically as she pounded on his shoulder to get his attention, but then without warning, he cast the weave and it went into motion. Two thick streams shot out and enveloped him and Taurwin. There it seemed to churn a little as it shot through them before it slammed into Sylvy where it stopped. Then it was over. Sorram released some of the elements that remained in him, and the air warmed. She had no idea what he had tried to do because whatever it was, it was nothing like any healing weave she had seen in any book, not even close.

Sylvy felt as if she were waking from a nightmare. She was confused and tired, so tired, but Sorram and Taurwin were both there. "Your teeth are showing," she said as she reached up to grab one tooth sticking out of Sorram's mouth. She let out a giggle as he smiled at her and shook his head.

"I'm sorry, Sorram, did it hurt you much?" she asked with a frown but didn't wait for an answer. "I didn't mean to get hurt, but he was so much stronger than me. Did I save anyone? Did anyone get away?" she continued. She could see the answers on their saddened faces. "They will go after the others. What are you going to do?" she asked and felt as if she already knew the answer.

"Weesh huntttsssss," Sorram answered Sylvy as he looked her in her eyes. Then he looked to Taurwin and commanded, "Ffffindss . . . ttthheemmssh" with a sneer he couldn't contain to which Taurwin just grunted in response before he stood and bounded for the forest. He turned his attention back to Sylvy and growled something intelligible to her.

"I am tired, but I want to go with you. You should put your teeth away. It is hard to understand you like that. You do that while I get a short nap and then we will go hunting. Yes, we will hunt . . . ," Sylvy was saying before a yawn overcame her. Her eyes lids were so heavy. She decided to close them for just a second.

Daven couldn't see what Sorram was doing or if it was working for that matter. The way the two of them were kneeling over her, you would have thought they were trying to keep some sort of secret. The lightning stopped first, but right after that, the clouds dispersed and the air warmed back up. He knew that it was done. He still didn't know whether it had worked or not. Not until he saw Sylvy reach up to take hold of Sorram's . . . tooth? What the hell? What had he missed? No, it didn't matter. Sylvy was alive and talking. That was the important thing. He heard Sorram tell Taurwin to find them, and he knew that if anyone could, it would be Taurwin. He reached out for Taurwin as he ran past, but the boy just slipped past. "Wait, I want to go with you," he called but Taurwin didn't answer or look back. The boy didn't even acknowledge him.

"Stop them, Corney," Hoovar ordered with a glare.

"Really! Are you shit'n' me!" Corney protested vehemently. "Did you see what that boy just did?"

"They have to wait. They can't go off by themselves. You have to stop them," Hoovar explained in desperation.

"I'm not going to do anything. I'm not even going to try," Corney argued as he glared back at Hoovar. "I don't think anyone is going to stop them."

Hoovar turned away from Corney to watch Sorram trot off toward the forest where he would join Taurwin in the search of the perpetrators. He noticed that there was nothing graceful in Sorram's stride now. Hoovar saw the boy stumble and stagger to the point that he thought Sorram might actually fall a couple of times. "What is wrong with him?" he asked no one in particular in his confusion.

"He must be exhausted. He will need to rest before he kills himself," Corney explained with a shake of his head. Even after all these years, Hoovar still didn't realize that working magic was no different from any other work. The harder you worked with it, the more it took out of you. More magi were lost due to exhaustion on the battlefield than any other cause. Young magi would cast and weave until they simply fell over dead.

"No, he needs to feed," Sahharras corrected, which earned her confused looks. She found herself wishing she hadn't said anything.

SACRIFICES

He had risked death by his attempted suicides without hesitation. He had poisoned his colleagues and, in doing so, made one of the most powerful institutions man has ever known—his enemy. After all he had seen and done, there was nothing left for him to fear. That was what he thought until today. The disturbance was unlike anything he had ever seen or witnessed before today. It would have taken a circle of . . . he had no idea how many it would have taken to draw the elements as he had felt. It was such a magnitude that any mage with an ounce of ability could sense that anywhere in this hemisphere. To make matters worse, he knew that it was created by no circle of magi. There were no magi willing to defy the emperor with such a bold statement. Therefore, that only left one possibility to the cause of the disturbance.

It was the emperor. It had to be Danemon. There was no other living who could even come close to wielding the amount of the elements he had sensed. Krotus had seen Danemon wield the elements firsthand and it was always impressive, but this time it was beyond impressive. This time it was downright terrifying, and he was only a few days' ride away. Krotus wanted to turn around to run away, but it was too late. If the emperor had discovered his plot and killed the boys, there would be no place he could hide where he would be safe. Especially if Danemon could wield that kind of power now, and that was the point of all this in the first place now, wasn't it. He had set all this in motion to challenge Danemon.

Actually, he had intended for the boys to challenge Danemon, but how could he expect them to stand up to that? Sure, Sorram could wield the flows, but to what extent remained to be seen. Taurwin was resistant to elemental magic, to all magic to tell the truth, but he wasn't immune to all magical effects. Krotus would never have been able to make him as strong as he was in the first place if he was immune to all magic. Then again, both of those abilities were only side effects from the infusion of another species of blood. Neither of the boys demonstrated the side effects from the human blood infusions, but they did after that last infusion. Krotus's thoughts were interrupted as he shuddered at the price he had agreed to pay to get his hands on that blood. He hoped he had time before he had to pay that balance off. That had been the riskiest, most powerful, and possibly most beneficial of the blood magic he had cast on the boys.

Danemon had declared that the key to true power was the blood magics, and Krotus figured he was right. That was why he had altered the boys as he had. Both Sorram and Taurwin had been from the heartiest of stock. Of course, if they hadn't, they wouldn't have survived any of the enchantments. He had spent years planning all of their enchantments. He had planned for too long to give up. He would have to figure out a way for Sorram and Taurwin to defeat the emperor and his blood magic . . . the emperor's blood magic . . . Something was wrong. What he had felt was elemental, not blood magic. Blood magic was based on the power harnessed from captured souls, not the elements. Maybe . . . but if it wasn't the emperor, then who or what could it have been?

*   *   *

The disturbance was so strong that the emperor could feel it even at this distance. His head turned to the southwest as his gaze was drawn to it. He seized the elements and wove a shield strong enough to protect himself from any attack. Once the shield slammed into place, he realized what he had done. Anger swelled up inside of him immediately. Half of the girl's body lay outside of his shield while he still held the other half. He looked down at his unsatisfied form and at the now dead girl. She had been so young too. The young ones were always more fun to play with and torment. He liked the way they screamed in fear and wriggled under his intentions and ministrations Not to mention how sweet and untainted their souls tasted to him. That too had slipped away and was now beyond even his reach. He still had her flesh at least. Oh, these humans didn't realize just how fortunate they were to posses such gifts. He could feast upon her corpse at his leisure later. It would take a while before it was cold. He had more important things to deal with for now.

Finding out who had the audacity to form a circle and so close to his palace would be his first priority. He knew the magi still formed circles, but not near him. Nor did they dare draw on the elements as he felt. Whoever was doing this had decided to defy his wishes. It was a blatant nose-thumbing as he had ever seen. The circle was strong enough he would have been able to feel it anywhere on this plane. It may even be stretching onto parallel planes as well, but it wasn't just anywhere. It was only leagues . . . It was in Hoovar's province.

Surely, Hoovar and Corney had nothing to do with this. They wouldn't want to displease him. They had been loyal allies since the beginning. As soon as he felt the circle wink out and the elements return to normal, he released his shield. He used a flow of air mixed with a touch of spirit and water knotted just so, and he heard the familiar tones he had designated to summon one of his retainers. He thought of covering himself but decided against it. He never did like covering himself as these humans obsessed over. He was tired of covering up what he was for these humans. One day he would let them gaze upon him in all his glory. One day they will worship him and they will throw themselves at his feet for his pleasure.

Grumman felt it the same moment Brinnel did, and they rushed to their master's chambers. As the intensity of the disturbance grew, so did their urgency. Grumman was surprised when they had reached the emperor's private chambers before being summoned. He could feel his master drawing on the elements and wondered what was going on. He could tell by the look on Brinnel's face that his equal was worried as well. He let out a sigh of relief once the disturbance finally subsided. It was followed by the familiar tones of their master that signaled for their summons. It would be good that both of them were here for this, he thought. Normally, only one of them was required to be on hand to respond, but fortune had shone on him at both being nearby today. He wouldn't have to take all the blame at not knowing who was responsible for this outrage.

"You have summoned, Master," Grumman said as he knelt before the nude emperor. He could see the grotesque remains of a sacrifice lying on the floor, and he understood the delay. His master must have been entertaining himself before feeding when the disturbance began, but the shield he had woven had spoiled his sport. He knew the girl had gotten off easy. He had been in attendance outside that door to hear the torment of his master's sacrifices more times than he cared to count. Too often, the screams would last for hours.

"First you will explain that to me," the emperor demanded as he pointed to where the disturbance was only moments before. He had no difficulty pointing to it. The residues of a link that strong would be felt for years to come. They would fade over time as all residues do, but he would still be able to sense it for years. It would serve as a reminder of their disobedience for years. Such ingratitude after all he has done for them. His rage boiled until he had difficulty focusing his thoughts.

"I have not granted anyone permission to form a circle. Perhaps Brinnel has," Grumman answered to cast suspicion and any unwarranted anger in his counterpart's direction.

"No, Master. I have not," Brinnel declared immediately in his defense. "I will send out envoys to have the matter investigated immediately and order the arrest of anyone involved if it pleases m'lord," he added hastily as he bowed deeper. He knew what Grumman was doing, and he wasn't about to take the fall for this.

"I will be pleased when you present the perpetrators before me. I want them found and brought before me. I don't care who they are or why they thought it necessary to link, but I will make an example out of them so no one will ever think about linking again," Danemon declared as he struggled to control himself. He closed his eyes and took deep breaths to calm himself. If he changed forms now, these two would be scared witless and be of no use to him whatsoever. Sure, he would have enjoyed that immensely, but he needed them to . . . No, he didn't need them . . . He didn't need anyone. He wanted them to find his enemies for him. He would save his strength. Not that he needed to save his strength. He could have handled the circle he felt by himself, but there was no reason to risk getting hurt or wasting good souls when you could send someone in your place. Yes, send someone else to battle for him. Especially since good, powerful souls were a commodity. It is done that way. He would wait until the traitors were brought before him. Then he would strike them down and devour them. He could hardly wait to harvest them. Magi never tasted that good, but what strength their souls possessed.

"Bring me another sacrifice. This one has expired prematurely," he added as he signaled their dismissal.

"Two in one day, m'lord?" Grumman protested.

"Unless you would like to take her place?" replied the emperor.

"Oh no, m'lord, it's just that there are only so many and you are on a schedule. If you took two today, you will be short one later," Grumman pointed out. If the people only knew what happened in this room, there would be a revolt like never seen before; and the more the sacrifices, the harder it was to keep the dirty little secret. "If m'lord wishes, I could see if an extra can be harvested in a day or——"

The emperor raged at the man's stupidity. Thought he could deny him. He shoved a strand of air into Grumman's mouth to cut him off midsentence. "I think you just volunteered to be today's sacrifice. If you please me well, I may allow you to live to see another day," the emperor teased as he sauntered over to where Grumman was kneeling with his jaws spread open by the wad of air. He could see a tear form and run down the man's cheek. He realized this could be more fun than he had ever imagined. He had enjoyed the sport of male sacrifices before, but never one that knew what that entailed. He could smell Grumman's fears permeate the room, and it excited him. He looked down to see that his form had responded to the stimuli, and he smiled a toothy smile, which caused Grumman to whimper.

"If that will be all, m'lord, I have much to be about. You will want the search for the traitors to start as soon as possible, and I will see that the sacrifices you require are found and kept on hand in case such an emergency arises again," Brinnel offered nervously.

"I think you should watch and learn what happens to those who displease me. You may even learn how to redeem yourself if you find yourself in the same situation," replied the emperor as he licked his lips in anticipation.

*   *   *

"What the hell happened back there? Pruitt, I am talking to you. I thought you were an experienced battle mage. How could you freeze up like that?" Roaran yelled as he poked a finger at his chest. It wasn't as if it had been a complicated plan. All his men had to do was ride in and kill a bunch of useless farmers. They had even scouted all the farms and picked that one to start with because there were so few men there. There were only a handful of women and children at the farm, and he had twenty men and an experienced battle mage at his command. It should have been simple. The last thing he expected was casualties. He had lost three men, and the rest had required healing.

"I didn't freeze up. I keep telling you, but you won't listen. I held back for a reason. Wherever magic is used, it leaves a residue. The plan was to make it look like thieves, not start a war. Corney will feel the residue, and he will know it wasn't thieves who had attacked the farm. Your men should have—" Pruitt stopped midsentence to look back to the east toward the farm and stared. He felt someone else wielding magic now. Someone more powerful than he had ever dreamed of was drawing on the elements as he hadn't seen since his days with the northern army. He could see the clouds forming and feel the wind begin to blow as it rushed to fill the void created by whoever was drawing in the elements. The temperature dropped, even at this distance. They would have to leave immediately. There would be no camping here for the night. They were too close to that . . . that . . . What in the hell was going on over there? Would there be any place safe from it? He knew of only one person able to draw on that much, and that meant there would be no place safe for them in the empire.

"We got to go. We have to leave now. Pack up your things—no, there's no time for that, just leave it. Order everyone to their horses and let us be on our way," Pruitt declared in panic.

"What? If there is going to be a storm, we might as well sleep under a tent tonight. What is wrong with you? You look as if you have seen a ghost or something," Roaran scolded with irritation. He studied Pruitt and then the storm clouds in the distance. Then the lightning began, and it seemed as if the lightning didn't stop for some time. It wasn't one lightning and then another but some sort of unnatural lightning without end. When it was finally over, he felt a chill in the air and asked, "What was that?" to which he didn't get any answer. "Can you place a spell on camp to protect us if that lightning comes this way?" he asked.

The mage had lost his mind. He just kept staring in the direction of the storm. "That's strange. It seems to be over. I guess there is no need to worry about it now. We will camp here and hit another farm tomorrow," he declared as he sat down on a log and drew his sword so he could sharpen it.

"You fool! There will be no tomorrow for us! I told both you and your father the risks and now we will pay the price for your ignorance and greed!" Pruitt ranted as he continued to panic. He knew he was as much to blame, but there was no turning back now. There was so much wealth to gain that he let it cloud his judgment, and he knew it. There was nothing to do about it now but beg forgiveness when he came for them.

"What are you ranting about?" Roaran asked as his men started to gather to hear what had the mage ranting. "You men should be about your business. He is only shaken up because of the strange weather. You know how magi can be," he added, but the men didn't move. They were waiting to see what dangers lay ahead.

"*Who*, not *what*. I am talking about the emperor. He is here or there rather," Pruitt replied as he pointed in the direction of the ruined farm. "I told you how important it was to not get caught, but you continue to act like a fool. One thing for sure though, it is the last time you will disregard my advice," he assured Roaran with a mad laugh.

Roaran was back on his feet now, and his face was blood red with rage. "You are mad. The emperor doesn't visit farms in the countryside. He stays locked away in his fortress. No one is allowed to see him unless you have been summoned and then very few ever talk about it. You are the fool if you ask me. You jump at shadows and tremble at myth. You were even afraid of a little girl. I name you a coward," he spit out as he poked Pruitt in the chest. He wasn't afraid of any mage. Magi breathed, bled, and therefore died just as any man did.

"You still don't listen. I told you there is a special relationship between the emperor, Hoovar, and Corney. They know each other, have fought together from the beginning. The emperor is the one who appointed Hoovar lord over the central province after Bordeaux's mysterious death. It was rumored the emperor himself killed Bordeaux to clear the way for Hoovar's retirement. You just don't get it. The emperor does as he pleases. He comes and goes when and where he wants. He doesn't need to travel with guardsmen because he is death incarnate. He is the most deadly living thing known to man. He has killed more men than you may meet in your lifetime. He has lived hundreds of years, and it is rumored he is immortal. He doesn't travel by coach or by road for that matter because he doesn't need to. I don't know how he does it, but it is written how he fought in battles hundreds of leagues apart in the same day. I told you and your father that he may not let you have Lord Hoovar's land and nothing you do would change it. Nevertheless, you put your faith in the overlord. You had to listen to that moron, and I was foolish enough to listen to you. Now, we have essentially murdered Lord Hoovar's people and in one single act declared war with him. In response, Hoovar has obviously called on his old comrade and ally for assistance. Now, we will feel the emperor's wrath," Pruitt continued to rant in reply. He didn't back away from the arrogant fool, but he didn't dare seize the elements to prepare a weave either. The emperor may be able to sense the smallest weave at this distance.

"I have heard all of that before. His abilities are overrated. You know how the histories are distorted by those who write them. Besides, what makes you think the emperor gives a rat's ass about Hoovar now. The man has been retired for years. There are better younger generals leading the imperial army now," Roaran said in a lame effort to calm the mercenaries who were looking at him as if he was a rancid piece of meat.

"What? Are you blind and stupid? It was plainly visible from here. If you didn't see it, you could hear it, could you not? Are you deaf, blind, and dumb? If so, that would explain a few things," Pruitt screamed in his panic.

"You tread on thin ice, old man. All I saw was a storm. I have seen you form storm clouds to water the fields during a drought. Corney could have done that little storm easily enough. There is no proof of the emperor's involvement," Roaran replied as his knuckles turned white from the grip on his sword hilt. "Besides, there is no proof that we were involved in what happened on that farm. We are in our province now. We have been doing a little hunting. That is all. We know nothing and deny any charges directed at us. That is why we left none alive or have you forgotten. There are no witnesses. Father and I have planned it all out despite your nonstop whining," Roaran argued and was rewarded with looks of approval from the mercenaries.

"That wasn't a storm, moron. That was just the effects of someone drawing on the elements hard and fast. Corney couldn't draw a fraction of that. Corney and I linked together couldn't draw but a fraction of that. It would take a circle of at least . . . To be honest, I have no idea how many it would have taken to cause what we witnessed. I haven't seen anything that strong ever before in my entire life. I have only read stories that compare, and all the texts refer to the same man doing it. That is why circles are forbidden. The guild of the magi doesn't even teach how to link to form circles anymore. Even teaching how to do it is forbidden because if enough magi link, they could be a danger to the emperor. That is how I know he is here, and as for your lack of witnesses, who says the emperor needs one? Huh? He doesn't. We are guilty because we are the only people here. We could have blamed it on thieves we had trouble with and were trying to track down except for the fact that you ordered me to strike down the little girl. There may be others traveling through the area, but the odds of a group traveling with a mage on retainer are pretty damn slim. Don't you think?" Pruitt explained as he went over to the log Roaran had been sitting on previously and plopped himself down.

"There is no need to pack up to try and run. If I am correct, there is no place safe for us. If I am wrong, there is nothing to fear. Pray that I am wrong, or none of us will see home again," he added as he accepted his fate.

Roaran had ordered Pruitt to kill the girl, but he had no choice. The mercenaries had ridden in blades drawn per plan, but little balls of flame sprouted everywhere and nearly ruined the whole thing. The horses reared and threw nearly half of the men from the saddle before he even knew what was happening. Then the peasants began beating his men something fierce with sticks, of all things. The three men he did lose were run through with pitchforks so many times their clothes could have passed for cheesecloth. Those women were ferocious, and the children were nearly as bad. Pruitt had ordered the mercenaries to strike the girl down, but they didn't recognize her as a threat. They had no idea where the small flames were coming from.

Then the flames became less in number, but instead of simple lights frightening the horses, they were actually hot. They had been so hot that he had been burned bad enough to receive blisters in several places. It was like being stung by angry hornets while trying to fight. Roaran hadn't considered the possibility of Corney having an apprentice, let alone the possibility of the apprentice actually being at the farm they attacked. Then the girl wasn't as easily cut down as he thought she would be once he understood who was wielding the little flames. She was quick and nimble as a cat, not to mention that every time you came to close her, she would burn you something fierce with those little balls of fire. More than one man had been burned in places that . . . that . . . were just not proper for a little girl. Who had taught her that little trick?

Meanwhile, Pruitt just sat his horse, yelling, "Kill the girl!" Finally, Roaran resorted to ordering Pruitt to kill her, and even then the mage took his sweet time about it. Once the apprentice had been dealt with, the rest were easy to cut down—well, easier anyway. Very few had actually surrendered, and most of those were children. In his rage over being burned in unmentionable places and losing his men, of course, he had ordered the captives to be put on pikes and left to die a slow, painful death.

"The overlord told us that the emperor never leaves his fortress anymore and he is only granted an audience in person once a year. Any other communication goes through one of the emperor's two lackeys. I don't think the man would have lied about it. He had as much at risk as the rest of us if caught and less to gain, I might add. All of your scripts and books are of ancient history. The overlord has the most accurate information on the emperor's current habits. Now, I'm not going to act as if I know what the story is with that storm, but I am positive it had nothing to do with the emperor. We have nothing to worry about, but if it makes you feel better, tomorrow we will actually do a little hunting. We can even wait a few days before we hit the next farm," Roaran conceded reluctantly.

* * *

Hoovar had counted off two men to escort Sahharras, Garnet, and Sylvy to the next farm while he led the rest of his men into the forest to catch the vile criminals. No one spoke as the group departed. Thommaus and Daven had volunteered to track the men as long as the daylight held, but there was no need for tracking. The boys left a trail a blind man could follow. There were deep gouges cut into the trees to mark their passing. The group hadn't ridden far before they came across what was left of a small deer. Its hind legs had been torn off, and most of the meat along the back straps had been eaten down to the bone. There was blood that was still dripping from what remained of the carcass That left no doubt that it was a fresh kill. The boys had been here, with Sahharras's words "he needs to feed" hanging heavy on their minds. They continued on their way without comment. They came upon the remains of a second deer within an hour of the first. This time, there was barely enough left of the carcass to identify the remains as a deer at all. Still no one commented about it.

It was nearly dark before Hoovar decided to stop for the night. They had come to a small clearing with a spring to the side, and two rear quarters of larger deer were hanging from a limb in the trees. It was as if the boys had picked out the site for them and was saying "camp here." Their horses had been ridden hard before they had arrived at the farm, but now they were played out. If he didn't stop soon, one of them was bound to stumble and come up lame. No one said a word while camp was being set up, but once the men began to gather around the fire while the venison roasted, the silence was finally broken.

"You know I don't often ask questions. I haven't questioned you two about much before, but damn it. What the hell? What in the hell did we witness? What the hell are we following? Why are we following for that matter?" Thommaus questioned with frustration and could tell by the nervous looks on Markus and the rest of the men that he wasn't the only one who wanted some answers. Those carcasses left on the trail were not eaten by a human, but he was not about to bring that up. He was sure no one wanted to discuss those any more than he did.

Hoovar didn't have the answers. He had some ideas, but he didn't know for sure how to answer nearly any of those questions. He did know the answer to one of the questions and so he answered it. "The reason we are following Sorram and Taurwin is to see that justice is served to those who have broken the law. It is our responsibility to uphold the law. I have explained it to both of those boys, and I hope they remember what I told them. They cannot act on their own or they will be breaking the law," Hoovar tried to explain. He did not want to look at Daven because he knew how the man would feel. Nevertheless, he had to do it. He had to let Daven know that he would uphold the law. He wouldn't stand for vigilantism. That way led to anarchy.

"Damn it, Hoovar, those boys will tear the bastards to shreds, and I for one don't blame them. You know how they feel about Sylvy. Let them have at it. Whoever put those women and children on the pikes deserve whatever they get and probably worse if you ask me. Not once did we do anything like that, and that was during war. I have seen you sentence men to the gallows, ordered men to the cross, and even turned them over to the questioners for less barbaric acts than that. I don't see it any different," Thommaus protested as he stared into the fire. He couldn't force himself to make eye contact with his longtime mentor. He wasn't used to talking to his friend and boss like that, and it was a new and uncomfortable experience. He couldn't force himself to meet Hoovar's eyes, but he could look at Daven where he found support and approval.

"Damn it, Thommaus, do you think I don't feel the same way? But sometimes you have to do what no one wants to do. If I have to declare those boys criminal, I will. It is my duty," Hoovar declared in disgust. Although he couldn't decide what disgusted him more—the fact that he may have to declare them criminal or the fact that they would dispense the justice that he desire to do personally. He took a few breaths in an attempt to calm himself and clear his mind before he continued.

"I can't even decide if it makes any difference what I do. Corney, what in the hell did we witness at the farm? You must know. I haven't seen you this quiet in decades. What thoughts are rolling around in your skull that has kept you from rambling all the way here?" Hoovar inquired not only because he wanted to know but it was equally important to change the subject.

"I am not sure yet . . . I do have a couple of ideas though," Corney answered as he stared at what appeared nothing to everyone else. It was the carcasses that had him worried the most. It was obvious that those two were not human, but that didn't tell him what they were either.

"Well, out with it, man. If you were waiting for the right moment to enlighten me, now would be good as any. You couldn't possibly confuse me any more than I am already," Hoovar told his old friend.

"Well, I'm not even sure where to start. Well, I guess I will just tell you what I noticed. Then I will proceed to what it could mean or what I suspect it means. No, I should start with explaining to the newcomers what some of this knowledge could mean," Corney said as he looked at Markus and the new men before he continued.

"Shit, it does involve him, doesn't it?" Hoovar spat as he shook his head. He could remember how much it took to feed Danemon. He was like the boys in his insatiable appetites. The worst part was how "fresh" he liked to eat his meat.

"Not sure, but it does appear that way. I'm just not sure how it can be possible. I don't think they could be his offspring. That would be . . . improbable," Corney replied carefully. "I don't think he would be able to find a mate suitable for his needs on this plane, and his species isn't naturally transplaner," he explained what he felt was obvious. He was confident Danemon would be reluctant to bring any of his own kind to this plane as well. The monster wouldn't risk the possibility of having to share rule with an equal.

"Who?" Markus asked in his befuddlement.

"The emperor. I wish you would pay attention," Corney snapped.

"What? Why would the emperor burn a farm and kill a few farmers? That makes no sense," Markus said in his confusion.

"Because that is something he would enjoy, but that isn't what we are talking about," Hoovar explained. Danemon was a true monster who enjoyed that sort of sport. It was one of the things that made him such an effective weapon.

"Just listen for a moment while I think this over. First Sorram can wield magic and maybe Taurwin, but the ability can't be felt by other magi. The same can be said of the emperor, but that doesn't make them of the same blood. Sorram and Taurwin can change forms, but to what, I don't know for sure. I don't think we saw their full transformation, but I did see claws on both, not to mention what appeared to be the beginning of snouts. That would explain their hideous teeth. Remember, the emperor always had the hardest time getting his teeth to look human. It took him decades to perfect his human form. They may be too young to control their forms as well as the emperor can, or they have not been infused with enough human blood to stabilize their transformation. If they are not like the emperor, I don't know what else they could be," Corney explained until he stopped to stare off in thought.

The fact that they were not human was probably the explanation to why it was possible to ward them without killing them. If they were a hardy creature like a dragon, they could heal themselves while the ward changed their makeup. If the pain didn't drive them mad, they survived. It was brilliant but also sick and cruel, if the texts he had read were even remotely accurate. What he didn't understand is why anyone would want to try to ward them if they were something like a dragon. That alone would make them dangerous beyond most people's imagination. The only purpose he could think of was that you could. It would be the only way to conduct successful warding of live tissue. It made him wonder who could be that cruel.

"Change forms? What are you saying? How can they change forms?" Markus asked without waiting for the answers. "Don't answer me. I'm not sure if I want to know the answers. Maybe I . . . we should be on our way. We don't have to be part of this," he added as he stood up. He had no idea where he would go, but right at that moment, he felt as if anywhere else had to be better. He didn't sign up to fight monsters, things that could change shapes, or whatever these crazy men were talking about now.

"I'm afraid it is too late for you to turn back now," Hoovar told him. "You might as well sit down and listen to a story. A long time ago, a group of magi was convinced to capture a young dragon. The plan was to use it to fight and defeat their enemies. Then they used elemental magic to infuse human blood into the dragon so the dragon could change forms and appear human. It was the closest thing to true blood magic the human race had ever attempted. That young dragon became older, and as he matured, so did his abilities. This very powerful individual slew their enemies and became a very powerful individual. Now he is known as the emperor," Hoovar told them. That was relatively accurate to how it went anyway. He couldn't see the point of dragging out the story with all the details.

"Yeah, that's pretty funny. You had us all going there for a minute," one of the men said as he laughed. "I will have to remember that one. That is definitely a bedtime story to scare the bejeebees out of a little rascal," he added nervously.

"He wasn't joking," Markus corrected with a shake of his head.

"There is no such thing as a dragon," the man protested.

"You are correct, at least not on this plane of existence. That doesn't mean they don't exist on other planes though. The knowledge of other planes was taught to humankind by the elves in the beginning of what we would consider modern histories. When the dragon was brought to this plane, the elven and dwarven kingdoms brought to this plane of what became known as the devourers, very resilient creatures. The elven and dwarven nations had brought the beasts here to this plane to train and use as guardians. Only later did they learn that they couldn't control them, which was a bad thing to learn when the creature was nearly impossible to kill. Anyway, the reason they couldn't control them had something to do with the lunar cycle, which drove the creatures mad. Can you imagine being driven mad by the moon? I can think—" Corney was saying before he was interrupted.

"Anyway, that isn't what is important. What is important is the fact that the emperor isn't human. What is important is the fact that Sorram and Taurwin have enough in common with the emperor that I believe they may not be human either, but . . . but . . . I'm not so sure whether or not they are young dragons like the emperor or something else altogether," Hoovar told them as he ran his fingers nervously through his thinning hair. "There are very few left alive who know the truth about the emperor, and you will live longer if you can keep it a secret that you now know as well," he warned Markus and the rest of the men.

"I don't understand, you are supposed to be personal friends with the emperor. You have fought . . . ," Markus began but paused as the pieces began to fit together for him. "You . . . you were the ones. You were there. You were part of bringing him here in the first place, weren't you? That is how your name is throughout the histories. You are the great general because you have lived . . . how many lifetimes. That is why you were given lordship because you kept his secrets, not because of your service," Markus mumbled to himself as much as for anyone else's benefit.

"Yes and no. Yes, the great general was me, but I was made lord of the central province to keep me close. Not because of any secret I held over him," Hoovar corrected.

It wasn't the whole truth, but it would suffice. He was too old for all this crap. He had wanted to retire, get some rest. "Corney, what was that spell Sorram used?" Hoovar asked to redirect the conversation.

"I am not positive, but it was awful similar to the one you, Krotus, and I had witnessed so many years ago," Corney answered cryptically. Then he picked up a stick and began to scratch in the dirt with it. Actually, the flows Sorram used were nearly identical except the fact that they ended in Sylvy. The flows they had used with the emperor weaved through all of them. That was how they received the gift or curse of immortality from Danemon. Danemon received the ability to appear human in exchange. By that reasoning, Sylvy should have received attributes from the boys but returned nothing to them. The problem with that reasoning was the fact that any weave of the flows if altered even slightly could have completely different effects. Hell, there was one detonation weave, which was nearly undistinguishable from one of the most effective healing weaves known. That was why that particular healing weave was never taught to any but the most experienced and skilled healer.

Hoovar knew only one spell that would be of any significance that all three of them had witnessed. It would be the one spell that had changed them, their fates, and the lives of countless others until the end of time. "Blood magic then? Nevertheless, why did he draw on the elements as he did? Then again, how he knew how to do any of it in the first place is what I want to know. It has been forbidden for . . . before we——" Hoovar stopped himself before he said more than he intended. It wasn't true blood magic because technically it used the elements. However, its effects were all the same. He knew and understood why this assimilated blood magic had been forbidden since the beginning of time itself. Generations have paid the price for their dabbling in blood magic use and were still paying the price to this day.

Daven had remained quiet and listened to their conversation. He had come along to see justice done or at least try to keep anyone from interfering with Sorram and Taurwin while they dispensed it. He had no idea how to go about it or how to help those two. However, the more they talked the more, he thought about what he knew about those two strange boys. There was no denying the fact that they were different, but not human. Could they be that different? How could they be monsters and yet be so good to his family? He doubted if there was anything Sorram and Taurwin would hesitate doing if it would help Sylvy. They had healed her with this blood magic, and he couldn't understand why such healing should be banned. Once again, he felt as if he was out of his depth. How was a simple farmer supposed to understand events such as these?

"If blood magic can be used for healing, why is it completely banned?" he asked and wondered if he would be able to understand the answer.

"It is called blood magic, but that isn't a very accurate description. Blood magic's true source of power is in the soul. Sorram didn't heal Sylvy with magic. He passed on part of his and Taurwin's soul to her. They have infected her with their blood and soul. They must have a natural ability to heal themselves, and that was what healed her. Her healing had nothing to do with the spell itself. The ability to heal oneself at will is a great gift indeed, but there is no telling what other attributes she may have gotten as well. She will live. However, she will not be the same, and there is no way to tell how this will affect her," Corney explained with regret. "I am sorry, Daven. There are some—" Corney started to say.

"That is enough, Corney," Hoovar interrupted. "We don't know for sure if there will be any side effects. Look how long we have survived," he added and realized he had said too much.

"He needs to know. He will have to watch for signs," Corney argued vehemently.

"Need to know what? What should I watch for?" Daven demanded. He was alarmed now.

"Madness. There have been those who went mad after—" Corney tried to answer.

"Stop it, Corney. You said yourself that you didn't recognize the spell. We don't know for sure what even happened. We don't know if those others went mad from the spell or from other influences," Hoovar scolded. There was no reason to torture the man. "I am sure your daughter will be fine. She just may be a little different," Hoovar tried to reassure the Daven; after all, the man looked like he was about to go mad.

"Different, different how?" Daven demanded to know. He was on his feet and scared.

"I don't know exactly. You know those boys better than we do. I know they don't appear to require sleep. She may not sleep anymore or just require very little of it. I have seen Sorram run, and she may be able to run as fast as him now. On the other hand, she may be as strong as any man because Taurwin is so strong. It could be both or neither. It could be a little of both or a lot, but one thing. One thing I think I can be sure of is her strength in magic has just increased. If she got anything from Sorram at all, that will increase. By the time she reaches womanhood, she will be stronger than me or any other human. I am sure of that," Corney explained.

"Well, that doesn't sound too bad. What are you not telling me?" Daven probed further.

"She may receive any or all of their traits or nearly none as far as we know, but not every trait you get is beneficial. For example, both Sorram and Taurwin appear coldhearted at times. They had told that sergeant of the city guard that he needed to be put down like a rabid dog. Then despite my interference, the man never made it back to the city. I don't know how he managed it, but I believe Sorram killed him. The boy didn't show any remorse over it either. I had actually believed that he had failed to accomplish his task, but I think I was wrong," Hoovar answered reluctantly.

"That isn't all of it, damn it. In the past when humans first discovered the power of blood magic, they experimented with it a lot. Some of the participants couldn't handle their new attributes. Some committed suicide while others went on murderous rampages," Corney admitted as he stared at Hoovar in defiance.

"What? Murderous rampages . . . You can't be serious. I hardly doubt Sylvy is going to go on a murderous rampage, and to think that you actually had me worried," Daven replied with a smile. The whole idea was laughable, but the looks Corney and Hoovar gave him told him that they were serious. "But that don't make sense. Why would she do that?" he protested.

"She should be fine," Hoovar said again, but he couldn't even convince himself.

"Why didn't you say something before? I left her with her mother and Sahharras. Now, you tell me she could be turning into some sort of monster. Are you shit'n' me?" Daven shouted with outrage.

"Calm down, Daven. It isn't as if it happens overnight. The others took decades before they went mad, and I only know of two of them who murdered anyone as a similar application of the magic. Most of the people who had difficulty adjusting to their new lives just took their own life, but only after decades of struggling with their new attributes," Hoovar informed him. "Sorram and Taurwin may not realize what they have done, but they did save her life. This is no different from any other aspect of life, Daven. With every good thing, there is always a price to pay. You take the good and hope you don't regret paying the price later," Hoovar told him.

"There is just no—" he began but cut off midsentence. There was no mistaking what he heard, and he knew everyone else had heard it as well. He heard the scream of a man off in the distance. He knew Sorram and Taurwin had caught up with their prey. The others had heard it as well. They all stood and watched the forest as if their worst nightmares had come true. More screams followed the first and then they didn't stop.

"What do you plan on doing with them?" Thommaus asked Hoovar as he nodded into the darkness where Sorram and Taurwin were evidently dispensing their idea of justice.

"I don't know what I can do. If they were like the emperor, even as a young dragon, it would take a small army to arrest them. If they were somehow related to the emperor, I wouldn't have the authority. The only thing I do know at this point is that I am going to eat my share of the venison whether it is done or not. Then I am going to try to get some sleep. It will most likely be a long day in the saddle tomorrow," Hoovar answered as he got up and cut a chunk of venison off the roast over the fire. He was glad the others followed his lead. Then again, who could talk while the screams continued?

* * *

Sahharras was worried, but she tried to hide it as best as she could from Garnet. She doubted if her act was very convincing. She tried to comfort Garnet and reassure her that Sylvy would be fine in a few days as much for herself as for Garnet. The truth be told, though, she had no idea what was going to happen. Sahharras had no idea what Sorram had done to heal Sylvy or why it had even worked at all. She didn't have a clue as to the purpose of the weave Sorram had created nor could she understand why he had drawn on the elements as he had. The weave she had seen only used a fraction of what he had drawn. Then there was the blood. Why did Sorram's blood seem to be absorbed by Sylvy? What did it mean? Sahharras had so many questions, and Corney wasn't there to answer a single one of them—a typical male trait. If those were her only questions or worries, she could have coped better, but they weren't.

She worried about Sylvy's unnatural sleep. The girl needed sleep to recover from her injuries and that was normal, but the way she tossed and turned while she slept wasn't. Sahharras thought Sylvy was just having nightmares about the attack on the farm, but something made her think there was more to it. The way Sylvy whimpered and cried in her sleep reminded her of the times the boys had been unconscious after their more severe injuries. She never asked Sorram and Taurwin about the nightmares, and they never talked about them either. Whatever the nightmares were about were vivid enough to make Sylvy thrash until she fell out of the litter they were transporting her on more than once. Sahharras and Garnet both had tried holding Sylvy's hand to comfort her while she slept, but she struck out and clawed at them until they retreated to nurse their own wounds. The boys were even worse when she had watched over them as they slept. That gave her an idea, and she started to hum a lullaby to Sylvy as she had the boys. Almost instantly, Sylvy responded to the sound of the song and began to calm down. From then on, Sahharras and Garnet took turns humming the lullaby until they finally reached the next settlement.

RECKONING

Thommaus was exhausted. It had been all but impossible to sleep while listening to the screams of the man in the distance. He knew he wasn't the only one who had trouble sleeping as he examined the faces of the other men across the morning fire. He knew Hoovar would lead them on toward the source of the screaming after they ate, and he for one was in no hurry. He had wanted to be there in person to see Sorram and Taurwin dispense justice, but now he was having second thoughts. He wasn't even sure if he wanted to see what they had done to cause the screams to last all night.

Hoovar was anxious to be on the trail to put a stop to the torture of whoever had screamed all night. He should be on the trail by now, but he wasn't. Instead, he sat by the fire as he watched fresh venison roast over it. He wasn't hungry and doubted if anyone else was either. The looks on the faces of his men told him that the distant screams had ruined any sleep and killed all appetite they may have had.

So why did he still hesitate? Why was he still here instead of on his way? Hoovar asked himself repeatedly. His duty demanded action, yet he was reluctant to leave camp. He moved over slightly on the log upon which he was sitting to make room for Corney who had finally arisen. He would have been relieved to hear the old mage ramble under his breath if it hadn't been for the disgusted look on his face and angry shaking of his head. "What's the matter, Corney?" he asked the old mage and half wished he hadn't. He was afraid of what the answers might be.

"Something is wrong. Sylvy was struck down by a mage, but I haven't felt any activity. I should have felt something when Sorram caught up to the mage. Those screams could be farther away than I think, of course, but I doubt it. If I can hear the man screaming, I should be able to feel the mage draw on the elements, if not feel the weaving itself. I may not feel Sorram draw on the elements—Creator knows the boy already holds enough in him to burn a small city to ash—but I haven't felt him release it or try to weave anything either. I should have felt him do something. There must be something wrong with me. Have I gotten so old that I am losing all of my senses?" Corney asked as he looked at his old friend. "Or is there something more dangerous that we still don't know about that boy? Either way, I don't look forward to today. I am too old for this shit. My adventuring days are long gone. Hell, my time has been gone for decades. I am tired. Are we ever going to be able to rest?"

Hoovar saw a tear roll down the old mage's cheek. Hoovar understood what he was complaining about and how he felt. "I think our time for rest is closer than you think, old friend. For good or bad, I think the signs show that we will rest soon," he assured Corney.

They would not survive this world much longer. After a little thought, he wasn't sure if humankind would survive much longer. What was it the good book had said, "The blood of man will run bridle deep on a horse" or was it "The rivers will run bridle deep with the blood of man"? *No, it was . . . Ah hell, it didn't really matter now, did it.* The simple fact of the matter is it said that the blood of man was going to flow. Well, if there were now three dragons on this plane, the blood of man would be sure to flow as it never has before.

Daven was relieved to be on their way, finally. Listening to the man's screams all night was more than disturbing. He didn't know what Sorram and Taurwin were doing to the man, but he was sure the man had earned it. The man had murdered women and children. Was there anything viler than that? Daven had decided that Sorram and Taurwin were not the monsters Hoovar and Corney feared they were. They couldn't be monsters. He had seen them show compassion, and he believed they loved Sylvy as a sister. Monsters didn't show compassion or feel love, or did they? Even this morning while it was still dark, one of the boys had slipped into camp to put more wood on the fire and set fresh venison to roast over it. They may be torturing the man in the distance, but they still cared for those people close to them—not monsters. He decided that the boys had to be right in their actions. Maybe they had been carried away with punishing the criminals who had murdered their friends, but who could say they wouldn't have done the same if they had the ability to do it for themselves? He for one couldn't. When he saw his little girl burned and lifeless, he wanted the pleasure of personally delivering them to the fires of the Fallen One.

Thommaus took to the lead as usual, but there was no need for his tracking skills. The way was clearly marked. Sorram and Taurwin were not trying to hide any of their actions. Thommaus had the duty of tracking down criminals before, and this wasn't the same. A criminal tries to hide everything. Tries to hide what he has done and where he is going. Not these two, they left marks on the trees a blind man could follow, which were not necessary either. He could follow those distant screams easily enough. No, these two didn't see that they were doing anything wrong. That didn't make whatever they were doing to the man acceptable, of course. It just meant that the boys didn't know better or maybe they didn't care. Thommaus wasn't sure which it was and was even less sure if he wanted to find out. He liked those two. He had known questioners in the army, and he hadn't liked any of them. There was always something "off" about them. He always assumed it was a requirement in that profession. He tried to convince himself that Corney and Hoovar were wrong about Sorram and Taurwin. Those two were not monsters like the emperor was, but as he rode closer and closer to the source of the screams, he became less sure of himself.

Hoovar had his men dismount and hobble the horses at least a hundred paces from their destination. He also had one man stay with the horses to keep them from spooking and running off. He had seen Sorram and Taurwin have that effect on horses before, and he didn't have any desire to spend the afternoon trying to round them up again. He had Thommaus take the lead once again, and they slipped through the woods as quietly as possible to the clearing where the screams still camefrom. He didn't know what he expected to find, but what he did find was beyond his imagination.

The camp wasn't set up much different as theirs had been set up the night before. Bedrolls still covered the ground around the center campfire, and there was what remained of a tether for their horses. The tether was downwind from the camp by a small spring, but those were the only things that were as they should be. The rest of the camp was something out of a nightmare. There was a line of corpses lying off to one side of the fire—what was left of the corpses rather. He wasn't sure what exactly the source of the screams was though. Sure, it was obvious what the source was, but what was it? He approached it slowly and carefully while trying to understand what he was looking at.

"Corney, can you help me out here? What in the hell? What am I looking at?" Hoovar asked him.

"If I was a betting man, I would say it is what is left of the mage, Pruitt," Corney answered as he too studied the invisible box.

"That isn't very helpful," Hoovar replied with a frown. He reached out with a hand carefully until his hand rested on something solid. It felt solid as . . . as a stone box, but he didn't see anything. He wouldn't have known anything was there at all if it wasn't for the flailing, burning, screaming Pruitt? He wasn't even sure if it was Pruitt. The screaming entity inside the solid invisible box had the shape of a man, or human anyway, but it was covered with flames. Even when it opened its mouth, all Hoovar could see was more flames; no flesh could be seen anywhere. It was as if the entity itself was made of flame. "What makes you think it is Pruitt?" Hoovar asked with doubt.

"Process of elimination, those corpses are obviously wearing mercenary garb, and Roaran, or what is left of him, is propped up against that tree yonder. That leaves Pruitt. It makes sense in a way. After all, he would be the only mage here. He would have to be the one who burned Sylvy," Corney concluded.

Hoovar nodded his head in agreement, as he ran his hands along the side of the barrier until he found the other corner. He decided the box was approximately a pace and a half square and held off the ground about knee high. He couldn't find the top of it though. "Does it have a door or seam or anything?" Hoovar asked.

"I'm not sure how it was made, to be honest. It is made of the elements, but the threads are so fine I can't seem to make the individual threads out, let alone find a seam. What are you thinking?" Corney replied.

"I'm thinking that there should be something you can do," Hoovar replied with disgust. "I mean, besides just watch the man be tortured," Hoovar answered. "How is he still alive anyway?"

"I don't know. The weave that contains him is so fine that I am unable to reach him. Probing him is out of the question until I get rid of the box that contains him. I am unable to untie the weave for obvious reasons, but I should be able to cut the weave which forms the box open with spirit. I don't know what will happen after that though. I may have to act quickly or he could set the forest on fire. If you wish me to remove the box, I suggest everyone else to step back to the edge of the clearing. There is just no telling what will happen next," Corney told Hoovar as he scratched his head.

"You heard the man. Step back and be ready for anything," Hoovar commanded as he distanced himself and waited. "What about you, Corney?" he asked with concern.

"Don't worry about me," Corney replied as he began to draw on the elements. He didn't need anything but spirit to cut the threads that formed the box, but he wanted to be ready with a weave of his own to confine the burning Pruitt if it was necessary. He used spirit to form the shape of a blade and then stiffened it with mineral. Then he pressed the knife edge of spirit against a corner of the box. The weave that formed the invisible box began to fray almost instantly. The next thing he knew, the threads were dissolving as the weave came apart at an alarming rate. It had taken no effort at all, which made absolutely no sense. A child could have mustered up enough spirit to remove the box. Corney caught himself before his mind wandered too far from his task and prepared a weave of his own to seize the fiery Pruitt if need be. He began to study the weave of fire, air, and spirit of the "fire suit" as soon as the box threads weakened enough to allow him to see the threads that made it. The threads were not as hard to follow as the box, but he was still impressed at the skill required to create the fine weave.

The fiery Pruitt continued to flail at the weakening box as it deteriorated, which didn't make Corney's job any easier. It isn't as easy to pick out individual threads on a weave when it moves around all the time. He thought about restraining the burning mage, but he wasn't sure what effect that may have to the existing weave. It is generally best to restrain someone with air, but the added threads of air could intensify the heat of the already existing flames. Water would be the obvious choice in this case, but threads of water are used in almost all detonation weaves; if they became tangled into the existing weave, he could be in an even bigger mess. The real solution lies in unknotting the existing weave before the box dissolves completely. He didn't want to have to resort to cutting the threads that formed the weave because it was generally a bad idea to allow that many threads of fire to dissolve at once. That was generally the trigger for all detonations, and there were enough fire threads in this weave to result in an impressive detonation. He realized he was running out of time as the top of the box finally gave way and disappeared, which was followed by the bottom.

The whole thing was coming apart rather quickly now, but there was something else going on at the same time. Corney had expected the grasses to catch fire once the bottom gave way and the fire was exposed to the ground. That didn't happen. It didn't happen because Pruitt didn't land on the ground. He seemed to be sinking into some sort of darkness. It looked almost liquid but lacked the shiny surface. It was as if he was looking at the absence of light in liquid form, and Pruitt's fiery form was now knee deep into it. Pruitt's struggles took on a new urgency as he slid deeper into the darkness. To Corney it looked as if the fiery mage was trying to hold on to the top edges of the dissolving box to climb out of the darkness, but the box kept crumbling under his grip. As Pruitt slid deeper and deeper into the blackness, he began to claw at the ground to try to get ahold of something, anything, to save himself. Corney had never witnessed anything quite like this or read anything for that matter. What petrified him though was the fact that the liquid darkness didn't consist of any elemental threads. He was positive that the dark pool wasn't the work of any mortal. That meant it must be the work of either the Creator or the Fallen One. The Creator was the creator of light while the Fallen One diminishes light Being in the presence of the works of the Fallen One was enough to make him empty his stomach. He dropped to his knees and emptied himself until he thought he had thrown up everything he had eaten since he was a child.

"What the hell was that?" Thommaus screamed over the sounds of men retching. "What . . . that wasn't what I thought—"

"I think we all have a pretty good idea what happened," Hoovar replied as he wiped sweat from his brow.

"I don't . . . Sorram must have . . . That would explain the box, but not even . . . there are so few who can—" Corney stammered.

"Corney, I need you to talk to me in complete thoughts, buddy. I have no idea what you are trying to say otherwise," Hoovar said as he helped his old friend to his feet. Hoovar had seen men die by the thousands on the battlefield, and not once had he ever seen anything that even came close to what he had just witnessed.

"I believe Sorram created the transparent box with a weave so fine in order to keep Pruitt from finding refuge in death. Pruitt had burned in that box even after there was no flesh left to burn. The man's soul was trapped and on fire until I broke the weave that formed the box. However, when I broke open the box, his soul . . . Well, you saw. I don't believe he got any refuge where he was going," Corney concluded.

"At least we know now that Sorram is the same as Danemon," Hoovar stated as he shook his head. Humankind was surely doomed.

"I didn't say that," Corney corrected. "I'm not so sure if Danemon had the ability to do what I saw. It was hard to learn much about the box, but I am sure it was made entirely of the elements. I have been there when Danemon harvested a soul, and he uses something else. Something I can't see or detect. I don't know how or where Danemon stores those he has harvested, but I do know it has nothing to do with the elements. Most species that can wield what we consider as magic do no more than affect the flows of the elements to achieve a desired effect. It is more science than magic. What makes it magic is the fact that most people can't see or understand it. Dragons like Danemon and a few other creatures can do the same with the souls, or life force, as we do with the elements. The so-called blood magic that was used to make Danemon appear human was actually elemental magic to mix the souls. It wasn't real blood magic. For it to be true blood magic, we would have had to have the ability to mix the souls without the use of the elements," Corney explained. "Now do you understand?" he asked a confused-looking Hoovar.

"No! How could that make things any clearer?" Hoovar complained.

"Sorram may be something different because he had to use elemental magic to trap Pruitt's soul. He didn't use whatever Danemon uses. There are other possibilities to consider as well," Corney explained.

"Okay, I think I get the soul-trap thing, but what other things could there possibly be to consider? I mean, if he isn't at least part dragon, then what is he?" Hoovar continued to question.

"There are other creatures—not many, but a few—who can trap souls and wield true blood magic," Corney told Hoovar.

"Yeah, but they are all of the lower planes of existence. That doesn't bode well for humankind either. It will not matter who wins the battle of superiority. Mankind will lose," Hoovar countered and spat on the ground.

"Not all of them are of the lower planes. There is one or two of the higher planes," Corney corrected.

Daven's head was spinning again. "What are you two talking about? What lower planes?"

"It doesn't matter. We can't do anything but go on as we should," Corney advised to redirect the conversation.

"Go on as we should. What kind of advice is that? What are you suggesting exactly? I should chase Sorram and Taurwin down and arrest them for torturing Pruitt, but I don't even know if that was Pruitt. I could arrest them for murdering and mutilating the men, but I don't even have any proof it was them. There are no witnesses. If there were a witness, I still would never be able to sentence them. Even I half believe their actions are justified, and to make matters worse, you are telling me that they could be here on behalf of the Creator or the Fallen One. It doesn't really matter which one it is. I would still be a little out of my jurisdiction here. Don't you think?" Hoovar ranted as he rubbed his temples. If his head hurt any more, it would explode.

"That isn't what I said either. Well, forget about them then. Focus on something we can work on. Wasn't that always your strategy? Whittle away until you had worn away opposition?" Corney replied.

"I'm sorry, Corney. I still feel a little lost here. What is it that I can work on? Huh?" Hoovar challenged. Hoovar was glad that Corney's mind was in the here and now, for the moment at least, because he was at his wits' end.

"Well, we could look at Roaran over there. See what we can do for him. On the other hand, we could try and figure out what started all of this in the first place. Maybe we will be able to figure out what those two will do next or at least where to look for them. Maybe by the time we see them again, we will have an idea what to do with them," Corney lectured. He didn't have any idea what to do with them, but if they were here in the name of the Creator maybe, they could be convinced to deal with Danemon.

It took a few seconds for Corney's words to sink in, but he eventually pulled himself together to ask, "He is alive? Why did they leave him alive?" He looked at what was left of the once great and mighty Roaran Pizolla.

He walked past the line of limbless bodies to where Roaran sat. The man's arms and legs were gone. Hoovar didn't know how it was possible to live through that kind of injury. He reasoned Sorram must have been applying a healing weave as Taurwin ripped the man's limbs off. Well, he could have cut them off, but somehow Hoovar doubted it. "What happened here, Roaran?" he asked as he approached the man.

"M-m'lord . . . ? Is that you, m'lord Hoovar?" Roaran stuttered as he began to cry.

"Yes, Roaran, it is I. Can you tell me what happened here?" Hoovar questioned as he knelt down beside the man.

"Yes, they said I was to tell what happened. I am to tell others what happened to me or they would come back. Don't let them come back. Don't let them . . . Pruitt has stopped screaming. What happened to him? Did you save him, or did they come back for him?" Roaran whimpered.

"Pruitt is dead and beyond their reach now. Please tell us what happened," Hoovar asked again as he tried to wipe dried blood off the man's face.

"I didn't know. I am sorry, but I didn't know. Don't let them come back for me. Promise you won't let them do to me what they did to Pruitt," Roaran rambled as he cried.

"Yes, I promise. Could you please tell me what you are talking about now? What didn't you know?" Hoovar replied.

"We only killed a few peasants. It was the little girl who attacked the men. We would have gotten away if it weren't for her. My men were killed because of that stupid girl. We didn't know you cared. I was just trying to scare them off. It should have been easy to kill a few peasants and the rest would have left. Didn't think you cared for them," Roaran rambled as he sobbed.

Hoovar looked over to Corney and Thommaus to see if it made any sense to them. All he got in return was a shrug of the shoulders in response. "Why did you want the farmers to leave, Roaran? What was there to gain from it?" Hoovar continued.

"Wanted the land, Father wanted the western quadrant. You must warn him. They will go for him next. You must save him. They made me tell them," Roaran replied before he began to sob uncontrollably.

"Who did you tell?" Hoovar asked but Roaran didn't answer. The man was a blubbering mess. Hoovar didn't blame the man for losing control of himself, but he still had questions that needed answered. One thing was for sure though, and that was Sorram and Taurwin were not finished. They would go after Roaran's father if they knew he had ordered the murder of their friends, and who could blame them? Hoovar knew it was against the law for a commoner to lay a hand on a lord, but that wouldn't matter to them. They had already broken more laws than he cared to count by taking the law into their own hands and killing these mercenaries and torturing Pruitt. He still didn't understand why they hadn't killed Roaran.

"Pull yourself together, man. I can't help you or your father unless you answer my questions. Now look at me and tell me the rest of it. Who did this to you and why?" he demanded.

"Don't make me look. I don't want to look. Cut out my eyes. Cut them out!" Roaran shouted back.

Hoovar didn't know how to respond to that request. "Corney, can you tell if he is still sane or if there is something else wrong with him?" Hoovar asked with a shake of his head.

"Maybe, give me a minute to probe him," Corney answered and stepped forward to examine Roaran. The man's limbs were gone, but there were traces of magic over the wounds. That would be typical at an army camp after a battle. Well, at least men lost limbs in battle and magic was commonly used to heal the areas to save a man's life. Very seldom did anyone lose all of their limbs and live to tell about it. Corney's probing didn't reveal anything unusual except at his eyes, but he didn't know what was wrong with them. Roaran's eyes didn't have any apparent weave or magical residue about them, but Corney still suspected the man was blind. Corney got down on his knees and tried to open the man's eyelids to look into his eyes, but Roaran kept moving his head and screaming about cutting out his eyes.

"Hold still, man, I am trying to help you," Corney shouted at Roaran. That calmed Roaran down some, but once Corney got the man to open his eyes, he wasn't sure what he saw. It was as if there was a dim light coming from within the man's eye. He could see it moving around, and then he made out an image of a fiery Pruitt flailing around in a transparent box. There were some other images, but he couldn't make them out, and then it returned to the image of Pruitt once again. "What in the hell?" he mumbled in his bafflement.

"Cut them out. I don't want to watch it anymore," Roaran shouted as he slammed his eyes closed.

"Well, what is it?" Hoovar asked impatiently.

"I'm not sure, but I think somehow the image of what happened here has been burned into his eyes. Well, maybe burned isn't a good word, but I do believe that is what he sees and nothing else," Corney answered.

"What?" Hoovar exclaimed in disbelief.

"It is hard to tell. The images are so small, but I definitely saw Pruitt burning in that box. I think Sorram may have made it so he will see those images for the rest of his life as punishment for his role in what happened to Sylvy," Corney tried to explain.

"Yes, my punishment to live through it again and again. Cut out my eyes, I have seen enough. I won't do it again. I will never kill any of your peasants again," Roaran, pleaded.

"Can you heal him or at least remove the images so we can get some coherent answers out of him?" Hoovar asked with a shake of his head. How the hell did the boy manage that? "Is there any way to watch what happened here for ourselves?" he added as an afterthought.

"Are you kidding me? How the hell am I supposed to do that? I don't even know how the boy managed to do whatever that is," Corney replied. "As far as healing goes, I can't find anything wrong with his eyes. No magic has been used on them, at least that I can tell. I swear this is more and more like one of the stories in the good book all the time."

"Don't go there. If I remember correctly, the last time the Creator took a hand in man's wicked affairs, we had a small flood," Hoovar said in disgust.

"If you would have read the good book, at least once you would know that isn't an accurate statement," Corney scolded.

"Well, it's a little late to start reading it now that all of them have been destroyed," Hoovar said sarcastically. How many years had it been since Danemon had banned those? He wasn't sure which was worse, the fact that the crazy bastard had actually banned them or the fact that no one had even noticed the absence of the books. No one even questioned why there were no more holy men.

"What are you two talking about? Have you lost your minds? What does the good book or the Creator have to do with any of this? Just find out what happened so we can decide what to do next," Daven shouted at the two crazy old men.

Hoovar wanted to laugh at Daven's ignorance, but he felt like crying instead. So much of the histories have been lost or rewritten over the centuries. Hoovar had learned too late that the battle of light versus the darkness was real. There were too many things disregarded as bad luck or poor politics when it was all about the souls of man. The battle would last until the end of time, and if Sorram and Taurwin were what he thought they were, the end was near. They would bring destruction and death as foretold in the good book: "The rivers would run with the blood of man." The question whether they were there on behalf of the Fallen One or for the Creator remained.

"Yes, you are correct," Hoovar lied. It was easier to lie than to explain what he really suspected was going on. "Roaran, you said you and your father wanted the land, but for what?" he asked again.

"He didn't tell me. I just had to get rid of the farmers,"
Roaran answered and began to sob once again.

"Okay, Roaran. That is okay. Now tell me who did this to
you," Hoovar pushed on while the man was still coherent.

"Not *who*, *what* did this. I don't know what . . . I awoke
to Pruitt's screams. He was trapped and on fire. The rest of
my men were fighting the shadows. It was so dark. I didn't do
anything. I couldn't move. I was held in place by something
I could not see. I was forced to watch as the shadows pulled
my men apart as effortlessly as pulling the wings off a fly.
Their arms and legs were thrown into the fire, and they were
consumed by the flames. Then they came for me. They said
that they had saved me for last. Said I was to watch and tell
others my fate so they wouldn't ever have to do this again.
Then . . . then they ripped my arm off and threw it into the
fire so I could never lay that hand on anyone again. Then
when that was consumed by the fire, they did the same with
my other arm for those I had already laid a hand on. They
made me watch my arms be consumed in the fire as those of
my men had before mine while I listened to Pruitt's screams.
Then the dark shadow tore off my leg to prevent me from
spreading my evil across the land and threw it into the fire.
Then my other leg was torn off and thrown into the fire for
the evil I had already spread across the land. Said they would
come back if I didn't do as they instructed. Now, all I see . . .
cut out my eyes. Kill me! Have mercy, I didn't know! It was
only a few peasants! Kill me! Please kill me!" Roaran cried
hysterically.

"Who did this to you? You must have seen them," Hoovar
tried again. He didn't know why he kept asking. He knew
who it was, but there was no proof. Why did he care if there

was proof if there was nothing he could do about it anyway? Roaran had reaped what he had sown and that should be the end of it, but it wasn't.

"I don't . . . I thought . . . you sent them. You sent them. Why did you do this to me? They were only peasants. Why did you do this to me?" Roaran sobbed.

Thommaus had heard enough. He didn't care who did it. Roaran was lucky to be alive, but then again, maybe being alive like this was a more suitable punishment for him. The proud man wasn't proud now, was he? He wouldn't be able to push others around or poke them in the chest and intimidate them. He would be lucky if he could intimidate a child now. The real problem as he saw it was what was they were supposed to do with the man. They could leave Roaran here to die, but he doubted whether Hoovar would be so callous. No, Hoovar wouldn't leave the man to die. Hoovar would insist on taking Roaran back to his family, but the man sure as hell couldn't ride a horse now. They would have to make a litter and drag him behind a horse all the way back to his family's estates. That would take days. Days of listening to his bawling and blubbering as if the man didn't deserve his fate.

Daven should have been happy to see that those who had hurt his little girl had been punished, but he wasn't. It wasn't that he disagreed with the justice that Sorram and Taurwin had seen fit to bestow on the murderers, but somehow he still felt empty. He didn't need to be there to witness these punishments, and he would have been sick if he had done it himself. Then why didn't he feel satisfied? Was there any punishment those two could dish out fill the hole in his soul after what he had seen at that farm? He wasn't angry anymore or sad—just flat. He felt dead inside. He wondered if he would ever feel as he had before that day when he saw his daughter dead and his friends and neighbors slaughtered. No, Sylvy wasn't dead, he corrected himself. She is alive and will be fine no matter what Hoovar and Corney said. Maybe he will feel better when they arrive at the Pizolla hold to find Roaran's father like his son. After all, his plan and orders had set Roaran into action. He was as guilty as anyone else was. Surely, Sorram and Taurwin were well on their way there by now.

Hoovar had ordered the men to break up into pairs to find the mounts belonging to Roaran's men. They could use them as remounts. They would be able to travel faster that way, in theory. He knew he wouldn't arrive in time to save Lord Pizolla, but he still had to try. It was the right thing to do, wasn't it? He still couldn't decide. He couldn't even decide if Sorram and Taurwin were the monsters he thought they were. The torture of Pruitt was a little excessive, but didn't the good book say, "Live by the sword and you will die by the sword" or something? Well, Pruitt had used fire instead of a sword and he was burned alive. There, the crime justified the punishment, but it still didn't justify them taking the law into their own hands.

Then there was Roaran, who evidently hadn't killed anyone but had ordered the deaths. Hoovar couldn't decide which was crueler. Letting him live, or killing him for following his father's orders. Whatever had been done to Roaran's eyes was definitely over and beyond justifiable, but he doubted if Daven or anyone back in the western quadrant would agree with him. Roaran's men had been killed for their roles in the deaths at the farm, and there was no doubt about the justification of that. However, the tearing of their limbs off to torment Roaran wasn't justifiable. He could tell by the lack of blood around those wounds that they had already been dead when their limbs had been torn off. He could be wrong, but that was what had made him draw the conclusion that it had probably been done to torment Roaran. It could have been done to get him to tell what he knew. There was very little done that couldn't be justified but under what authority of the law. Why couldn't Sorram and Taurwin have waited for him? He could have deputized them and given them the authority to police the entire western quadrant if he wanted. He could have given them orders to find the criminals. He could have . . . no . . . No . . . He wouldn't have done anything of the sort. He wouldn't have given those two the authority to do anything. They were too young. A young man's blood runs too hot for that kind of responsibility. He realized he was trying too hard to justify their actions, but why was he doing it? Was it because he didn't want to have to do something about them? He didn't want to face them, arrest them, as if he could. Then to make matters worse, he had at least three days to contemplate all of this on the road to Pizolla's hold.

*　*　*

Sylvy had been asleep for far too long, and Garnet was worried. Something was wrong. Nothing Sahharras said would convince her otherwise. Garnet had stayed by her daughter's bedside since their arrival at the nearest group of farms. It had been almost two days gone since Sylvy went to sleep, and she had not eaten or quenched her thirst in that time. Garnet didn't know how long her daughter could live without taking nourishment, but she believed that if she didn't wake soon, she never would. Sahharras had assured her repeatedly that Sylvy would wake up hungry and thirsty when it was time and not before, but that didn't tell her squat. She wanted to know when her daughter was going to wake, and until then she would not stop fretting. She would sit at Sylvy's bedside and be the first thing she saw when she did wake if she did. No, she wouldn't think that way. She had to believe Sorram had known what he was doing. Sylvy had been awake then. Garnet had heard Sorram talk to her afterward. He had talked to her and she had witnessed it. He . . .

"Mommy, oh, Mother, we must pray," Sylvy said as she sat bolt upright in bed with a pained look upon her face.

Garnet leapt from her chair to the bed to engulf her daughter in a bear hug. "I will get you something to eat and drink. Sahharras said you would need to eat. You have been asleep a long time," Garnet whispered in Sylvy's ear. She didn't want to let go, but she had to get Sylvy something to eat. She reluctantly let Sylvy go after one more smell of her musky-smelling hair and wiped the tears from her eyes. Then she realized Sylvy was crying too.

"It's okay, honey. Everything will be all right now," she tried to reassure her daughter as she sat back on the edge of the bed to give Sylvy another embrace.

"We must pray for them. We must," Sylvy whimpered to her mother.

"We had service for those that died yesterday, honey. I'm sorry you weren't there, but as I said, you have been asleep for a long time. You were burned badly and . . . ," Garnet tried to explain, but she stopped to calm herself before she began crying once again.

"No, not them, Mommy, we need to—" Sylvy tried to tell her mother.

"Sorram and Taurwin are okay. They will be back before you know it. You should know better than to worry over those two," Garnet answered with a weak grin. Now that was an understatement. She shouldn't have doubted Sorram. He has done so much for her and her family but she still doubted him. Those two really were her family's guardian angels.

"Not them either," Sylvy said with impatience in her voice. "We need to pray for those men. The men who hurt me . . . ," Sylvy said and stopped to raise her hand to feel her now disfigured ear and run her hand through her hair where she had been burned badly only days before. "And killed the others, we should to pray for them," Sylvy told her mother as she looked down and pouted.

"You need not to worry about those men. Sorram and Taurwin went to hunt them down and . . . so they can't hurt any more people," Garnet said coldly. She wished she hadn't said it after she heard how it sounded off her lips, but it was justified.

"No, Mother, Sorram and Taurwin, they didn't go to kill the men. They went to make the men pay for what they had done to . . . ," Sylvy said with a sniff. Then she looked up to her mother as tears flowed freely down her cheeks and explained. "We should pray for them because Sorram and Taurwin know how to make them pay." She paused to wipe her nose on her sleeve before she continued.

"Oh, Mother, I saw all of it. I saw it all as if I were there. Oh, Mother, the things the magi have done to them. I didn't want to see it, but I couldn't stop it. It hurt so bad . . . How did . . . How could she? She was there, Mother. She was there to see it all. How could she live there while they were being tortured so? She knows what they did to them and . . . She knows what they are," Sylvy ranted before her sobbing made her unintelligible.

Garnet was having difficulty hearing her daughter's words because of her sobbing, and what she did make out made little to no sense at all to her. Those men should pay for what they have done; she would not pray for them. She looked into Sylvy's . . . green . . . eyes? Why were her eyes green? What had happened to her blue eyes? They weren't only the wrong color, but they looked too large. They reminded her of . . . Sorram and Taurwin's eyes.

"I'll be right back, honey. You really need to eat, and Sahharras should be here to check on you," she said before she made for the door. She would find Sahharras as soon as she saw to Sylvy's nourishment and then she would get some answers.

Sahharras didn't know what to do with herself. Sylvy didn't need her now that she was awake and eating anything put in front of her. Sahharras had seen to all the animals and crops this cluster of farms had for her in which to administer her magic. She had even walked the pastures and grazing areas while weaving her way along. There just wasn't anything else for her to do. It made her wish someone would be injured to give her a reason to be there. It wasn't as if she was wishing for something serious, but a sprained ankle or a smashed thumb would have been nice. Even someone needing her to mix up some herbs for a bad headache would have helped, but she didn't even have that. The only thing she had to do was to avoid Garnet. That woman was tireless. Why couldn't the woman accept the fact that she did not have the answers the woman sought? Sahharras had questions of her own when Sorram and Taurwin returned. Sahharras knew they would return before Hoovar and the rest did. She knew that they would never be able to keep up with the boys. Being on a horse would help, but it wouldn't be enough. The trouble was they should have been back days ago. She wouldn't have expected them to be gone more than a day or two at the most, but it had been nearly a week already. What were they doing? She would have thought Sorram and Taurwin could have caught up to those men by daybreak at the latest. Those men didn't have that big of a head start to get any farther than that. If they decided to wait until the cover of darkness the next night, it would have surprised her. That would make two days' travel and two days back. What have they been doing for the last two days?

She was beginning to worry about whether they would return at all. Maybe they were having trouble controlling their form. It had happened before; it would happen again. That was one reason she had spent so much time weaving the more distant pastures. If they were having trouble, they could approach her while she was alone and she may be able to help them. If Hoovar returned before they did, she would know they were in trouble. If that happened, she would ask Sylvy if she could borrow her horse to use as a packhorse and go looking for them herself. She would have to figure out how to find them.

She would want to ask Corney a few questions before she went, but she wasn't sure if he would answer all the questions. It wouldn't matter; she would go and do her best for them. She owed them that much. Sahharras paused for a moment to reach out to see if she could sense any other magi in the area. She didn't find anything, but of course, she wouldn't have been able to sense Sorram or Taurwin anyway; no one could sense them.

Sahharras woke with a start, leaped from her bed, and formed a light orb. She could sense a mage approaching, and he would be there soon. She hastily threw on her dress and made her way for the door. The mage was strong as Corney; it could be Corney returning but she didn't expect Sorram and Taurwin returning with Corney and Hoovar. She decided that didn't matter, not now. What was important was she would be able to hear news of what had happened, or at least she could have an update on current events. Once she made her way outside, she looked to the west where she felt the other mage's presence and waited.

Within moments, she could hear the plodding of a single horse coming closer. She was overwhelmed by her excitement as she ran out to meet him. "Corney, where is everyone? Where are the boys?" she asked with a grin.

"Good question. Where are the boys?" was the answer she heard, and she froze in her tracks. She wasn't smiling any longer, and as the man dismounted, she seized more of the elements. She drew on the elements as hard as she could. The mage turned on her the instant he sensed her drawing and prepared himself for battle as well. She knew that voice and to whom it belonged.

She had little chance to stand up to anyone with such strength and experience. His attack came quick and strong. She tried to knock his flows away with a club of air and spirit, but they were on her in an instant. She duplicated his weave and launched her own attack. He countered by using spirit and mineral to cut her flows as she had her shield. She cursed herself for not thinking of it first. She formed her own knife and began hacking at his flows before they completely engulfed her. She had some success, but she couldn't cut the threads as fast as he could form them. She duplicated her weave, forming two knives, and continued to cut her bonds away. She found that she couldn't keep both knives going as his weave began to form a shield around her and choke her off from the elements. She didn't have any idea how long they had been fighting, but she was starting to feel it wear on her. The sweat that had beaded on her forehead now began to run down the side of her face. Her legs ached, and finally her knees buckled as she fell to the ground.

"Stop it before you kill yourself! You only have so much spirit, girl!" he shouted at her.

Sahharras was nearly used up, and she knew it as well as her adversary. She had all but given up until she saw a small figure loping along in the darkness toward the mage. If she could keep his attention for a few more . . . Yes, she saw the shadow attack with incredible speed. First, it hit the man in across the knees with its pungi sticks. The man fell to his knees immediately, and Sahharras felt his weave quiver. Then the shadow darted off into the darkness and circled behind the patiently awaiting horse. She was close enough to see the man's frustration as he prepared another weave to catch her accomplice with a shield of her own on her next strike.

"No, Sylvy, it's a trap, he will catch you!" Sahharras shouted. She didn't want Sylvy to be caught, but she needed more of Sylvy's help if she was to have any chance to escape capture herself. She wasn't even sure if the two of them together was much of a match for someone with his experience. What she saw Sylvy do next was as much of a surprise to her as it was to the man.

Sylvy circled around the backside of the man's horse to attack again, but this time she didn't use her pungi sticks. This time she seized the minerals from the ground to strengthen her small blades of spirit and cut at the flows rolling over Sahharras. She cut away and then darted off into the darkness once again.

Sahharras was surprised at how successful the attack had been. While Sylvy's knives of spirit were smaller than those she had made, they looked more solid, sharper, faster, and essentially more effective. Sahharras was now able to draw more of the elements in to strengthen her own attack on the man because Sylvy had nearly cut half of her bondage away in one single attack. She shortened her reach, made her own knives smaller, and began to work on small sections of the walls trying to form around her. It was more effective than it had been before, but she was becoming exhausted. Her renewed strength forced the man to return his attention on her. He struck out with more flows than she could count.

There was no way Sahharras could defend against them all. She had to give up her attacks on him to put all her efforts back into cutting at the wall that was once again trying to form around her. She saw Sylvy darting toward him again. This time the man diverted the threads from her and directed them at Sylvy. Sahharras saw that Sylvy didn't even bother trying to cut the threads that engulfed her. Instead, she threw everything she had at the threads holding Sahharras. She was almost completely free when Sylvy was finally completely cut off.

"Finally I got you, little troublemaker," she heard the man say in triumph at shielding Sylvy. Sahharras drew as much as she could and was disappointed at how little it was in her weakened state. She launched everything she had at the man, and he cut away at her flows effortlessly. She had to do something quick. Not only was he cutting away her threads now, but also he had renewed his attacks on her once again. She increased her efforts, but she was getting nowhere. Then she saw Sylvy grin before she leapt at the man who had disregarded her as a threat. Sahharras watched as Sylvy drew her pungi sticks in flight and struck at the man's head with a vengeance.

Sylvy continued to strike the man until all of his threads winked out and Sahharras knew the man was unconscious. She was so tired she couldn't move, but Sylvy quickly formed a weave to form a barrier around the man once her own barrier fell away. Sahharras was more than grateful to Sylvy for helping her up off the ground and over to the man who now lay unconscious on the ground.

"Why have you come, Krotus?" she mumbled in her exhaustion at her one-time teacher.

"Sorry it took me so long, but I couldn't beat him," Sylvy admitted begrudgingly.

"Looks like you beat him senseless to me," Sahharras replied with a smile. "I wish I could have been the one to do it." She thought about kicking Krotus, but she figured it wouldn't be as satisfying since he was unconscious.

"Yeah, but I think I cheated a little. I couldn't beat him in a straight-up fight. I wasn't sure if the two of us together could take him either. That is why I made sure all of his attention was on you before I struck at him again. I know it wasn't right to let you take the brunt of the attacks, but it was the only idea I had at the moment," Sylvy explained as she nudged Krotus with her shoe. "What does this weave do anyway?"

"It cuts you off from the elements. It is called shielding," Sahharras answered. "Let's see if I have enough strength to show you how to tie it off. Then you will make at least another ten shields around this one," Sahharras told Sylvy as she reached out for the elements once more. "I don't think we want him to get free. I don't want to have to do that again." She rubbed her throbbing head. She knew what the pain meant, but she had no choice. They had to finish what they had started.

"Sahharras, who is he? Why did he attack you?" Sylvy asked innocently.

"That is a long story," Sahharras replied as she demonstrated how to tie off the shield.

"I can do that," Sylvy said as she began to repeat what Sahharras had shown her. She could remember seeing the man named Krotus before this. She felt as if she should know who he was, but couldn't remember. She had been having that sensation all too often recently. She thought the feelings were being caused by memories that were not her own, but why did that make sense to her?

"Well, I got plenty of time. It seems that I can't sleep anymore. Oh, don't tell my mother I have been sneaking out at night, but I get so bored pretending to sleep at night. Honestly, I don't know how Sorram and Taurwin find anything to do at night. Of course, they are allowed to go hunting all night. I would practice my magic, but Mother won't even let me practice my magic in the house. She said I shouldn't practice anything that uses fire in the house and that kind of excludes everything I know how to do. At least tonight turned out to be pretty exciting," Sylvy admitted with a giggle.

*　　*　　*

Hoovar had pushed them for speed until the last leg of the journey to Pizolla manor. Now he led them slowly and carefully because he didn't want his presence to be taken as a threat, not that the Pizollas should have reason to fear from him. He hadn't been very sociable with the Pizolla family recently, but he hadn't been exactly hostile either. He just wasn't sure what kind of mess he was riding into, was all. If Sorram and Taurwin had already been here, then Lord Pizolla would be dead or worse. That would leave a grieving widow in command until the other Pizolla son could prove himself man enough to replace his father. Well actually, that responsibility was to fall on the eldest son Roaran. However, Hoovar doubted if Roaran would be able to fill that role now. Hoovar knew Roaran had been groomed for that purpose since the day he was born, but he wasn't so sure about the younger son. He had only met the boy in passing once or twice. Therefore, he was probably riding into the Pizolla stronghold with the heir to the province crippled and tied to a litter being dragged behind a horse to return him to a distraught and recently widowed woman. Damn, if this wasn't one of the most dangerous and insane things he had ever done. He would be lucky if she didn't order all of them put on a pike. Well, it had to be done, nevertheless. He would have to be very cautious. Any sign that she may turn on them, and he would have to lead the men back to the forest and into hiding.

As they rode closer, Hoovar noticed newer blockhouses built on the grounds outside of the manor wall. He knew they had not been there the last time he had been here, but that was no surprise since it had been . . . it had been . . . Wow, he had no idea how long it had been since he had been here. It had to have been since he was made lord of the neighboring province. What was a surprise though was the size of them. A small army could be housed in those blockhouses. Why would the Pizolla family need a small army? Their province was mostly farmland with small farms spread across it as his was. There was no point in having such a large workforce like those houses suggested in one centralized area. Even more alarming was the large number of armed men patrolling around the blockhouses and walls of the manor house. Even if he had arrived during shift change, the Pizolla family had more than double, no, triple the number he had at his manor. Not to mention he had only Thommaus, Corney, Daven, and a handful of untrained men with him. If things went sour, he doubted if even Corney's magic would do them much good.

Once they reached the main gate, Thommaus was supposed to announce Lord Hoovar and his request to have an audience with Lord Pizolla; but when they reached the gate, it swung open while Lady Pizolla urged them inside from the wall. It wasn't what Hoovar expected, but what was anymore?

"Come inside quickly, now. I hate to leave the gate open for long," Lady Pizolla urged desperately.

Hoovar led his men into the large courtyard behind the gate and dismounted, where he waited on Lord Pizolla. Two groomsmen came to take their horses away, and Hoovar hated to let go of his animal. It wasn't as if he would be able to ride back out now that the gate was closed behind them, but he felt as if he was giving up his key to his freedom.

"M'lady Pizolla, I am afraid I must be the bearer of ill news," Hoovar said as he made his best leg for her. It was not necessary for him to bow to her or her husband for that matter, but he would do nearly anything to comfort the woman—well, anything within reason, that is.

"I'm afraid I have ill news as well, Lord Hoovar," Lady Pizolla replied and was surprised to see the old man wince as if she had slapped him. She didn't think anything could faze the old codger. She had been present when Hoovar had come to visit her husband before, and Hoovar had tolerated her husband's arrogant remarks without a single comment. She had been impressed, to say the least. The old man never even acknowledged her husband's posturing. She wasn't sure what circumstances had brought Hoovar to her now, but she wouldn't let this opportunity pass. She wasn't sure what had gotten her husband killed, but if she read the books in his study correctly, she was in serious trouble.

"Let the grooms take your horses and come. There will be someone to see to your wounded man shortly. We can discuss the dangerous countryside after you freshen yourselves. Maybe we will be able to come up with a plan to return you to your estates safely in a week or two," she added while her mind raced in search of a viable solution to her problems. That would give her plenty of time to convince Hoovar it was in his best interest to come to her aid if she could come up with a plan.

"I don't . . . I'm sorry, my lady, but that isn't one of my men. It is . . . it is your son, Roaran," Hoovar stammered. The woman was . . . a woman, and Hoovar was sure she was up to something. He had no idea why, but she scared him. Hoovar decided that it might be worth the risk to fight his way out instead of letting her keep him here for two weeks. Damn it, if he could make it here, he sure as hell could make it back home. Besides, the only real danger in the forest was Sorram and Taurwin, and they were not after him now, were they.

"What? No, that is not . . . He is on a hunting trip. He is safe far away from here," Lady Pizolla responded and shook her head in denial.

"I am sorry, m'lady, but we found him this way. He can tell you more about what happened to him than we can. Although I must warn you, he seems a little traumatized by his experience. He doesn't always talk coherently or make much sense," Hoovar warned. He wasn't sure what else he was supposed to do. Damn, he should have thought to bring a woman along to comfort her. No, the lady should have her own maids in attendance for that sort of thing, right? Besides, how did he expect himself to find a woman in the wilderness to comfort her? It wasn't as if his little trip to escort Sahharras and Corney to the farms had turned out the way he had originally planned.

It couldn't be her son. He wasn't here. He said he wouldn't be back for weeks. She walked slowly to the horse that had the litter behind it to look at the man. She tried to calm herself, but there was nothing for it. Her hands trembled, and her voice came out more a croak than anything else. "Who did this to you, son?" She closed her eyes and tried to picture the little boy she remembered playing in the courtyard. Nevertheless, the image of the broken man on a litter came back to her despite her efforts. She opened her eyes to take in the vision once again and tried to talk to her son. Her voice cracked at the stress she was feeling, and she knew he hadn't understood her. She tried to ask him what had happened to him, but instead her voice made an unintelligible moan to which Roaran turned his head.

"Mother, is that you?" Roaran asked as he turned his head around as if his eyes were capable of locating her.

She was standing close enough to reach out and comfort him, to answer him, but she didn't. She was stunned. He had lost all his limbs and his sight. Who could do this? She would . . . She shook her head in an effort to clear it. Suddenly she felt hot and clammy. She put her hand to her brow to wipe off her perspiration and realized how dark it was.

Hoovar hadn't known what he was going to tell Lady Pizolla about her son. He thought he would come up with something polite and proper when the time comes, but what had come out of his mouth disappointed him. "Not my man, it is your son" wasn't impolite, but it was callous. He felt ashamed at his lack of sophistication, but there it was. He couldn't take it back. All he could do is stand there like the fool he was while she went to her son. He watched with sympathy as she saw her broken son. He saw her face twist and heard her as she tried to speak. He had never liked the Pizolla family, but he felt the pangs of guilt for her pain. It wasn't her fault that her son was a piece of . . . Hoovar tried to catch her as she crumpled and began to fall to the ground. He was too late, of course, but Corney wasn't. Hoovar could see her clothes being held by what had to be air.

"Well, I guess I handled that rather poorly," Hoovar admitted to no one in particular.

"Do you think?" Corney teased. "You never were much of a diplomat. Too direct and to the point," Corney added with a shake of his head.

"Yeah well, I guess we will have to figure out what is going on around here without her help," Hoovar said. He grabbed one of the groomsmen and asked him to have everyone and anyone in charge to report in to him. He instructed another groomsman to have the other Pizolla boy to be brought to him as well as soon as the first ran off. He grabbed a third man and instructed him to find the lady Pizolla's maids so they could attend to her. The fourth man Hoovar saw he ordered to stay with the lady and assist the maids when they showed up. This left them standing in the courtyard with half of their mounts. He asked Daven and the rest of the men to see to the horses and meet him inside.

ANSWERS

Hoovar vaguely remembered the layout of the manor house from his previous visit and found what he was looking for quickly. There was a small receiving room off to the right of the main entrance furnished with a small desk and a couple of chairs. By the time he sat behind the desk, the Pizolla boy was there as requested.

"I don't have any desire to usurp your authority, son. I am only here to help you in your time of transition," he assured the boy as he stood back up and motioned the boy to the chair behind the desk. "Sorry about that, it is a matter of habit, I guess. Go ahead and sit. I have asked for everyone to report in. If you need any advice or have any questions, feel free to ask." But the boy stood, giving him a blank stare for what seemed like forever.

"Um, I think you have me mistaken for my brother. He isn't here at the moment. He will be back in a week or so, but until then my mother can see to your needs," the boy replied rather sheepishly.

"I'm afraid your brother has suffered some rather severe injuries and will not be able to fulfill his duties, and your mother . . . Well, she has enough to cope with at the moment," Hoovar explained. The boy blinked and stared as the news began to sink in. "I must apologize m'lord, but I can't recall your name," Hoovar added. He was beginning to think the boy was a little slow before he finally responded.

"My name is Rieckurt, but they just call me Kurt. Just call me Kurt. My . . . my mother, is she all right?" he stammered as he fought the feeling of being overwhelmed.

"Your mother will be fine, Kurt. You may call me Hoovar. Now, sit down and we can get down to business and figure out what is going on. Okay," Hoovar said as he guided Kurt to the chair behind the desk. He was anxious to hear the reports from the men waiting. Once he had Kurt seated behind the desk, he signaled the first man forward to report.

"M'lord—" the man started before Hoovar cut him off.

"Not to me, man. You will report to Lord Kurt," Hoovar instructed as he thumbed in Kurt's direction.

"M'lord Kurt—" he started again.

"Don't call me that, Joshua. Just . . . ," Kurt replied but looked over to Hoovar and asked, "Is that okay if he still calls me Kurt?"

"Of course, it is. I don't go by Lord Hoovar all the time either," Hoovar answered with a smile.

"I am sorry, Kurt, but there is nothing new to report. I haven't been able to figure out who or how your father was murdered. I really wish I did have more," Joshua said sincerely.

That was a little less informative than Hoovar had wished for under the circumstances. He gave Kurt a bewildered look and hoped the boy understood. He received a shrug of the shoulders in response. "I don't mean to pry, son, but I really don't have any idea what has transpired here. I will not be able to give very useful advice unless I have a little more information," Hoovar explained with a sigh.

"Well, three nights ago, my father was murdered and Joshua was trying to figure out who had done it," Kurt informed Hoovar as if that would explain everything.

"I understand it is hard for you with the loss of your father, but would you mind if I asked the . . . Joshua, was it? Would you mind if I asked him a few questions so I can understand the current events?" Hoovar probed cautiously. "Or maybe you could be a little more specific as to the events surrounding your father's death." He was out of his jurisdiction here, but he wanted to know what had started this mess in the first place. This was where it started, or at least he hoped this was where it started anyway. Besides, the boy may actually want his advice.

"Ask any questions you like," Kurt answered.

"Thank you, Kurt. Joshua, could you please tell me any information regarding Lord Pizolla's death, including what you have found in your investigation into the culprits?" Hoovar questioned and felt proud of himself for his diplomatic-sounding request.

"There isn't much to tell, I'm afraid," Joshua admitted. "There wasn't anything unusual that may have occurred on the day Lord Pizolla disappeared or anything to suggest foul play. He had retired the previous evening with the lady to their suite, but in the morning, he was gone. We searched for him, but he couldn't be found anywhere. His horse was in the stable so he couldn't have gone far, and no one on the night watch reported seeing him at all. The search lasted all day and into the night. It was finally decided to hold off the search until daybreak, but when morning arrived, his head was discovered on a pike in the center of the courtyard. I still don't even know how it got there. I have been a tracker for the Pizolla family for most of my adult life. Yet I couldn't find the tracks of the perpetrators anywhere. I have even failed to locate the lord's body. I just don't understand it!" Joshua exclaimed. He paused to take a breath and calm himself. Lord Pizolla hadn't been the most amiable master. However, he had been generous to Joshua over the years, and it frustrated him to no end at not being an adequate tracker.

"I'm not sure whether you will be able to find it. I have a story to tell you as well. Now keep in mind that some of this story isn't really mine to tell. A good bit of it was told to me by young lord Roaran. My part of it starts last fall on my visit to Pua Dar. During my visit there, I was instructed to develop the western quadrant or I would have to forfeit the land to your father. Well, I'm not one to give up anything. Therefore, I hired some farmers to develop some of the land into farmland and grazing pastures. There were two extremely talented hunters who traveled with the farmers, and I brought them to the western quadrant with the farmers. Everything was going well. It looked like I wouldn't have to give up my land, but about a week ago, I was on an inspection visit to these farms in the western quadrant when I found out that one of the little settlements had been attacked. There were mostly women and children at the farms because most of the men had moved north to build the next settlement. All of them were dead except one, and she had been burned severely. Only through healing did she survive. I still don't know if she will recover fully or be the same as she had been before the attack. You see, she was still unconscious on our departure. Those two hunters had seen the smoke from the buildings that had been set on fire and arrived about the same time as we had. If I said they looked upset at what they found, it would be an understatement. We set out to find the murderers, but our horses were about played out and we were unable to keep up with the two hunters. Now I don't have any proof, but I believe those two attacked and killed all but one of the men they were hunting.

"According to Roaran, he and his men were responsible for the murders in the western quadrant. Upon his request, we traveled here to warn Lord Pizolla that he was in danger because Roaran had told his attackers that Lord Pizolla had given the orders to kill the peasants. Once again, we have arrived too late. Now, Lord Pizolla is dead and we may never know what had started it in the first place. I understand that we haven't exactly been cordial, but to attack and kill each other is unacceptable. We are not barbarians. He has had to have a reason to attack and kill those peasants," Hoovar explained. He knew his story wasn't entirely accurate or complete for that matter, but he figured it should suffice for now, or at least he hoped it did.

"You mean your men have killed Lord Pizolla!" a stunned Joshua exclaimed in disbelief at the man's audacity.

"I believe that is correct, but I don't have any proof nor did I order it. I am truly sorry I wasn't able to prevent the incident," Hoovar replied.

"Incident! Incident! Are you kidding me! Your men murdered my master, and you act as if you have spilled a pitcher of milk!" Joshua shouted back as he stroked the hilt of his sword. He couldn't believe the nerve of the man to come here and claim responsibility as if there would not be consequences.

"You forget that I have five men in the western quadrant that will never see their wives or children alive again. You forget that Roaran himself has admitted to be under orders from your lord while he stuck a six-year-old little girl on a pike and left her to die. I did not start this. Hell, I haven't even been a participant up to this point. I am only trying to clean up this dog's mess that was made by your lord and tracked all over by those two hunters that I don't even have on my payroll," Hoovar countered. This wasn't his fault. There was nothing in his power in which he could have done to prevent these events.

"You lie! You lie! He wouldn't have—" Joshua shouted.

"That is enough! Stop it, Joshua!" Kurt interrupted. "This is easily verified. You have talked to Roaran, Lord Hoovar. If I am correct, that means he is still alive. Joshua can ask him if these accusations are true and take any actions Roaran seems fit if they are not," Lord Kurt declared. "I don't understand why you even brought this to me instead of him in the first place."

"Well, as to that. There is a good reason. It appears that Roaran may have been tortured to get him to divulge what he knew. I don't think he has yet regained all of his mental capacity. For example, I can't get him to tell me even a simple description of the men who had done it to him. He is completely incoherent at times. We have ridden with him for days and I still don't know or understand what is even going on completely," Hoovar told them.

"What have they done to him?" Joshua shouted and looked to Kurt for help, but he knew he would not find it there. "He was your father. Roaran is your brother. Are you so callous to feel nothing, boy?" he added desperately as Kurt squirmed in his chair.

"They reaped what they have sown if what Lord Hoovar says is true," a sultry voice from the door said. "And if what he says is true, Roaran will hang before the sun sets this day. The murder of women and children will not be tolerated no matter who commits such a heinous crime." Lady Pizolla sauntered into the room.

"My apologies, m'lady. I have handled the situation poorly. I didn't wish to cause you any more injury," Hoovar apologized. "I thought I gave orders for the maids to see to your comfort," he added nervously.

"I'm not as fragile as you might think. I may have given in to weakness for a moment. However, I am obviously needed, or what is left of my family will be destitute and in chains by year's end," Lady Pizolla declared.

"You may be overreacting a little. Your estates should provide wealth for your family for generations to come. The spring planting to harvest doesn't stop because of the death of one man. The cycle will continue whether your husband is here or not," Hoovar assured her. He hadn't lied about that. He had only collected taxes on a small portion of his estates, and he was able to make ends meet. The Pizolla estates were as sizable as his were. Actually, they were the lands of a former kingdom that had been overrun by the empire generations ago.

"There is more to this story than either of you, know. I have been in my late husband's study to search for clues to his untimely death. I thought I would then be able to understand why he was murdered," she told them.

Hoovar was taken back as she glided across the room and into an open chair next to her son. To him, she didn't look like a woman in mourning but a she wolf on the hunt for a formidable mate. By his reckoning, she was several decades, no, many decades late to catch him in that trap. "I have no proof of any of my story besides the words of Roaran in this bizarre tale, but maybe you know the missing pieces. Maybe we will finally know what really happened," Hoovar replied. Had she changed dresses since the courtyard? No, that would be absurd.

"Yes, Mother, don't hold us in suspense. What is this all about?" Kurt agreed. He was never included in any of the business discussions the way his brother had been. This was a new and unexpected experience for him.

"My late husband has been buying up slaves. He had those two blockhouses you had to have noticed on your way to the gate built to house all of them. He has kept them here for nearly a full year. He hasn't set them to work clearing new ground or planting any crops. Meanwhile, feeding those slaves has been rather costly. I have read records showing that he has borrowed large sums of gold to invest in his little venture. I assume it has something to do with his desire to posses your western quadrant, but I didn't see anything to suggest why it would be of value. I also suspect that if we were to inquire about the lack of staples here of late, it was due to the lack of funds and not a failing of the servants as he had assured me," she added.

"Joshua, is there a leader amongst the slaves? A spokesman or something like that," Hoovar asked as an idea began to form in his mind.

"Yes, nearly every day, one or two of them petitioned the lord for more rations. Well, until his disappearance," Joshua answered reluctantly. He did not wish to answer this man's questions. He didn't even wish to be in the same room with the man who had been responsible for his master's untimely demise. Maybe he would be able to talk Kurt into giving the order of Hoovar's execution. If he could only get the boy alone, he would be able explain to him what needed done.

"My lady Pizolla, I request that you summon those leaders here so we can ask them of their former employment. If they are farmers, then we will know he wanted to farm the western quadrant, but I suspect that is not the case. There has to be something of more value there to make it worth all the risk he took," Hoovar suggested. At least that made more sense to him anyway.

"Make it so, Joshua," Lady Pizolla ordered. "Now sit down, Lord Hoovar, while I have refreshments brought for you," she added as she glided out of the room after Joshua.

Hoovar was stunned. It couldn't have been an hour past since she had fainted in the courtyard at the sight of her crippled son, and now she gave Hoovar chills down his spine. He looked over at Kurt who had noticed his mother's odd behavior as well. He shrugged at Hoovar to indicate he didn't have any idea either.

"Remember this little advice, Kurt. You can be a fair and decent ruler with just a little effort if you want, but it requires a gift of the Creator to understand the fairer sex. In all of my years, I have yet to meet one I truly understood. If you ever meet one you think you have figured out, don't you believe it. She probably has you right where she wants you and you had better run like the Fallen One is after you," Hoovar told him. That earned him grins from the remaining men in the room.

"I will try to remember that," Kurt replied as he tried to hide his blush.

"Remember what?" Lady Pizolla asked as she sauntered back into the room.

"Hoovar was just giving me some advice," Kurt answered as his face reddened.

"That is Lord Hoovar. Kurt, don't show such disrespect," Lady Pizolla scolded.

"That's all right, I told him to call me Hoovar. Friends don't call each other by their titles," Hoovar explained. Hoovar didn't think anything about his statement at first, but then he realized that he was still calling her by her title. "You may feel free to call me Hoovar as well. After all, we are neighbors," he added awkwardly. He wasn't sure how she took that as she studied him with one hand on her chin and one finger taping her pouty lips. Damn if he knew how women learned that look. "Or not if you wish," he added and realized he really didn't know anything about women.

"Yes, Lord—I mean, Hoovar, and you may call me Sopheala," Lady Sopheala Pizolla replied as she walked over and ran her hand along his cheek.

Hoovar knew he was blushing like a schoolboy, but thinking about it just made it worse. All he could do was stand there like an old fool. Joshua saved him any further embarrassment by announcing his presence and the slaves he had brought with him.

"M'lady, the slaves you have requested," Joshua announced as he ushered in two nervous men.

"Thank you, Joshua. Lor—" she started but cleared her throat before continuing. "Hoovar, would you do the honors by taking lead in the questioning?" Sopheala asked with a grin that made Hoovar begin to sweat but not nearly as much as the slaves that had been brought forward.

"M'lady, we thought you had decided to grant our request. We would not have taken it if we knew it wasn't for us," the men exclaimed over each other as they fell to their knees to grovel.

"Whoa, relax. It isn't that kind of questioning, fellas," Hoovar informed them. "I am not a questioner, and we only have a few simple questions. Well, we did rather. Although I am sure she would like to know what has you two feeling so guilty, now that you have brought it up," Hoovar explained with what he hoped would be taken as a friendly smile.

That left the two men speechless for a moment as they looked around the room dumbfounded. "You're not one of them. You know, cruel—" one of the men finally began until the other man hit him on the shoulder. "Of course, you are not. I knew that from the start. You are the great general Lord Hoovar. Everyone knows that name," the other man said while glancing from Hoovar to Lady Pizolla as if he wasn't sure whom he was to address. It was custom to address the highest rank then the most senior or who had jurisdiction over the territory. The man couldn't decide who was or had which and was afraid to offend anyone, so he did what he could do—change the topic.

"We would like to take this fortunate opportunity to thank the lady Pizolla for her gracious gifts. The meat has filled bellies, and we have smoked and salted enough to last for some time if we ration it. However, it would help us in our rationing if we knew how long we need to ration it for or whether more meat was on the way," he said, addressing Sopheala.

"What meat are you talking about?" Sopheala asked. The puzzled look upon her face was genuine. They had petitioned her husband daily for better rations, and by what she saw in the study, she couldn't afford to purchase any rations, let alone meat.

"My apologies, m'lady. I . . . we thought that the meat was from you, but it must have been something your husband arranged before his untimely tragedy," the man responded quickly.

"Has there been a shortage of meat?" Hoovar inquired.

"Ah . . . no, m'lord or m'lady provides all we need, to which we are grateful," one man answered.

"Listen, we are trying to figure out what happened here. We are trying to figure out why Lord Pizolla was murdered, and we can't do that if you don't answer truthfully, damn it!" Hoovar replied with disgust. "Joshua has already told me you petitioned him nearly daily for more rations." He saw that glimmer of fear in their eyes. "Now, this meat, do you know where it came from? It is obvious Soph-er, . . . Lady Pizolla had nothing to do with it." The two men glanced around, looking for a way out or some sort of lifeline, but found none. "Come on, meat doesn't just show up on your doorstep. Is that what you took? Meat?" Hoovar prodded. The truth of the matter was that he suspected Sorram and Taurwin were the source of the meat, but he still had no proof.

"Well . . . actually, it did show up on our doorstep. Well, the woodshed actually. It was hanging there in the morning. No one said that it wasn't for us, so we assumed it was the increased rations, which we had petitioned for from the lord Pizolla. It wasn't until later that we heard that the lord Pizolla was missing. Then we assumed he had done the hunting himself. We intended to thank him personally when he returned, but then it was announced that he had passed. However, there was fresh meat hanging there every day since the first," the man explained.

"Well, I don't care where it came from or see the relevance of it. Be grateful someone has taken to hunt . . . It was your men, wasn't it! Those hunters of yours," Sopheala said as she put the pieces together.

"Well, that is what I was trying to determine. They have been known to hunt game for no other reason than to give it away to those in need of it. Now if—" Hoovar was saying when Sopheala interrupted him.

"Well, how noble of them. It is nice of you to make the murderers of my late husband sound so just," she said heatedly. She quickly realized that she had lost control of her emotions. She tried to recover, but there was no taking her words back. She wondered if she could use her outburst to her advantage somehow. Maybe she could portray herself as mentally unstable . . . No, that wouldn't get her anywhere. Maybe she could . . .

"They may have murdered your husband, but I have no proof of that, at least not yet. Now if you could tell me about your mysterious benefactors, I may be able to identify them," Hoovar replied as calmly as he could manage. He understood the stress she must be under, but he couldn't allow himself to become upset as well.

The man looked back at Lady Pizolla before he continued. "Well, no one actually saw who placed the game there, but the first morning, there were three whitetails hanging from a beam on the side of the woodshed. We butchered them, but no one came for the meat so we used some of it for stew. The rest of it we began to preserve. It was obvious something was going on in the manor, but no one bothered us about it. We thought that either it was meant for us or it was forgotten about. The following day, there was a total of five deer and one bison, and today there was two more bison. We have been busy trying to cure all of it, to be honest. We knew the lord had passed, but this is the first time we heard he had been murdered. When you said he could question us . . . Well, we thought maybe someone remembered the game and thought we stole it. Technically we were only doing what needed to be done," the man explained to justify their use of the meat.

"Bison. No one hunts bison. I have heard that even the big cats of the plains only take the calves and sickly ones," Kurt chimed in.

"These two do," Hoovar admitted.

"That is proof enough for me. Now what do you plan on doing about it?" Sopheala directed at Hoovar. She wondered if she could demand some sort of restitution to be paid for the wrongful death of her husband.

"Well, it certainly proves they are or were here in my eyes," Hoovar agreed. "Only they would risk life and limb to feed those they felt who were in need of it," he added with a wince at his praise of their behavior.

"Who cares if they were here or not? I for one don't," Daven spoke up and glared at Sopheala in defiance.

"Who is this that dares to speak to me so in my own hold?" Sopheala asked as she glared back at Daven. The man was well dressed for a peasant, but there wasn't any lace to indicate he had disposable wealth.

"That, m'lady, is the father of my apprentice," Corney replied dryly with a frown for Daven and his outburst. "She is rather gifted for her age. You see, she had been traveling with an escort to visit the farms in the western quadrant to apply her studies to their private gardens when young Roaran attacked the farms in question. She was nearly burned to death by Pruitt who was under command of Roaran at the time. She has been healed, and she was alive when we left. She should have woken up by now, and she should be back on her feet by our return. She will, however, carry the scars and whatever side effects such a drama will cause a young one for the rest of her days," Corney elaborated as he frowned at Joshua who had taken to stroking the hilt of his sword and glaring at Daven.

"I fail to see what difference that makes. If these two hunters are responsible for my husband's death, they should be dealt with accordingly. Roaran will hang for his role in this, and these peasants should be treated no differently," Sopheala replied coldly.

"What difference does it make? Are you kidding me? Your husband is responsible for the deaths of a dozen innocent women and children," Daven challenged. "He was the son of a bitch that ordered—" Daven shouted back.

Joshua's anger had reached its limit as he slid his sword from its scabbard. The sound alone was enough to make the man hold his tongue in the lady's presence, at least. As he stepped forward to deal with the man, he felt the air cool, and he walked into an invisible barrier.

"That is enough! Joshua, put up your weapon. Corney, if you would be kind enough to release the elements and drop the barrier after he sheathes his weapon, please," Kurt commanded. He waited until he was sure both men had complied before he continued. "We are supposed to be above this. The man has a legitimate point, Joshua, but my mother is correct also. Two wrongs do not make a right," he added.

"An eye for an eye and a tooth for a tooth," Daven countered.

"I am not saying that my father wasn't at fault. I didn't say that your two friends were guilty of murder either, but they are guilty for abuse of the law," Kurt explained as he tried to cool their blood.

"Abuse of the law! I have never even heard of such a thing," Daven countered.

"*Ignorantia nomen excusate*," Kurt said as if it would explain something. Then he remembered who he was talking to and realized that it explained nothing to the man. "*Ignorantia nomen excusate* means 'ignorance of the law excuses no one in the old tongue,'" Kurt added for the man's benefit.

"Are you suggesting that they deserve a simple flogging for the death of your father?" Sopheala exclaimed.

"I am sorry, but we can't ignore my father's role in this no matter how we feel emotionally," Kurt told her somberly.

"I do believe you have the makings of a fair ruler," Hoovar said in agreement. It was obvious the boy had received some education if he was able to speak the old tongue to quote the law. That was more than he could do.

"I do believe you are right, but none of it matters. No matter what you decide, there is nothing we can do to the two hunters responsible," Thommaus declared as every eye in the room turned to him.

"What are you talking about?" Kurt asked in his confusion.

"These two hunters are better woodsmen than I have ever seen or heard of before this. Think about it. They have not only slaughtered your mercenaries and your mage, but they hunt bison and drag it to where they can hang it while you have, unless I am wrong, a double guard on the wall, without being seen. Not to mention they took Lord Pizolla from the manor without being seen and then managed to sneak away without leaving a trace. They have managed to outrun us and arrive here several days ahead of us. Let's face it, we will not be able to find them unless they want to be found. I have to be truthful about it. If we did find them, I wouldn't want to get them into a corner. You haven't seen what they are capable of," Thommaus explained with a shake of his head. Why were they wasting their time even talking about what to do with those two was what he couldn't understand. Was he the only one that could see it?

"You are right and I should have seen it sooner, but I am not sure where that leaves us," Kurt admitted. He felt inadequate and wished his brother were there to handle it so he could go back to his books.

"Well, I for one would like to understand what started this in the first place. Your husband had to have some reason to act as he had," Hoovar suggested as he tried to redirect the topic.

"That brings us back to the original reason for bringing you two to us in the first place, I believe," Kurt told the two slaves who looked as confused as confused could be. "Do either of you know what my father had planned on doing with all of you?" He leaned forward in anticipation.

"I . . . we don't have any idea. If you will forgive, m'lord, but he didn't exactly confide in us often," one of the slaves responded.

"What occupation did you have before you arrived here?" Kurt probed further. There had to be answers here somewhere. They just had to find them.

"I was just a laborer, the same as many here," came the answer from the other man.

"Did either of you have a trade at any point in your life, or is there anyone else in your barracks that has a trade that could help us decide what he intended?" Kurt continued. Maybe he should let Hoovar handle this; he was getting nowhere.

"Well, before the empire invaded my country, I ran a mine in the northeast," answered the first man.

"How about that, I worked for a mine as well. Actually, I was their structural engineer," the second man added.

"Now we are getting somewhere. I bet if we asked, we would get similar answers. Now, all we have to do is figure out what he planned on mining and where," Hoovar declared. "I guess the western quadrant is a logical place to start looking. Corney, you are strong in the minerals elements. How far can you sense something like a gold deposit?"

"What? Are you serious? I can't go riding all over the western quadrant trying to sense a gold deposit," Corney protested.

"Why not? How hard could it be?" Hoovar replied. It seemed logical when he thought of it.

"Because it would be hard! You don't understand. I can sense pure gold if it is a fair amount at maybe a hundred paces or so, sometimes even double that. However, if there is something hiding it like, oh, let's say several hundred feet of dirt, it cuts the distance drastically. Even then, it is sometimes difficult to identify what you sense. Some elements are very similar. Garnets are very similar to rubies, and one is quite expensive while the other isn't. The same can be said of gold and lead. Not to mention the western quadrant isn't exactly a small area to search. We will have to search his private office and hope to find some sort of map with the location marked," Corney explained. Search the western quadrant, how absurd. You would think after all these years he would know better.

"I have turned his office upside down over the last couple days, and I can assure you there is no map of any sort there," Sopheala admitted. Even thinking about owning her own gold mine excited her.

"Diamonds are mined, are they not?" Thommaus asked with a grin.

"Of course they are. Now tell us what you know," Sopheala demanded. *A diamond mine!* she thought to herself as she struggled to contain her excitement. Hoovar was looking more attractive by the second.

"I don't have any idea where to find what you are looking for, but I suspect it will be diamonds. I am sure I figured out who does know," Thommaus answered.

Daven began to laugh. It was ironic. They would really want to talk to the boys now. "Thommaus is right. They will know where you should mine," he declared for his own amusement.

"Who? Just tell us already," Sopheala nearly begged. She had to clam herself. She couldn't come across as overeager.

"Sorram and Taurwin," Daven answered with a smug grin that caused Hoovar and a couple of the men to groan.

"Who is this Sorram and Taurwin?" Kurt asked curiously.

"That is the names of the two hunters whom we suspect killed your father and tortured your brother," Hoovar admitted. "They would be the last to talk to your father," he pointed out.

"How can you be so sure my father told them the location of the mine?" Kurt asked with doubt. He could be wrong, but he doubted if his father would depart with that knowledge no matter what they had done to him.

"He didn't have to tell them. They already knew the location. Do you remember the bets I told you they placed at the Arena? Remember, the bulk of their wager was in raw and fresh-cut diamonds? They are even partners with the gem cutter," Thommaus reminded Hoovar. Those two must have made trips to the countryside to dig the things up. It wouldn't have been that far from the plains north of the city to the southern edge of the western quadrant. The trip would have taken some time for them, but they could have made the trip easily, depending on where the diamonds were located. Then again, since they could travel so far so fast, it was hard to guess how long it would have taken them.

"It could be true. More than once, Sorram disappeared for a week or so and when he returned he would send for Jordain," Daven added with a laugh.

"I don't see why you find this humorous," Sopheala scolded. She didn't find it humorous at all.

"Don't you see the irony? You want to punish those two, therefore, you will never see them again. Yet you need them. You need them to show you where you can locate your mine," Daven pointed out. Those two seemed to have that effect on people all too often. It was an odd love-hate relationship. How many times had those two done something wondrous for his family, only to scare the bejeebees out of him? How many times had he wondered if having them around brought benefits worth the danger they brought to his family?

"The worst part is that they are very good at this," Hoovar added and shook his head in disgust.

"What do you mean? Good at what?" Kurt asked.

"Chaos, they create chaos. I haven't traveled with them for long, and I have contemplated sending them away on more than one occasion. They are so damn gifted though. Then I start to think about all the good they can do, and they really do some good. Then they do what they want to do instead of what you want them to do, and you are back to where you started. You find yourself wishing you had sent them away in the first place," Hoovar tried to explain.

"I have to admit that I had thought about going a separate way more than once myself," Daven admitted and felt guilty for saying it.

"Really?" Thommaus said in disbelief. "But I thought they had done a lot to help your family out," he added as he tried to understand.

"They have and I am grateful for most of it, but they are so . . . so different. It makes you wonder if maybe it would be safer . . . I don't know, anywhere else. Life was a lot simpler when all we had to worry about was whether it would rain," Daven elaborated as he scratched his head.

"I don't really care how strange they are at this point. Hoovar, who is it that has authority here? I mean, who is to decide their sentence in this instance. Is it you because you are senior lord, or my mother because of jurisdiction?" Kurt asked. It was time to close this up and move on. There was nothing he or anyone else could do to bring his father back. If his brother admitted to his role in the death of women and children, there would be no saving him as well. Maybe the information those two hunters had could save his mother.

"Well, actually it would be between you and I, Kurt. Lordship over the land is generally handled by the eldest male of the bloodline unless he is deemed unfit. Your brother by no means is in any shape to rule, and there is still his penalty that needs set as well. You are old enough for the job, and you seem fit for it. At least I would vouch for you and back your decision. Therefore if you wish to set the penalties, that is fine with me," Hoovar told him.

"All right then. I will," Kurt declared as he stood up behind the desk. "You there, what is your name?" he asked as he pointed to Daven.

"Daven," he answered.

"Daven, how much could I fine these two hunters without running them off?" Kurt asked and waited. "How much can they afford? Ten or twenty gold crowns if I allow them to make payments?" he added.

"I don't think you heard me when I said they are partners with a jeweler," Daven replied and knew the man still didn't understand. "They have wealth. We call them hunters because that is what they seem to like doing, and they are very good at it. By no means do they need to do it. They not only own one business in Pua Dar but also own stakes in multiple businesses. I kept their accounts for a while until it became beyond my abilities. I assure you if you fine them a fair fine, they can afford to pay it. Therefore, you should ask yourself how much could you fine them without offending them. Does that make any sense?" Daven tried to explain.

"Then I set their—" Kurt began.

"Wait, don't set their fine just yet. Let's think about this. Somewhere in the western quadrant, there is a deposit of diamonds, which is good for me, but I don't have any means of mining it. We could collaborate since you have a ready workforce, but according to your mother, your finances are tapped out. We will need some capital to get things started. I have some capital, but I doubt if I have the kind of resources we will need to take on this venture. We will not only need them to tell us the location of the mine, but we will also need them to partner up with us because they evidently have the means to provide the start-up capital," Hoovar pointed out.

"What are you suggesting?" Kurt asked.

"I am suggesting that you first figure out approximately how much capital we need or at least enough to pay off your debtors and then fine them that amount. Then grant them an equal share in the profits," Hoovar suggested.

"They will not invest in any business that uses slave labor. You would have to pay all of your workers," Daven informed them.

"What? You want us to pay our slaves. That is absurd," Sopheala exclaimed.

"That is the way they do business. They buy slaves, set them free, and then pay them a fair wage. In return, the freed slaves pay back the cost of setting them free. This way you don't have to pay any armed guards and the workers are motivated. I have seen it work more than once. You may not make quite as much profit, but how would you notice on a diamond mine?" Daven explained. "Besides, it sounds to me that they will be putting up nearly all of the initial costs."

"Well, what do you think?" Kurt asked Hoovar.

"What other options do you have? We could look for other investors, but that will take time. The longer we take, the more the interest piles up on the debt you already have," Hoovar reminded him.

"All right, I agree, but how do we find them in the first place?" Kurt asked.

"We won't. I will leave that up to my daughter," Daven said with a smile. "If I were you, I would worry about getting the workforce ready to move. Hoovar can send word to where they are to go as soon as we find out where it is. He can also send some gold along to get the ball rolling," Daven told him.

* * *

Brinnel read the reports one last time before he entered the emperor's chambers. He didn't want to suffer the same fate as Grumman. He still had nightmares after witnessing that. He took another deep breath and formed the tones that announced his presence and waited for a response. The chime sounded, and he entered the emperor's chambers. He didn't realize the emperor had been entertaining himself with another sacrifice or he would have come later.

"M'lord, pardon for my interruption, I shall return when you are finished," he offered while he hoped to be sent away. He could hear the little girl whimper under the emperor's attentions. He would rather be anywhere else except here to witness the man's sick and twisted perversions. At least this one was a female, he told himself. He would use the potion he carried with him everywhere before he would let it happen to him. A quick death would be better than what he had to witness too often in these chambers.

"Don't be silly, I was ready for a break anyway. I can play with her for hours later," the emperor said with a wicked giggle. The statement rewarded him with renewed cries for mercy from the little girl, who was wiggling in her bonds of air. He swatted her on her bare skin and said, "Now, you behave or I will not be so gentle when I get back to you." He was delighted by her squeal and cries. "Now, as for you, I hope you have something to report to me. My patience wear thin," Danemon told Brinnel.

"Yes, m'lord, I have finally received a message from the guild of the magi. The report says that they already had a party in the vicinity scouting for new beginners and they have already begun searching for the criminals. They have also sent reinforcements to the area that will hook up with the forward team upon their arrival. I hope to report more updates as they arrive, Master. If there isn't anything else you wish, I will leave you to your sport," Brinnel said and wished for dismissal.

"That is odd to have a party looking for students in that area, don't you think. No matter, I guess I should be grateful for some good news for a change. I do have one thing for you before you leave," the emperor said as he strolled over to his desk and retrieved a book from it. "Here, take this and have it printed and distributed," he ordered as he tossed the book to Brinnel.

"If you don't mind me asking, m'lord, but what is it?" Brinnel asked as he tried not to look at the sick man. If he had any decency at all, he would at least cover himself, but

Brinnel knew that there was nothing decent about him. The emperor was sick and vile, and one day the emperor would be the cause of his death one way or another.

"It is the new version of the good book," the emperor answered.

"I thought, I mean, those are banned by you. Forgive me, but I don't understand. It is punishable by death for me to just hold this," Brinnel said as he held the book as if it was poison.

"I did, but this is my version. I have made some changes and you may now call me the Prophet," the emperor answered. It was obvious Brinnel didn't understand anything. "I banned the good book how many centuries ago, yet people still worship the Creator. I have rewritten the book and named myself as the Creator's prophet. Only through me can they receive forgiveness from the Creator. See, now I will get the worship I deserve," he explained with satisfaction.

Brinnel was stunned. He didn't know how to respond to this madness. All he could manage to do was stand there and gape like a fish out of water.

"I see you are impressed with my genius once again. I had finally realized that no matter how much I enjoy my sacrifices, I will never collect enough souls to challenge the Fallen One, let alone the Creator by collecting one at a time while they divide all those who die. Sure, I can collect large numbers during battles, but there are so few countries to declare war with anymore. This will be much more efficient. I have added some things that many will like too. You should read it. No, you will read it and make sure I haven't missed anything," the emperor commanded.

"I will do as you command, m'lo—ah . . . Prophet. Is there anything else?" Brinnel asked as he stared at the book. This was evil. He was mad. Challenge the Fallen One and the Creator? That was not possible, was it? Someone had to do something. Someone should kill this . . . this . . . Brinnel realized he was still standing there when he heard the girl's scream. He looked up instinctively to see the emp . . . prophet's bite tear away a small piece of the girl's flesh.

As he turned and ran for the door, he could hear the laughter of the "Prophet." He didn't stop to see if the laughter was for him or for the poor girl he left in the chambers with that rabid animal. He didn't care. If he weren't such a coward, he would take that medicine now and end it.

*   *   *

Hoovar promised himself a long hot bath when he returned to the manor, and if he had to ride his horse again in the next year, it would be too soon to suit him. He was too old for this traipsing all over the countryside, but the sooner he returned, the sooner he could be done with it. He even promised himself to stay at the manor until all the books were balanced and all of his paperwork was done, no matter how restless he became. He was returning with more men than he had left with, but that just meant that he wouldn't have to send one of his own men back to the Pizolla manor to let them know how his meeting with Sorram and Taurwin went if he found them. It would be a lot easier if they would show themselves so he could talk to them. He knew the boys had remained close enough to keep an eye on his little party as they made their way home. It was either that or forest fairies were leaving them fresh meat in the mornings, and he didn't believe forest fairies was the most likely source. He almost laughed at the ridiculous thought.

"What is it?" Thommaus asked as he studied his old boss.

"Oh nothing, my mind was wandering and I had a ridiculous thought, is all," Hoovar told him with a grin. "Don't worry, I am not losing my mind yet. I'm not that old."

"I lost mine once. I never did find it. After a while, I had to break down and buy a new one. It cost me a pretty penny too," Corney chimed in. "Of course, it wouldn't have bothered me if you weren't so tight with the pay," he grumbled.

"What are you talking about? I don't pay you at all," Hoovar protested.

"See what I mean? And with what that blacksmith charged me, it will take me forever to pay him back," Corney complained.

"Are you trying to tell us you had a blacksmith make you a new mind?" Thommaus protested. Corney's stories were sometimes bizarre, but usually they made more sense than this. Well, or they were funny anyway.

"What kind of foolishness are you up to now?" Corney scolded. "I haven't heard such a ridiculous tale in all my years," he added. "Blacksmith making a mind . . . How absurd." He continued grumbling and shaking his head.

Hoovar and Thommaus were dumbfounded as they looked at Corney and then at each other. They were laughing so hard they nearly fell from their horses as they left the forest trail and entered the meadow in which the farms were located and where they expected to find Sylvy and Sahharras.

It looked as any farm would with people attending gardens, fields, or livestock. A few people gathered to greet them and ask questions, but no one said a word when a door opened and Krotus stepped out of one of the houses.

"Corney, tell your apprentices to release me this instant," Krotus demanded. The statement caused a round of laughter, which made Krotus wish he hadn't said anything at all.

Corney dismounted and walked over to where Sahharras and Sylvy stood defiantly with their shoulders back and their chins up. "You didn't attack him, did you?" he inquired with a frown. Sahharras and Krotus answered as one, but Corney held out his hand until they were done and said, "One at a time, apprentices. How am I supposed to make heads or tails of anything while you jabber over one another like that?"

"I have not been your apprentice in ages. I am a full mage and demand the respect I am due," Krotus declared angrily.

"Then act like one. Shut up and wait your turn patiently," Corney scolded before he turned his attention back to Sahharras. "Sahharras, did you attack a full mage?" Corney asked again.

"No, I did not," she answered confidently.

"She lies!" Krotus protested as he crossed his arms for emphasis.

"I did not attack you. I just seized the elements to protect myself. After all, if you don't remember the last time I saw you, it was when you were weaving my shield," Sahharras pointed out and then stuck out her tongue at Krotus. She was shocked when something grabbed hold of it so she couldn't put her tongue back in her mouth. Then she saw the stream of air emanating from Corney. She had only stuck it out for a second. The crazy old mage was fast. She had to admit that.

"Since you can't control your tongue, I thought I might help you with it," Corney chastened her. Then he turned his attention to Krotus. "Is what she said true?" He could see the guilt in Krotus's eyes. Krotus was never any good at lying. He was about as straight as an arrow as apprentices came to be honest. "Why, Krotus? You know how serious an offense it is to attack another mage's apprentice?" Corney asked in disbelief.

"I wasn't thinking. Let's go inside so we can talk, and we do need to talk," Krotus admitted begrudgingly.

"Good idea. Let's all go in for a long talk," Hoovar suggested as he pushed past Krotus to lead them all inside. "Are you coming, or are you going to stand out there all day?" he added.

"You may release him if he promises to behave himself," Corney told Sahharras as he released her tongue.

"Actually I didn't capture him," Sahharras admitted as she looked at Sylvy.

"How the—never mind. You are right, Sahharras, the proper etiquette, if you can call it that, is to allow the victor to release his or her catch," Corney said with a chuckle as he ruffled Sylvy's hair.

Once everyone was inside, Hoovar asked, "The first thing I want to know is what exactly are those two boys."

"No, you don't. Trust me on this one, you really don't," Krotus corrected as he slumped down in his chair.

"Then why bring them here. Isn't one of them enough for you? I thought you hated the emperor," Hoovar started and he just knew he was right. "Then why in the hell would you bring more of his kind to this plane? Damn it, boy, what were you thinking." He got up from his chair and began to pace as he ranted. "Of all the foolish things—"

"No no, they are not like him. You are right, I do hate Danemon. He is evil incarnate and you two know it. He is the mistake we must erase from history. That is why I brought Sorram and Taurwin here. They are one of the few things I've ever seen him fear. That is why I brought them here, but I only brought one of each of their kind. I enhanced them some, of course," Krotus said in his defense. "That doesn't matter. Where are they? I have to get them out of here. They are not mature enough to face him yet. Once they are adults, they may have a chance to kill him with our help. If the human race was to stand with those two, there is a chance, but they have to live until they are fully grown," he explained.

"Devourers, don't tell me you brought devourers here. Damn it, not even the elves could control the devourers. That was the reason for the covenant, remember?" Hoovar reminded him.

"Yes, I do remember. Do you? Do you remember why they brought them here in the first place? Yeah, that's right, because of him. They couldn't control the devourers because they wouldn't use blood magic. All of the devourers went mad, but I gave these two the blood of humans not only to make them look human but also as the means to keep their sanity in check. You have met them. They have loyalty to a fault. I have witnessed it. They desire to please. They are rock steady. I don't recall one instance that they had lost their temper or acted out of rage. I couldn't have expected them to turn out as well as they had. I have to admit that Sorram's capability with the elements were unexpected side effect. Taurwin's resistance to the elemental magics was just as unexpected, but that makes both of them that much more valuable as an ally," he told them as a proud father would boast of favorite sons. "Which reminds me, who made that little disturbance that put this whole province under the glass?"

"First of all, that was one of your slightly modified creations at work. Then your sane, steady-as-a-rock child was upset and healed a friend of his. Then your creations proceeded to kill a bunch of mercenaries. Between the two of them, they have killed at least twenty men that I know of, and that don't include mage Pruitt. They tortured and dismembered Roaran Pizolla. Then they stole Lord Pizolla out of his manor house in the middle of the night to murder him. That is only what I know they have done. I suspect them of other crimes, but I don't have any proof. Now, what do you have to say for your steady-as-a-rock creation now?" Hoovar told him.

"What, Sorram did that? Was he in a circle? Why did you let him do that, Sahharras? The search is on for them now. What in the world did he do anyway? Why did he draw the elements like that? He could have hurt himself, ya know," Krotus asked with a scowl. "I half expected to find a chasm where someone split the planet's crust."

"That's not fair," Daven interrupted. "Tell him the rest of it." He waited, but it was obvious that Hoovar didn't know what he meant. "What he didn't tell you was that they have healed the injured, fed the hungry, clothed the poor, and sheltered the homeless. Not everything they have done has been an act of violence," Daven protested.

"You don't even know what we are talking about, do you," Hoovar challenged. "Yes, they fed the poor. The devourers got that title because they would hunt down and eat anything. Their drive to hunt eventually overtakes them until they no longer hunt for food. They will hunt and kill for no other reason. That is what they are and that is what they do. On their plane of existence, they are at the top of the food chain, and only the harshness of their environment and their savagery toward one and another keeps their population in check. On this plane of existence, there is very little they have to fear. As they mature, the drive to hunt will drive them mad," Hoovar explained.

"No, they won't. I fixed them. I gave them . . . ," Krotus began and stopped short to shake his head. "There is a weave that can help them if they start to be overcome by their instincts. Corney, you know it will work. I will monitor them as they mature to make sure they don't go mad. We have to give them a chance or mankind will have no chance," he begged.

"I have heard enough. I don't care what any of you say. Those two have done right by me and mine. I will stand by them, and I refuse to stand here while you talk about them like this. They are not the monsters you make them out to be," Daven said before he turned to stomp out the door. The door slammed behind him to emphasize his statement.

Hoovar looked around the room and saw strange faces looking back at him. Corney looked so old he barely recognized his old friend. He looked at his hands, and they were the hands of an old man. They were wrinkled and covered with sunspots as well. "Where have all the years gone?" he said as he reached out to pat Corney on the shoulder. "I remember when we were young. We were going to change the world. We thought we could make it better. I can't remember how long it has been since I thought I was doing something to make the world better."

He noticed the tears running down Sahharras's cheek. "If there is anyone who could watch over them, it would have to be you. I think they love you as a mother. Corney can teach Sylvy if he needs to have an apprentice. You should go with Krotus and make sure those boys get to safety. Take them south and out of the empire. I will write out orders to give you rights to pass to the border unhindered," Hoovar told her. Then he turned to Sylvy. "I think you better go get them and ask them to come here. Tell them I said—no, tell them Sahharras said they are to behave and come in," he instructed Sylvy.

"I don't—" Sylvy began, but she saw Sahharras frown and point her to the door with a wink. "Fine, I will go, but I am positive they don't like him at all," she protested as she pointed at Krotus.

"Good, they should hate me. If they don't kill me, then they have strong control of themselves still," Krotus said with a nervous quiver in his voice. He watched her bound for the door and then disappear through it. "Corney, you will have to tell me your secret on finding such gifted apprentices if I survive this next encounter with the boys," he joked nervously.

Hoovar was relieved when Sylvy returned with both boys in tow. There was too much riding on those two for him to feel comfortable, and he wasn't thinking about the mining. It was insane to let the fate of humankind ride on the backs of those two young boys. No, they were not boys, he corrected himself. They had returned to their human form except for the odd tooth peeking out, but they were still demons who were doomed to go mad. They were the hounds who were expected to hunt down, kill, and eat the most dangerous prey on this plane of existence. It wouldn't matter if those two actually accomplished their task because it would be up to mankind if there were any of mankind left alive to execute the victor while they were too weak from the battle to defend themselves. He once again felt the guilt of his responsibility weighing on his shoulders. Would their cruel fate been any different had he died in his cradle so many years ago?

Thommaus wasn't sure what had happened to Hoovar, but when Sylvy returned with Sorram and Taurwin, the man changed. He closed up and barely spoke a single word. The man wouldn't even look either boy in the eye or acknowledge their presence. This left him to negotiate the terms of their partnership with the mine. To make matters worse, Sorram and Taurwin spent most of their time staring Krotus down. They paid nearly as little attention to him as Hoovar did. At least Daven was willing to step in on Sorram and Taurwin's behalf. It still took longer than he expected to negotiate the terms. He thought he did fairly well considering the circumstances, but he doubted if the Pizollas would be pleased with the boys' insistence that all diamonds were to go through the same jeweler. Thommaus wasn't sure how this Jordain would take to the news that he would be responsible for overseeing the polishing, cutting, and sales of all the diamonds a mine could produce either. He wouldn't have agreed if it hadn't been for Daven's assurance that Jordain was more than a fair man.

FLIGHT TO FREEDOM

Sahharras didn't even know where to begin. She was supposed to pack her things and then see to the boys' packing, but there wasn't enough room for all of her stuff. They were going to be riding horse and not a wagon, so she could only take with her what she could pack in her satchel or roll up in her bedroll. She would barely have enough room to take two changes of clothes. The boys had paid for dozens of them for her. How was she ever going to decide which to leave behind?

"What seems to be the holdup, apprentice?" Corney asked as he entered the room behind her.

"I was having trouble deciding what to take and what to leave behind," Sahharras confessed.

"Really? I can't believe a woman would have problems with that," Corney teased with a chuckle. "I am sorry that I haven't had the time to teach you properly. I only . . . I . . ."

Sahharras waited for Corney to finish his statement, but as he continued to stare off at nothing, she became concerned. She let the elements seep into her, and she reached out with spirit and air to probe the mind of the old mage. She couldn't find anything broken, but that didn't mean there was nothing wrong. She would have to read more of the books on diseases of the mind before she would even know what she was looking for in order to heal him.

"Oh, stop it. I am quite fine. Grab your satchel and come. I have something to show you, and I suspect it may be advantageous to others as well," Corney commanded abruptly before turning to leave.

Sahharras followed Corney outside where he immediately seized the elements. He continued to draw on them slowly as he walked past the barn. She nearly ran into him as he stopped as suddenly as he had taken off. She looked around until she saw what he had been looking for until now. It was Sorram and Taurwin. They were just beyond the corral for the horses waiting for the men to mount up. They were supposed to lead the men to the location of the diamonds today. Actually, Sorram said it would take him several days for him to lead them there and back.

"Hand me your satchel," Corney commanded but stared in Sorram's direction. He took Sahharras's satchel from her and emptied its contents upon the ground, which caused some grumbling. "This weave I show you can be very useful. You have to figure out the uses for yourself." He prepared the elements in an intricate pattern and wrapped them throughout the fabric of the garment. "This allows you to carry much more than you could have otherwise. Think of it as an inner-planer pocket. The objects you place in here will no longer burden you down. You can put as much as you like in here as long as it fits in the opening. You should watch putting something too valuable in here due to the fact that if something damages or destroys the weave, it becomes more than difficult to retrieve your items," he concluded before he turned his attention back to Sahharras.

Once Corney's words sank in, she was ecstatic. "Are you serious? That is wonderful," she exclaimed as she leaped up to give the startled mage a kiss on the check. "I could take all of my dresses."

"You could, but I wouldn't recommend it. It would make unpacking or finding one particular dress rather difficult, but you could easily take nearly a dozen or so," Corney corrected as he glanced back at Sorram.

"That will be plenty, I think," she said as she kissed him on one cheek and then after a brief pause kissed him on the other cheek as well.

"What was that for?" Corney asked as he rubbed his cheek.

"The first was from me. The others were from the boys. Sorram and Taurwin thank you too," she said with a grin. That had to be why he wanted to do his demonstration in front of the boys. They would have things they would want to take with them as well. She did not blame them. There had to be things that would remind them of their time among friends. Those would be the things she should try to use first if they began to have difficulty holding to their human forms.

* * *

"Where is Taurwin?" Thommaus asked Sorram as they prepared to camp for the night.

"He has other business to attend to this night. He should return to the farms shortly after we do," Sorram answered.

"Really, I thought you both would be here," Thommaus questioned with concern.

"Should it take two of us to show where to dig?" Sorram asked with a confused look.

"No no, it's just that . . . Well, I thought he was coming with us. Wait a minute, you said he had other business to attend to tonight. What is he doing?" Thommaus began to protest.

"He's probably out killing someone," Joshua provoked as he squared up to Sorram.

Sorram sighed, shook his head, turned his back to the fool, and began to walk off in disgust.

"Don't turn your back on me, boy," Joshua sneered.

"If we had thought you were guilty as your master, you would already be dead, but your taunts will not provoke me. Your words mean nothing to me. I have no desire to kill you. Nor do I wish to fight you. I don't even have any reason to hurt you," Sorram replied as he studied the man. "If you continue to look for a way to provoke me, I fear you will find it. If you insist on this, I guess I could spar with you if you wish. Then maybe we can move on," Sorram added in a sad voice after some thought.

"What, spar with those stupid sticks you carry? I don't play with sticks, boy," Joshua taunted again as he stroked the hilt of his sword. Real men don't play with sticks. Real men used swords.

"Use what you wish. I will use my hands," Sorram answered calmly.

Joshua blinked at the answer. He couldn't figure out what angle the boy was playing. Then it hit him. "Don't think that I will hold back just because you haven't shown us the location of the diamonds, boy. I will cut you to pieces given the chance," Joshua threatened.

"If you follow that stream to the south, you will come to where it feeds into another stream. Look to the western bank of that stream until it reaches the river and you will find all the diamonds you wish," Sorram told the man.

"Wait a minute. I didn't ride all the way out here to watch you two kill each other. Joshua, I expect you to behave yourself. You leave Sorram alone. He has agreed to the terms set by your master," Thommaus interceded.

"Not my master, my master is dead," Joshua said as he slid his sword from its scabbard.

"Here are my terms. I spar with you. You can use any weapon you choose while I have none. If you win, I will be dead. If I win, you ride on tonight. You will continue riding with no master. You will have no home, no family, constantly moving. The only time you stop is to help someone in need of your services. You will lend a hand to any who required it, in my name or Taurwin's," Sorram challenged as he faced off in front of Joshua.

"Fine with me. None of that will matter because you will be dead in—" Joshua said as he thrust his sword at Sorram.

Thommaus wasn't surprised when the man's blade missed its mark. He saw Sorram slide around the blade and toward Joshua where his open palm found the underneath of the man's chin in one fluid motion. Thommaus could swear Sorram hit the man hard enough that his feet left the ground before he was thrown backward to the ground. Sorram just stepped back and waited. He didn't think the boy looked angry, but the boy wasn't grinning as he did when he sparred with someone like Sylvy or Taurwin. He couldn't help but think on Krotus's words about the boys not losing their temper and wondered if they killed the mercenaries, tortured Pruitt, and Roaran with the same lack of emotion. No, that would be impossible. No one could have done that.

"I take it that you are in agreement then. Your men will be witness and judges then. We can begin as soon as you can get up," Sorram stated calmly over Joshua's curses and groans.

"I wasn't ready for that, is all. We don't need any judges to tell me you are dead. I will know when I remove your head from your body," Joshua declared as he dragged himself to his feet. He launched his next attack without warning also. He hadn't expected the boy to pose such an inhuman speed. He would not make the same mistake twice. This time he didn't overreach. He kept his strokes and jabs to just that. He wouldn't leave himself open to a counterattack. Just because the boys said he wouldn't use a weapon didn't mean he was without resources.

Thommaus watched as Sorram easily dodged the man's slow long sword. After a few careful and conservative forms of the sword, the man began to look more confident. Then Sorram started batting the sword away with his open hand on the flat of the sword. The look of disbelief on Joshua's face was priceless as far as Thommaus was concerned. Soon it became a contest where Joshua was not doing much more than trying to turn his blade quick enough to get Sorram to cut himself. He had abandoned the forms altogether to achieve this one objective. It was if the man thought it would be all over if he could just cut Sorram once no matter how small or insignificant the cut. The sparring had become a farce where Sorram had made a fool of the man. The shame of it to Thommaus was the fact that the man didn't look half bad while he stuck to the forms. Now, he looked like a fool, and judging by the looks on Joshua's men, he wasn't alone on that assessment.

Joshua couldn't believe what he was seeing. It was simply impossible for anyone to do that. The boy was batting his sword faster than he could even turn it. How long had it been since he had even actually tried to attack? This was ridiculous. "Why don't you just kill me?" Joshua begged as he sank to his knees and presented his sword.

"I have no desire to kill you. You have shown loyalty to a fault to a man that didn't deserve it. Your master was a cruel and greedy man and he died for it. Those at the farm were murdered because there was no one there to protect them. Why don't you ride out, find others like them, and be their protector, be their avenger. I don't care whose name you claim to glorify. Do it as reparation of your master's sins. Do it in the memory of the master as he should have been or as the master you remember him to be. Do it for the honor of doing the right thing. I don't care what reason you pick, but you need to do it for yourself," Sorram lectured before he turned and trotted off into the darkening hills.

Sorram's words had stirred something in Joshua and his men. It was all Thommaus could do to convince the rest of the fools that Sorram's instructions were for Joshua and Joshua alone. The rest had work to be about in the morning. He doubted if he would have had any of the Pizolla men left to ride with him to find the diamonds by morning if Joshua hadn't agreed with him. Even more shocking was the fact that the man was on his horse swearing he would return for the others as soon as he could before he rode off into the oncoming darkness. Thommaus couldn't believe the change in the man. He also believed the man would take Sorram's charge as seriously as he took his loyalty to his former master.

*   *   *

Brinnel rushed to his master's quarters to answer his summons while he fingered the small vial he carried at all times now. He had planned to report to the emper . . . prophet after he finished with his new toys. He was always more pleasant afterward. Brinnel had even sent two sacrifices today in an attempt to ensure a favorable mood before he gave his report. However, if he were to drink the potion now, he would not have to give the report at all. The door opened before he even rang for admittance. He took a deep breath and entered. "The great prophet has summoned," he said as he knelt on the floor.

The smell of fear emanated from Brinnel so thick he could almost taste it. "Puzzle me this. For years I have been kept on a strict schedule of sacrifices, but today I receive two for no apparent reason at all, two children at that," the prophet said as he ran a finger through a puddle of blood on the floor and then proceeded to lick his finger clean. "Don't get me wrong, it isn't as if I didn't enjoy them immensely, despite their premature departure. That is the problem with the younger ones. So much fun but so short-lived." He giggled.

Brinnel was sure his ruse had worked. The "prophet" was in a rare mood. "I have been puzzling over a report and I am not sure what it means. I wished to ask for your help understanding it. I thought you might be more generous with your wisdom if I was able to please you first. I saw the two children huddled together in the cells, and I thought they were the perfect surprise to lift your spirits," he replied cautiously. He had probably condemned his soul for it, but then again the odds were in favor, of it already being condemned. Then again who was to say the emperor would not consume him as he had countless others.

"And you were correct. The prophet is in a generous mood. Tell me what troubles you, Brinnel, and I will see if I can shed light on it for you," Danemon answered as he wrapped himself into a robe. He hated clothes, but this robe was relatively comfortable. If he remembered correctly, it too had been a gift from Brinnel. Maybe he should think about giving Brinnel a little something in return. Then again, he did cover himself in front of the man. That should have made the man happy. Why did these humans obsess over such trivial things? Still it wasn't as if he couldn't afford something a little more substantial as a gift.

"You are most gracious. The report comes from the guild of the magi. The report states that they don't have any suspects in custody yet. They are expecting news soon though. Then it goes on to list items that are missing from the guild's vaults. I don't understand what one thing has to do with the other. It should be listed as separate events, but the way it reads makes me think they meant the two events are related," Brinnel explained. It was more than obvious the prophet was in a good mood. He would have to remember that little trick for the next time he thought he might have bad news.

"That is strange," the prophet replied curiously. "What two items have the fools lost?" he asked with a grin. This man had been in his service for . . . well, a long time. Brinnel had probably outlived any other attendant that had served him.

"It says they lost a dwarven hammer and an elven book," Brinnel answered with a smile. He watched as the smile slid from the prophet's face. That couldn't be a good sign at all. "What is it, m'lord? I mean, m'prophet. Are they valuable?" he asked as ice formed on his spine.

"Are they valuable? Well, they were valuable enough for me to go through all of the trouble to steal them in the first place. I went through a lot of trouble stealing them. Then they misplace them. Those . . . incompetent . . . ," he ranted as he began to pace. The man was loyal, but he didn't know anything. Are they valuable?

"I have never even heard of them before this. What is their purpose? What do they do?" Brinnel asked nervously. He could feel the mood change.

"I have no idea what they do, but they are the source to the elven and dwarven magics, or so I was told. Even if one could not wield them, they could lead the elven and dwarven nations against me," the prophet explained. Those were two boils that he had yet to prick. It wasn't as if he wasn't working on them, but they could still cause him trouble. Those elves were dangerous enough without their stupid book, and the dwarves were as dangerous as the elves, maybe even worse with their machines.

"Why didn't you have them destroyed? If we can't use them, wouldn't it have been better to destroy them and deny them from your enemies," Brinnel inquired. His curiosity was getting the better of him. He couldn't help but get excited over something the prophet seemed to fear.

"I couldn't. They were a gift of the Creator. I wasn't strong enough to destroy them. I need to destroy the Creator first, but then their power would cease to exist anyway. Damn! How the—who lost them?" Danemon demanded. All he had to do is find out who had them and take them back. It wasn't as if there was anyone who could stop him. At least there wasn't now. He was too powerful for anyone to think he could be denied now. He would crush whoever stood between him and what he wanted.

"I have a copy . . . huh, that's strange," Brinnel mumbled as he studied the notes and papers and then shuffled them again.

"What is strange, damn you? Don't keep me in suspense, Brinnel, you wouldn't like my reaction to it," the prophet shouted as he struggle to contain himself. That was what he would do. He would take those artifacts back before anyone realized their value or figured out how to use them against him.

"Well, I thought I did have some good news, but I am not so sure now. This report claims a skirmish between the culprits, and the magi recruiting party ended in the deaths of several magi but the mage in charge received reinforcement from Lord Hoovar and is in close pursuit of the criminals. That is why it is suspected they would be in custody soon, but this copy of the vault records show the same mage was the one who reported the items missing. It could be a coincidence, but I don't think so. That has to be the connection. Why couldn't they just write that? Why did they have to be so cryptic about it? I think I figured it out, m'lord. This mage has stolen your artifacts and left the tower under pretense to search for apprentices. Then he must have tried to use them in some way killing some or all of his party in the process. Now, with fresh reinforcements and orders giving him authority to do nearly anything, he is roaming the countryside. No, that still doesn't make any sense," Brinnel concluded as he scratched his head. "I thought I had it there for a minute." What if this mage figured out how to use the artifacts, and he was the one who caused the disturbance? What if the disturbance everyone felt was in fact this mage while he was killing the rest in his party? What if this mage, armed with these artifacts of power, were as powerful as Danemon?

"Let me see that damn report," the prophet demanded as he snagged the papers from Brinnel's hands. One name leapt off the page at him. "Krotus . . . ," he fumed. "Have orders written for the execution of the battle mage Krotus on sight. Have orders written to capture all with him and have them brought before me." He set the papers to burst into flame. He will kill Krotus as he should have done years ago. He can find someone else to replace Krotus.

"Yes, m'lord, immediately," Brinnel said as he ran for the door. The flames had been his sign that he was dismissed. He would live to see another day. He hoped that he wouldn't regret it.

The prophet stood there and brooded over what he had read. Maybe he had underestimated Krotus. Krotus hadn't been allowed to leave the tower in ages, but he had figured a way to get out. What angered him the most was according to the report, it was his orders that Krotus had used to get out. His orders kept Krotus from any harm after a few suicide attempts and the magi thought fresh air and different surroundings would heal Krotus's failing mental health. Then all he had to do is check out the hammer and the book from the vault and walk right out of the tower. Then he somehow used them to cause the disturbance and then convince his old mentor to give him reinforcements to battle an enemy that doesn't even exist. The whole plan was quite cunning, but it wouldn't work. He would go to the west and wait for Krotus there. Krotus would never live to see the elves or the dwarves.

General Basserus was delighted at the appointment of lord of the city. Now, he would be able to stay in the palace permanently, and with that would come all the posh benefits associated with it. He had no idea what he had done to deserve his good fortune, but he wasn't going to complain. This appointment didn't even seem to have a downside. The hardest thing he had to do all day was to sit here on his "chair of judgment" and pretend to listen to these reports. Most of the time he didn't even bother to do that much. Like now, for instance, he wasn't listening to the clerk ramble on about the tax collections. Instead, he would think about his next visit from one of Sharletae's girls. Now there was a benefit he didn't ever want to give up. If he ever went back to the military, he would have to take Sharletae up on her deal to send girls to "keep up the morale" among the men. Hell, he was even considering contacting one of the other banner generals on her behalf to suggest just that. He had to admit her idea did have merit even as ridiculous as it sounded. He wondered if General—"What was that you said?" he asked the clerk that he hadn't been paying attention to since the man started the morning report.

"Which part, m'lord? It has been a lengthy report, m'lord," the clerk responded dryly.

"The part about the overseer," Basserus told him. The man knew what he was talking about, damn it. He was just jerking him around because he hadn't listened to anything today. "See, I do listen," he lied.

"The part about the overseer not been seen for two days, or the part where a search for him found him dead and beheaded in one of the towers to his fortress, m'lord?" the clerk asked dryly.

"He's dead?" Basserus exclaimed.

"Yes, m'lord," the clerk repeated.

They had traveled across country and avoided the roads and towns where there may be any soldiers. Of course, Sorram and Taurwin ran constant scouting forays ahead of them. They would run back and check the back trail as well as check the flanks. No one was within a league or two without the boys knowing about it. Krotus would have preferred it if they would just tell him instead of them telling Sahharras as if he wasn't right there though. Then again, maybe he should be grateful they didn't simply drag him off in the night to cut on him a little as had been done to them on more than one occasion during their stay at the tower under his authority. He wasn't sure how much of that "following orders, name of the emperor" crap they believed, and he decided not to press his luck.

Sahharras was sure there was something wrong with the boys. She understood why they didn't like Krotus, but there was something else going on. She noticed them checking their teeth too often. Even worse was the times she saw their teeth when they hadn't checked on them. They never did get to the point where they could make their teeth look human, but at least they could hide them as long as they didn't smile or growl. For some reason, ever since the incident with Sylvy, she was sure they were having more difficulty holding their human forms. She didn't want to say anything to Krotus about it, but she was worried. To make matters worse, that wasn't her only worries.

She wasn't sure how Krotus planned to get the boys across the river into the Therresian kingdom either. Hoovar had written orders for them to hunt down fictitious criminals, but those were only good inside the realm of the empire. Those papers did nothing to help them cross over the border. Then the boys had no legal documents at all. That wasn't uncommon for a peasant or a farmer, but any tradesman would have at least a permit for their profession. Any militiaman, sellsword, or private guard would have not only a permit but would require at least a license issued by an imperial clerk. She doubted if it was hard to obtain the documents if you had time to submit a request for them, but time was not a luxury they had an overabundance of unless she was mistaken.

* * *

"What's bothering you, old man? Corney? Corney?" Hoovar asked his troubled-looking friend.

"What?" Corney responded as he shook his head to clear away the cobwebs.

"What is bothering you?" Hoovar repeated himself.

"I was just thinking—" Corney began but stopped to stare off into the night.

"Thinking what?" Hoovar asked as he got up and walked over to where Corney was sitting to see if the old man was ill. He put a hand to his friend's forehead. There wasn't a temperature, but the man's skin was clammy.

"Oh, stop that. You make me feel juvenile," Corney scolded as he swatted Hoovar's hand away. "I was just thinking about my apprentice, is all."

"Oh, is that little she devil giving you trouble?" Hoovar teased. He had heard a few of the maids comment on how nice it was to have a young one in the manor for a change. However, he had spent too much time going over books and reports since their return to know any more about how Corney's apprentice was doing.

"No, quite the opposite, she has changed and continues to change by the day. It has only been a few weeks since Sorram healed her, and I am not too sure if her own mother would recognize her now," Corney answered.

"What do you mean?" Hoovar replied in disbelief. Surely, Corney was exaggerating. Then again, maybe it was Corney who couldn't recognize his apprentice.

"Just that she is growing so fast the first maid can't keep her in dresses. I gave her the day off her classes today so the first maid could take care of her . . . her . . . you know, feminine issues. I didn't think that would be a problem for a few years yet. That could explain some of her miraculous gains in ability but . . . ," Corney was saying until he stopped to scratch his head.

"But what?" Hoovar asked with a sigh as he shook the old mage. Inquiring with the first maid would be easy enough to confirm his concerns or tell him if the old mage was losing it.

"It doesn't explain her knowledge. I mean, the other day she used a weave I know I didn't teach her. It was one of the higher forms of healing. Only the masters of healing know one of those weaves. There is only one way . . . Those two boys or devourers are actually a species of animal. They are not demonic in nature. They exist naturally on a few planes, but they are not necessarily of the lower planes, nor were they created out of malice by the Fallen One as the rest of the demonic species. That could explain it," Corney explained as he stood up and paced back and forth.

"What does it explain?" Hoovar asked. He was as confused now as he was before Corney began to explain. It sounded like Corney knew what was going on. It even sounded like he should be making sense. Hoovar had always believed the devourers were demonic, but did it really make any difference if they were not? A large male could grow to the size of a large draft horse. Demonic or not, that was a scary thought. He didn't even want to think about having a wolf or leopard the size of even a small horse running around. Add the intelligence to use weapons and magic into the mix the way those two could, and it was enough to give any sane man nightmares.

"Instincts! Don't you see? They can know things from instincts like any other wild animal. It is the human side that is unnatural to them," Corney answered.

"Okay, they have instincts, but what does that mean, Corney? I don't have any idea what you are even talking about," Hoovar complained. Times like these made Hoovar wonder if Corney had control of his faculties and it was he who was losing his faculties.

"Those two don't have to necessarily be taught. They may be able to learn from the blood of anyone or anything Krotus infused with them to make them what they are. They may be able to . . . that is probably why Sylvy knows weaves she shouldn't. She may know nearly as much about fighting as they do because they have infused her with their blood. Her instincts told her to use that spell. She probably got it from Sorram, and Sorram got the knowledge from whoever's blood he was infused with," Corney tried to explain again.

"Then why didn't either one of those two know any table manners if they knew everything those who gave their blood to them knew?" Hoovar asked doubtfully.

"It wouldn't have been important to their survival. For example, Sylvy had been summoned to help a woman with child. The woman had been injured from an accident involving a horse. The woman was bleeding, and it was believed that she was going to lose the child. I learned from probing the woman that not only was she bleeding internally, but the child was severely injured as well. There was nothing Sylvy could do to save either woman or child. It was beyond her ability, but Sylvy would not hear of it. She insisted on trying anyway. I watched as she drew on the elements until she held nearly as much as I can hold. Then she used the flows to weave a healing spell I have only seen in books. Thanks to Sylvy, both woman and child will be fine. When I asked her where she learned the weave, she told me she had to do it because it was the right thing to do. I am too old for this. I should have had her fix my head," Corney concluded while he rubbed his forehead. He turned and made his way back inside the manor to find his bed and rest his old bones.

Hoovar's head swam as he tried to wrap his mind around Corney's explanation. If the abilities of those two weren't enough to make matters worse, if Corney was correct, they would not only have the knowledge of those whose blood they were infused with but those individuals' ancestors as well. Krotus had bragged how the blood infusions would not only help them pass as human but also stop the boys from going mad at the same time. Hoovar thought the idea was sound at the time, but now he wondered what all of those memories or knowledge would do to their mental health. In the end, it couldn't be good.

*   *   *

"Tell me, Sergeant, is the captain of the guard available?" Krotus inquired as he approached the highest-ranking officer on the watch. He held out his orders to the sergeant so the man would know that he meant business.

"I will let him know you require his assistance right away, Battle Mage Krotus," the sergeant stammered nervously as he bowed and scrambled away.

"You will not mind if I ask your men some questions?" Krotus asked as the man was leaving.

"As you wish, m'lord," the sergeant shouted back as he trotted to the guardhouse.

"You men, come here and look at this," Krotus ordered gruffly.

The men checking papers at the foot of the massive bridge that led to the Therresian kingdom hesitated for only a brief moment before they complied. "Yes, sir," answered one of the men.

Krotus took several pieces of script out of his satchel and passed them around. "I want every one of you to look at these. They are drawings of very dangerous criminals wanted for crimes against the emperor himself. There is evidence that they may have been headed this way to escape the empire. Please tell me if you have seen any of these men pass here," Krotus said as he ran his finger along his nose. That was the signal for Sorram and Taurwin to take a stroll across the long bridge to the other side. "Speak up quickly if you think you have seen anyone of them," he barked to hold their attention.

"I-I may have seen this one before," one of the men spoke up nervously.

"Really?" Krotus said as he looked at the picture. "He is the most dangerous of them all. You say he passed through here, huh. If you can get someone to confirm your story, it will be worth twenty gold crowns, but I caution you men. These men are very—and I mean very—dangerous. Don't try to stop them even if their paperwork looks suspect. Send for at least a battle mage preferably two before you confront any one of them," he cautioned the guardsmen. Now, all he had to do was wait and let greed take its course.

"I was working the shift with him two nights ago. I too saw the man pass. We didn't try to stop him though. All of his papers were current, at least as far as we could tell," another man spoke up.

"Okay, that is one. What about the others?" Krotus declared as he started counting out coins for the two men who looked as if they had just won a lottery. It didn't take long before he had a witness stating every one of the dangerous criminals had passed through this very checkpoint within the last week. By the time the sergeant returned with the captain, he had all that he needed.

"You men return to your post!" shouted the captain as he stomped over to Krotus. "What is the meaning of this?" he demanded.

"I have orders to apprehend these criminals from Lord Hoovar on behalf of the emperor. Danemon wishes to witness their deaths in person," Krotus stated as he started shuffling papers to the captain.

"Danemon who?" the captain asked as he took the orders from Krotus's outstretched hand to read them.

"Oh sorry, Danemon is the emperor's name," Krotus answered. "Anyway, that doesn't matter now. What does matter is—"

"Hoovar . . . Mage Krotus . . . Cornelius's apprentice?" the startled captain mumbled to himself. "I thought you were dead . . . I-I'm sorry. What can I do for you, Battle Mage?"

"Krotus will do fine. What I was saying was that these men have testified to me that they have witnessed and confirmed the passing of these criminals. I will need your blessing to cross because my orders stop at the edge of this bridge. You will need to send word to your superiors, of course, and I would personally appreciate it if you send word to Danemon, I mean, the emperor, that I am close to the trail of the traitors," Krotus told the captain.

"Yes, sir, I will immediately," he answered as he quickly scanned the papers shoved into his hands.

Krotus signaled to Sahharras to join him as he started for the bridge.

"Wait! Who is this?" the captain inquired.

"Why, she is my apprentice," Krotus replied with impatience.

"Where are her orders?" the captain asked suspiciously.

"She has none. I assure you it was a minor oversight in our haste to be after the traitors," Krotus assured the fool.

"How do I know she is an apprentice?" he asked with a quirk of the eyebrow.

"I could have her set you on fire," Krotus teased with a laugh. "She is rather skilled. I could have her explode that stone over there if you wish." The sad part of it was that the fool still wouldn't know if it was she or Krotus wielding the elements.

"No no, that won't be necessary," the captain replied nervously.

That was how Sahharras left the empire and entered the Therresian kingdom with Krotus and both boys. They were free of danger as long as no one came looking for them. Sahharras would be able to raise the boys and watch them grow into adults. She would have Krotus there to help keep an eye on their sanity. Well, if she could keep the boys from killing him, she would. If she couldn't, she wasn't sure whether the man would be missed. She was confident; all she really needed now was the boys. Now that Krotus had gotten them across the border.

There was considerable traffic on the road this close to one of the two bridges that crossed the massive river that served as a natural border and barrier to the empire. It was pointless for the boys to do any scouting with so many people in the vicinity, so they stayed close to Sahharras. Most of their time they spent glaring at Krotus, but they didn't say anything or do anything to draw any unwanted attention, at least.

The traffic on the road had thinned out significantly by the second day on the road in the Therresian kingdom. However, as they came upon a small bridge crossing a small tributary, what traffic there was backed up, waiting to cross. Sahharras could make out a few Therresian soldiers loitering off to one side of the road.

"Do you think we should try to find another way to cross?" Sahharras asked nervously.

"Don't be silly. We don't have anything to fear from them. We are no longer in the empire. Those men take their orders from a different king," Krotus assured her. He was surprised when she actually bought it. He would love to be able to find another way around, but he figured it would look suspicious if they turned around now.

Sahharras thought that what Krotus said made sense, but something still bothered her. She decided to see what Sorram and Taurwin thought, but when she looked over to Sorram, he had his head cocked as if he was trying to listen to the conversations up ahead. She decided to wait until he was done. Maybe he would know more by then. She watched and waited, but before she asked him anything, it was too late. She watched in horror as the expression on his face turned from curiosity to . . . to . . . She knew that look. If she hadn't recognized that, the teeth poking out of his upper lip were impossible to miss.

"Sorram, your teeth," was all she got out before he took off. She turned her head to see what Taurwin was doing, and he was following Sorram's lead, of course. "Krotus, we better follow them. There must be trouble up ahead," she exclaimed as she spurned her horse for more speed.

Krotus had no idea what Sahharras was talking about until he saw Sorram and Taurwin speeding toward the crowd at the base of the bridge. There was nothing for him to do but ride hard to catch up. It only took him a moment to remember just how fast those two were. They were just beautiful. It didn't take long before he and Sahharras had to slow down because there were at least a couple of dozen families blocking the road. They couldn't make their way through the crowd as easily as the boys did.

Coattus had escaped slavery with his family and carefully made their way across the empire. They heard of some soldiers that would allow slaves to cross the bridge at the border for a price. He made contact and waited along with some other families until it was safe to cross. Then they carefully made their way across the Therresian kingdom until they came to the first bridge crossing. There they found slave hunters checking all who wanted to cross. By the time they realized what was happening, it was too late. If they were to turn back now, they would just be ridden down. He didn't know what to do as they slowly made their way to the bridge.

"Who wants to go first? Don't be shy, now. All you have to do to cross the bridge is roll up your sleeve so we can see your shoulder. We are not here to rob anyone. Come on now," a man coaxed as he waved the crowd forward.

Coattus was within twenty paces of the slave hunters when the group of runaways came to a stop. No one wanted to go any further. No one wanted to be the first to be taken away. He looked around for some sort of escape or maybe a place to . . .

"You can check us first, if you can," Sorram challenged as he and Taurwin made their way through the crowd.

Coattus had no idea where the two young men came from, but it was obvious they were not part of this group. The two young men wore fine clothes that didn't show any wear. However, they didn't have any footwear. Most of the families like his own, which he was traveling with, couldn't afford footwear either, but those two didn't look like they couldn't afford it. He looked around to see where they had come from, and he saw two people mounted on horse trying to make their way forward. One was a woman who wore more lace on her dress than his wife had ever worn in her entire life. The man didn't wear any lace, but the fine material of his robes left no doubt about what he was. He still didn't understand what was happening, but then he heard the young man's challenge. He couldn't decide if this was his opportunity to take his family and run or if he should give the young man a hand. After all, there were less than a dozen of the slave hunters. If they attacked with numbers, some of them would get away. The sound of the man's sword sliding from its scabbard put an end to that train of thought.

"Big words for a boy, too young to be allowed to carry a sword," the man teased as he slid his sword from its scabbard. "See, boy, I don't play with sticks." He pointed to the boy's pungi with his sword, and he was rewarded with laughter from the rest of his men.

Sahharras was close enough to hear and see what was going on, but she wasn't sure what to do about it. She didn't want the boys to cause a scene to draw unwanted attention, but she doubted if it could have been any other way. Those men would have seen the scarring on the boys. She didn't know what the slave hunters would have done about it, but it didn't really matter, did it? Once the men saw the scars, they would remember them. That would have left a clue to their location for those who will come after them. "Boys, don't kill any of them," she ordered and wished she hadn't said anything at all because now she had drawn the attention of the soldiers.

"Sorry, m'lady, I didn't realize these were your retainers. That as it may, you should teach them to watch their tongues in the future," the man said as he knuckled his forehead. "You are free to pass, but I may not be as forgiving in the future, unless you wish me to discipline them for you now." The man slightly bowed.

"You misunderstand. They do travel with me, but they are not my servants although they do have their uses, if you get my meaning. We will pass along with all of these other fine people," Sahharras stated calmly and heard Krotus grumble.

"They will, m'lady. As soon as they show us their shoulders, they may pass. We are only interested in runaways. Honest folk have nothing to worry from us," he reassured her.

"They will do no such thing. Now, will you move out of the way, or do I have to have you moved?" Sahharras inquired while she tried to appear as snobbish as she could. If they couldn't hide, then she would make them appear as something else.

"M'lady, we are only trying to make a living—" the man started to explain.

"Boys, we have been waiting long enough. Remove them, but do not kill them. I want no trouble with the local authorities," she ordered and watched as the boys stepped forward.

Krotus couldn't believe his ears. What did she think she was doing? He was about to say something, but the look she gave him stopped him. Instead, he sat and waited for it to start. Sorram stepped up to the man who had done all the talking as the man brought his sword up in front of him. Krotus could make out the man's sneer as he rested the blade on Sorram's chest.

"What's the matter, boy, aren't you going to remove me?" the man teased.

It started so fast that Krotus nearly missed it. He could have sworn he saw Sorram hit the man's sword with both hands across the flat of the blade. One hand landed in the middle of the blade while the other hit the very tip from the opposite direction. He managed to do it with enough force to snap the man's blade in half. It was all Krotus could do—not to applaud as he watched the man gape at his broken blade.

"Kill them!" the man shouted.

Coattus stood there mesmerized after he saw the young man break the slave hunter's blade as if it was a twig, but the man's order to kill had brought him around quickly. He found his feet shuffling him forward in his desire to do something, but he wasn't sure if he desired to help or to make a run for it. He found himself moving towards the second young man, who looked built more like a blacksmith than a fighter did. He watched the biggest of the slave hunters charge with a studded cudgel raised over his head at the young man. Coattus tried to step up beside the young man, but the young man's arm swung around to push him back. He could have sworn the arm was as hard as steel, but it didn't matter. He would help. He wasn't going to stand by and let these young men fight for him. He was tired of scurrying around and hiding like some sort of roach. If they all stuck together, they could . . .

"I'll be——" he mumbled as he watched the young man leap forward with incredible speed. How did anyone built like a blacksmith posses that kind of speed was beyond him. It wasn't as if the man had been as lightning fast as the first man had been, but he was fast enough that the big man with the cudgel never had a chance. The big man never even started to bring the cudgel down to defend himself. The young man landed in front of the big man and planted his open palm in the center of the big man's breastplate. The sound the strike made was incredible. If Coattus didn't know better, he would have sworn he felt it.

Sahharras couldn't believe Sorram had taken such a risk. Sure, it was impressive, but it was equally dangerous. She would have to talk to him later about it. At least the man was left with no more than a stub of a sword. He wasn't out of the fight, but he all but was against Sorram and Taurwin. Then again, he really didn't stand much of a chance in the first place. She heard the man's orders to kill and waited for things to escalate, but it didn't happen the way she had expected. Only one man rushed forward. The rest remained where they stood and stared in disbelief at the first man's broken sword. Maybe Sorram was right to break it after all.

Her attention was drawn to Taurwin as one of the slaves approached him from behind. She nearly called out to warn him. Then she saw the man try to step up beside Taurwin as if he was going to help in the fight. Sahharras couldn't help but think, *Well, good for you, now get out of his way before you are hurt!* She saw Taurwin push the man back effortlessly before he leaped toward the oncoming man. She watched in horror as Taurwin hit him in the center of his breastplate with the open palm. She didn't want anyone killed here. It would complicate things.

"Mage, see to that man. Make sure he doesn't die," she ordered and was relieved when Krotus actually complied with minor grumbling. "I said don't kill anyone and I meant it, Ta-boy," she scolded. She cursed herself for almost letting Taurwin's name slip.

"Kill them!" the man with the broken sword shouted again before he looked around to see what his men were waiting for before they attacked. "You, you saw what they did. Arrest them!" he screamed at one of the soldiers standing by watching.

"Arrest them for what?" the soldier replied.

"For assault, you imbecile!" the slave hunter charged.

"Really, is that what you are going with? Assault? First, you deny people from the use of this bridge. Then you harass anyone who wishes to cross. Then you order the murder of these two. Now that you have had your ass handed to you by the first two who come along with a little combat training, you demand the army arrest them for assault when they were obviously defending themselves. No . . . no, I think it is you who should be arrested. It is you who should be escorted back to the border and have your license removed. If you can't do your job without harassing honest taxpaying citizens, then you have no business being here," Krotus lectured as he glared at the man.

"They are runaways!" the man shouted in his defense.

"Really, how can you tell?" Sahharras challenged.

"Look at them! They have no money to pay taxes!" the man shouted back as his face turned redder and redder until it looked as if he burst a vein.

"They don't appear to have any wealth. I will admit to that, but most common farmers do not acquire vast sums of wealth. I would like to ask you, where would this country be without them and those like them? Where would the grains come from that feed the multitudes in the cities? Who would raise the beef that feeds our armies? These are the unsung heroes who make all of those things possible. They are the poor and downtrodden laborers throughout our great country, that drives our economy," Sahharras lectured as she sat her horse proudly.

"It will be my pleasure to escort these men to the border at your command, m'lady. I will see to it that they may never again set foot inside our borders," one of the soldiers proclaimed as he stepped toward the slave hunters.

"Thank you, m'lady. We all thank you," Coattus declared as he made his best leg for the gracious lady as the soldiers started to herd the slave hunters north toward the border. "If you ever require . . . any of our services, . . . we will always be in your debt. You just send for me, Coattus, if you need anything at all," he added as he fought off tears of joy. They were truly free. He could . . . His thoughts were interrupted as he watched the lady exchange what appeared to be hand signals with the two young fighters.

"It appears that you have had some hard travels, my friend. Please allow me to extend this small stipend to you and your families in your time of need," Sahharras declared with a wave of her hand toward Sorram who quickly produced a small purse that clinked with coins from his satchel. She watched as Sorram lofted the purse to the Coattus. She could be mistaken, but she would be willing to bet anything that purse contained more gold than silver and copper put together. Hell, it might contain more gold than these people have ever made in their lifetime. She had no idea how much of their gold they had brought with them or how much they had to start with for that matter, but they were going to have to learn the simple fact that they wouldn't be able to afford giving their gold away to whoever appears in need.

Krotus was actually grateful for the boys' distraction. While the peasants were marveling over their newfound wealth, they would be able to slip away. "Come, m'lady, we need to be on our way," he whispered and was relieved when Sahharras put her horse to a fast trot. He couldn't help but shake his head as the two boys leaped ahead of her and took the lead. Damn, if they were not beautiful. Krotus spurred his horse to a gallop to try to catch up. "I do have to admit your idea to pose as nobility was rather ingenious, but I would suggest that you put your fine dresses away for the time being. You could switch to a mage and I could pose as a nobleman next time," Krotus teased with a chuckle.

"We should abandon the main roads as soon as we are out of sight as well. I think we should try to avoid as much contact with people as possible," Sahharras suggested after a little thought. "It wouldn't hurt if a certain two young men tried to refrain from helping everyone we meet as well," she added for the boys.

* * *

Sahharras was grateful for her short time spent among the women farmers. If she hadn't had that opportunity, she would not have known anything about camping in the rough. The preparation of wild game over an open fire always had a distinct taste that she appreciated, but armed with a few simple herbs, she could change eating for sustenance to a dining experience. She was amazed at the skill Krotus demonstrated the few times he volunteered to prepare dinner. He usually requested the boys to catch him particular game when he cooked though. This usually led to some minor confusion because the boys had spent so little time out of captivity. They had seen quail and pheasant, but they didn't know the fowl had names.

This frustrated Krotus to no end. He had spent a considerable amount of resources to see the boys educated. They had been taught in various weapons, from different disciplines across every culture he had access to. He had not realized how much common knowledge he had neglected. He hadn't thought it would be essential for their destiny. He tried to tell them what little he knew about the flora and the surrounding habitat as they traveled, but he realized he really didn't know much more than Sahharras appeared to know.

This frustrated Krotus, but it wasn't nearly as troublesome as the fact that both boys seemed to having increasing difficulty maintaining their human forms. He thought he had been imagining it, but he was now convinced of it no matter how often Sahharras swore the boys were fine. Even more frustrating was the fact that there wasn't anything he could do about it; at least he couldn't do anything about it for now. He would have to get them farther from civilization before he could even think about doing something for them. The amount of the elements he would have to draw to accomplish a blood infusion would draw the attention of every mage within a hundred leagues at least. It could even draw the attention of Danemon, and that was something he would rather avoid.

He was relieved to see that even as the two boys struggled to maintain their human form, they never did lose their compassion for helping others. They were consistently requesting detours and side trips to help people as they came across them. The reasons varied from tending to poor farmer's fields with enchantments to healing the ill. Sure, it was frustrating when they were supposed to be avoiding people, but it showed their true qualities. They were not afraid to sacrifice their own needs for those who needed their assistance. He just wished they didn't cause quite as many delays. The last cluster of farms the boys insisted on saving had been stricken down with the pox, and it took both him and Sahharras two days of weaving to clean the whole area of the disease. That was two days he was sure they could not afford. Then again, they still hadn't killed him. He was sure that he would be the first to go if they did lose control of themselves.

*　　*　　*

Brinnel read the report quickly again as he hurried to his master's apartments to make sure he understood the thing. The empe . . . the prophet will be very pleased to see this report immediately. He wouldn't be able to wait for him to finish with today's plaything. He paused at the doors to form his signature weave to form his tones to announce his arrival and waited for a response. He heard the tones that signaled his admittance and entered quickly. He kept his eyes down on the marble floor to keep from seeing anything to give him new nightmares, but it was futile. He could hear the groans of a man as visions of his onetime colleague came back to him despite determination not to see them.

"M'prophet, pardon my interruption, but I have a report here that you will want to see for yourself," he declared as he knelt down and buried his face to the cold floor.

"For your sake, it had better concern a certain traitor," Danemon warned Brinnel.

"It does, m'lord, I mean, m'prophet. It is a confirmed report on his location," Brinnel answered as he clutched his potion in his hand.

"Well, don't hold me in suspense, man. Where is he?" Danemon asked as he pushed his day's sacrifice aside. He had spent too many days and nights searching for Krotus on the western frontier of the empire.

"He is in the Therresian kingdom," Brinnel answered as he thumbed the stopper to the little vial.

"The Therresian kingdom! That is a very general location, don't you think. This news doesn't please me. It doesn't please me at all. Do you have anything to add, or should I consider adding you to the menu today," Danemon threatened as his temper flared.

"I realize it is a large area, but you said he would be headed to the land of the elves to the west. He still has to travel to the west through the Negron valley to reach them. I have dispatched a special squad to the southwestern border weeks ago. I already sent orders to the squad to intercept him before he enters the Negron valley. The maps only show one road through the Cursed Mountains. We have him. It is only a matter of time," Brinnel predicted with a triumphant grin.

Danemon was surprised by Brinnel's answer. The man was resourceful after all. Maybe he should stop tormenting the man and start thinking harder about giving the man that little reward. He may need a new donor if Krotus was killed. Yes, that would work. "Very good indeed, you have served me very well and loyally for years. Have you ever thought about retirement?" Danemon inquired.

"What? No, m'lord, I have not. What would I do?" Brinnel mumbled in his confusion. Fool, this was his chance to get out of the sick and twisted bastard's employ. Why didn't he answer yes?

"Well, there is that opening in Pua Dar," Danemon hinted as a plan came together.

"I thought you said retirement," Brinnel answered. What was the man trying to say?

"Yes, retire from this station to something a little less stressful. You could take the overlord position or the lord of the city if you wish. If you do choose to retire, I will have one parting gift for you," Danemon promised with a grin.

*   *   *

"What is that for?" Sahharras demanded to know as she glared at Krotus.

"It is a cart for transporting dangerous animals, obviously. I bought it from that menagerie up the road. It cost me dearly too. They had been using it to haul supplies around with them. Evidently the lion that it used to haul around had died a few months ago, and I was able to talk them into letting me purchase the contraption," Krotus answered cautiously.

"You don't expect the boys get into it, do you?" Sahharras protested. The man was out of his mind if he thought those two would go back to living in a cage.

"We have to do something with them. Taurwin can't talk, and half of the time I can't understand Sorram when the moon is full. They are losing control no matter how much you deny it and you must accept it. They go away for longer and longer periods of time. What will happen if they forget to come back the next time? We can't risk letting them run rampant across the countryside," Krotus ranted until he saw the tears running freely down Sahharra's cheeks. He understood that she had motherly feelings for them, but she had to try to remember that they were animals made to look and act human. It was the animal in them that made them special. It was also what made them dangerous. It was the human blood that gave them control over their instincts. He should explain to her about their original forms, but how could he tell her that the natural instinct of her "sons" was to kill and eat her? From what he understood, they were at the top of the food chain. They hunted in packs, but most importantly, they would kill and eat any dragon foolish enough to encroach on their territory. That was why he chose them as his platform to improve upon.

"You can't ask them to do it. You don't know what it is like. I hated living in a cage. You don't——" she was pleading as she saw Sorram trotting out of the forest. Taurwin wasn't far behind him, and both of them looked upset. She had better calm herself or they would kill him for making her cry. He wouldn't even have a chance to ask them to go in the cage. She wiped the tears from her face as she watched both boys inspect the caged cart. To her surprise, the horse hitched to the cursed cart didn't even react to their presence. Then she remembered that the animal was probably used to the smell of predators from its time with its previous owner. That did make sense, but the boys' reaction to the cart didn't.

"Rrnoo . . . rrrnoughrr," Sorram tried to say, but his words were intelligible. He shook his head and tried again, but all that came out was more growls. He walked to Sahharras and used signs to tell her what he wanted to say so she could translate for Krotus.

"He said that it isn't enough," Sahharras translated as Sorram wiped a tear from her cheek with his clawed hand. She noticed he even had difficulty forming some of the signs because of his deformed and clawed hands.

"What do you mean it isn't enough? What else can I do?" Krotus replied in disbelief. "That cage is built strong enough to hold a Minotaur. The man who sold it to me said so."

Sorram began to sign more, but Sahharras couldn't stand the thought of putting them in the cage. "You can't be seriously thinking about getting in that . . . that thing. Why, Sorram, why would you do it?" she protested.

Sorram tried to talk again but ended up shaking his head in disgust. He gave up trying to talk and resorted to using signs once again.

"What do you mean? You have to. No, you don't," Sahharras argued. She couldn't understand some of his signs but she continued arguing anyway. "Why would either of you?" she asked and waited for something that made sense. "What do you mean it is getting harder? All you have to do is concentrate. Come, I will meditate with you and we will have

you back to normal in no time. You don't have to go into—"
She stopped to wipe the tears from Sorram's muzzle. Sorram
continued to sign as she read what she could, but she didn't
translate for Krotus. He should have spent more time with
them and learned the art of sign as she had.

"The wilds call to me just as the moon calls to Taurwin.
Sometimes I think I can understand the big cats that run wild
and I want to join them. We have passed packs of wolves that
seem to have an interest in Taurwin and he swears he can talk
to them. I have heard them howl back to him, but the voices
that are not voices inside our heads are worse. We don't know
how to block them out or if they are real. How can we hold
conversations with something in our head?" Sorram tried to
sign to her.

"'Voices that are not voices,' that doesn't make any sense,
Sorram," she protested. She must have misunderstood the
signs.

"It feels like someone is sending pictures and scents to us,
but most of the time we understand what the pictures and
scents mean. The big cats send me their scents and ask me
for mine, I am sure it is how they introduce themselves. The
males never seem to like me as the female lions do. Taurwin
has had the same things happen to him but with the wolves.
Then when the moon is full—" he stopped.

"When the moon is full what, Sorram?" she asked
reluctantly.

"When the moon is full, everything smells like food, even
humans," Sorram answered. "That is why we must. When
the moon is full, we must be caged for the safety of others,
but the cage is not enough. We will need shackles, enchanted

ones. Something to keep me from accidentally wielding the elements." He balled his fists to prevent them from shaking.

* * *

Daven should have been happy and he was, but he felt as if there was something missing. He had more coins than he ever dreamed possible. Both of his children were doing well. Jerhod was busy in his smithy from dawn to dusk, and Hoovar's smith praised Jerhod's work on his last inspection. He hadn't seen Sylvy for weeks, but he had heard that she had saved a woman and her unborn child from certain death. He was told how much she had grown, which seemed odd. He was proud of both of them, but he missed them.

He tried to stay busy with the farm, but even that had changed. The crops looked better than they ever had before he had gone to Pua Dar. His chickens were laying more eggs than they could ever eat. There was someone from the mine nearly every other day to relieve him of the surplus eggs or extra vegetables from the garden. The other day, he had a tomato nearly perfect in shape and as big as a small child's head. It had tasted nearly as good as it looked too. He had no complaints about the farm except that with all the magical help Sahharras and Sylvy had given to his little spread, he had too much idle time on his hands. The fields didn't need weeded and the animals didn't get sick. There was a regular supply of rain. Sometimes, he thought he might be able to set his watch by it. Some had given that credit to Sylvy as well, but he thought Corney might have more to do with something that large. Either way, it had the same effect. If he checked with a neighbor to see if they needed a hand, he was informed that his family had helped too much already. This left him on his porch rocking in a chair like a useless old man. Everything was perfect, yet he still yearned for something. But he had no idea what it was.

*   *   *

This would be the last night the boys had to stay in that damn cage. It was the last night of the full moon, and they were nearly out of the Therresian kingdom. She didn't care how far they made it into the mountains before the next full moon. Either Krotus would weave the spell, or she would herself. She would not watch those two suffer another day in that cage. They looked miserable as they moaned and paced in the small confines. Occasionally Sorram would stop pacing to claw at the metal bars, and she would have to go to him to calm him down. She had to do the same when Taurwin would start biting at the bars of their cage. Now that she thought about it, she wasn't sure if the steel cage would last another month. Even with all the precautions Sorram had specified on those shackles, she still worried. If they did get loose, would she even be able to find them again to help them? Maybe they shouldn't wait until . . .

He couldn't believe the resources that had been dedicated to the execution of just this one traitor, but that would only make his job that much easier. He had no idea why anyone thought it would take this many magi to capture one single mage and a lowly apprentice no matter who it was or who had taught them. That just made the dark guard he had with him as more overkill. These were not just dark guard either. These were trained assassins as well. They had set up magical barriers to prevent their detection days ago, and everyone was in position. All they had to do is sit and wait to spring the trap.

Sahharras turned to the cage and began to hum a lullaby, but Sorram and Taurwin were doing their best to sign something with their clawed hands as they howled and roared in panic. She couldn't tell what—enemy . . . danger . . .

"Krotus," she said as she felt him reach for the elements. She let the elements fill her and prepared two knives of spirit and earth to protect herself, but a pain in her shoulder sent her to her knees. She could hear the boys clamor in a rage. She tried to reach out to them, but her arm didn't work anymore. She finally saw the arrow shaft jutting out of her shoulder, and she quickly weaved a shield of air, water, and mineral around her to protect her from any more arrows. She saw Krotus coming to her aid. No, he came to hide himself from the arrows as he defended himself from detonation weaves. She extended her weave around him. It took very little effort, but her concentration was slipping. She added two knives to fend off the attacks on her barrier while Krotus seemed to be battling weaves that filled the sky.

The sound of metal straining reminded her of the boys. "Let them loose. Help them, Krotus!" she screamed.

"I am busy, woman!" Krotus shouted back.

He watched as Krotus and his apprentice approached and was confident in his planning. He had no idea what kind of animals were in that cage or what their purpose was, but that didn't really matter now, did it? Then the clamor of the animals in the cage had caused Krotus to stop. It was too soon to attack. They were too far away yet. He had no choice. He had to begin the attack now or risk losing the element of surprise. He gave the signal, and the dark guard let their arrows fly. He realized that only one arrow found its mark when he saw the arrow strike the apprentice. Damn it, why couldn't the fools hit Krotus and miss the apprentice. No matter, he thought as he joined the other magi in their attack. To his surprise, the apprentice had formed a protective barrier that he didn't recognize and was impressed by its effectiveness. It had to have been something she had been taught by Cornelius. He was famous for his powerful protective wards. The real problem was that Krotus had taken shelter behind it as well. Krotus was impressive in his defense as he cut away detonation weave after another. He was still confident they would wear the man down. It was only a matter of time.

Then to his surprise, he saw Krotus make his last mistake. For whatever reason, the fool had diverted his weaves from defending himself to that of the cage that contained the strange creatures. It almost disappointed him to think that it ended so quickly without any real effort. All they had to do now was collect the apprentice and slip her back across the border into the empire. That was when he heard the cage give way.

Krotus must have weakened it or something to free those animals, but for what purpose? He watched as the animals bolted from the ruined door of the cage and slip into the darkness, but the sounds those things emitted were horrifying. He scanned the area to locate where they had gone, but he didn't see a thing. Then a fireball screamed past him, causing him to hit the dirt. He looked up to see one of the young magi he had brought with him flinging fireballs wildly in every direction. It took him a moment to recognize what was going on. The young mage had lost an arm and, in his pain and panic, struck out randomly in an effort to strike down his attacker. It had to have been one of those animals that had done it. They must have been trained. He hadn't even considered that.

He formed a large light orb to light up the road as he heard other men's screams in an effort to locate this new threat. It was obvious the apprentice was down and out of the fight. He prepared a detonation weave as he scanned the area and realized that nearly half of his men were missing. How the hell had that happened? "Where are they?" he tried to shout over the cries of his dying men.

Then out of nowhere came a flying object. He managed to duck before it hit him in the head, but when he looked to see what it was, he was horrified. Someone or something had thrown a leg of one of his men at him. He was stunned. He was still standing there gaping at the horrid sight when something came for him. It happened so fast he didn't even have time to react. He could have sworn that a large cat running on two legs had attacked him. He tried to call out for help as he tried to stem the flow of blood from his ruined throat, but it was no use. As he fell, he realized there was no one left standing. He thought it was so simple. All he had to . . . had to . . .

"Turn them loose! They don't stand a chance!" she pleaded. She saw the resignation in Krotus's eyes as he diverted his weaves to the cage. She saw him burst into flames as his weave reached the cage. Her barrier collapsed as the attacking magi turned their attentions on her. She lay flat on her back and stared at the empty black sky as she heard the cage finally give way. She could hear Taurwin's howls and the screams of men as they were ripped apart and died. The flows that held her to the ground became less and less as Sorram roared into the night. She was grateful for the storm clouds that obscured the light of the moon. She knew both boys would be in full fur with the moon and the rage in their blood. They would kill every one of their attackers in the mask of the darkness. Whoever had attacked them had made a major mistake thinking the boys were safe because of the cage. They would never live to make the same mistake twice.

She heard the boys roar, howl one last time before it went graveyard quiet. She realized that the threads holding her were gone. She winced when Sorram's lion-shaped head appeared in her vision. She didn't wince out of revulsion but out of sympathy. The boy had acquired a new scar. This nasty scar started in the middle of his long forehead and ran through his eye to the center of his cheek. She realized he was trying to get her attention. Of course, she had to use her key to remove his shackles. She tried to reach for it, but her arms didn't work.

She saw Taurwin reach for it. "No, Taurwin. Remember, it is enchanted. If you touch it," Sahharras cried. She had to get that key. Taurwin's face came back into view, and she saw that he had been injured as well. The side of his face was open from the corner of his mouth to his ear, and as she watched, it began to close up on its own. She couldn't help but smile. They will live. They will heal. They will figure out how to get out of those chains. It wouldn't matter that they were enchanted. They would figure out something. Then they would hunt. She hoped they killed as many of the imperial bastards as they could until they reached the emperor. The last thing she saw was her two boys crying over her broken body, and she just knew they would hunt imperialists until the end of days.